SEISHI YOKOMIZO (1902–81) was one of Japan's most famous and best-loved mystery writers. He was born in Kobe and spent his childhood reading detective stories, before beginning to write stories of his own, the first of which was published in 1921. He went on to become an extremely prolific and popular author, best known for his Kosuke Kindaichi series, which ran to 77 books, many of which were adapted for stage and television in Japan. *The Honjin Murders*, *The Inugami Curse* and *The Village of Eight Graves* are also available from Pushkin Vertigo.

LOUISE HEAL KAWAI grew up in Manchester, UK, but Japan has been her home since 1990. She previously translated Seishi Yokomizo's *The Honjin Murders*, Soji Shimada's *Murder in the Crooked House* and Mieko Kawakami's *Ms Ice Sandwich* for Pushkin Press. Her other translations include *Seventeen* by Hideo Yokoyama and Sosuke Natsukawa's *The Cat Who Saved Books*.

DEATH ON GOKUMON ISLAND

PUSHKIN
VERTIGO

Seishi Yokomizo

Translated from the Japanese by Louise Heal Kawai

Pushkin Press
Somerset House, Strand
London WC2R 1LA

GOKUMONTOU

Original text © Seishi Yokomizo 1971, 1996
English translation © Louise Heal Kawai 2022

First published in Japan in 1971 by KADOKAWA CORPORATION, Tokyo

English translation rights arranged with KADOKAWA CORPORATION,
Tokyo through JAPAN UNI AGENCY, INC., Tokyo.

First published by Pushkin Press in 2022

3 5 7 9 8 6 4 2

ISBN 13: 978-1-78227-741-5

Map hand-drawn by Neil Gower

Designed and typeset by Tetragon, London
Printed and bound by Clays Ltd, Elcograf S.p.A.

www.pushkinpress.com

CONTENTS

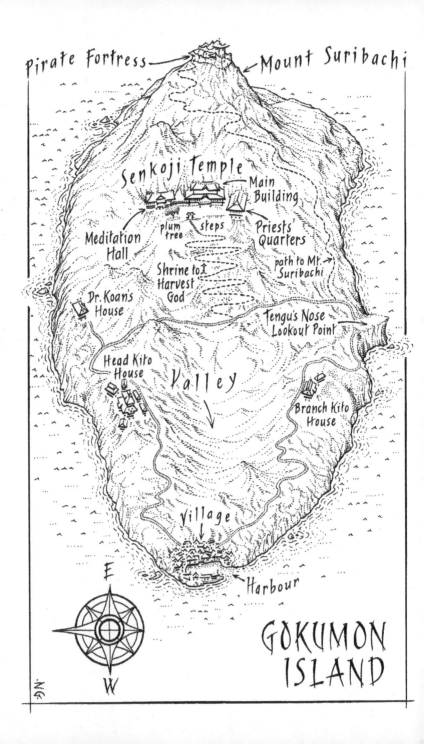

Pirate Fortress — ← Mount Suribachi

Senkoji Temple
→ Main Building
Meditation Hall
plum tree steps
Priests' Quarters
path to Mt. Suribachi →
Shrine to Harvest God
Dr. Koan's House
Tengu's Nose Lookout Point
Head Kito House
Valley
Branch Kito House
Village
Harbour

E

W

GOKUMON ISLAND

CHARACTERS IN GOKUMON ISLAND

THE INVESTIGATORS

Kosuke Kindaichi   private detective, just returned from the war
Inspector Isokawa   detective in the prefectural police depart-
                    ment, old friend of Kosuke Kindaichi's

THE HEAD KITO FAMILY

Chimata   Kaemon's grandson and Yosamatsu's son, Kito family
           heir, died in the war, Kosuke Kindaichi's friend
Kaemon   recently deceased head of the Kito family, was the
           most powerful fishing boss on the island
Yosamatsu Chimata's father and Kaemon's son; mad, imprisoned
           in the house, often referred to as "the lunatic"
Tsukiyo   Chimata's half-sister, Yosamatsu's eldest daughter
Yukie   Chimata's half-sister, Yosamatsu's middle daughter
Hanako   Chimata's half-sister, Yosamatsu's youngest daughter
Sanae   Chimata's cousin, younger sister of Hitoshi, runs
           the head Kito household
Hitoshi   Chimata's cousin, older brother of Sanae, not
           returned from war
Okatsu   Kaemon's former mistress, lives with the family
Sayo   ex-actress, second wife of Yosamatsu, deceased

THE BRANCH KITO FAMILY

Gihei	head of the branch family, second most powerful fishing boss on the island
Oshiho	Gihei's second wife
Shozo Ukai	handsome young man, ex-soldier

OTHER RESIDENTS

Ryonen	head priest of Senkoji Temple
Ryotaku	apprentice priest at Senkoji Temple
Takezo	shiotsukuri (tide master)
Makihei Araki	village mayor
Koan Murase	doctor of Chinese medicine
Sergeant Shimizu	Gokumon Island's police officer
Seiko	barber

Various islanders and investigators

PROLOGUE

Kosuke Kindaichi Arrives on Gokumon Island

Seventeen miles south of Kasaoka, falling right on the border between Okayama, Hiroshima and Kagawa Prefectures, in the middle of the Seto Inland Sea, there's a tiny island. Measuring barely five miles in circumference, its name is Gokumon-to, meaning Hell's Gate Island.

Many theories have been bandied about over the years as to how it got that name. The most credible is that the correct name was originally Kitamon-to, or North Gate Island. The evidence for this is as follows...

For as many as a thousand years, the Seto Inland Sea was famous for its bands of pirates, whose first leader was the notorious Sumitomo Fujiwara. Back then, trading ships from continental Asia sailing into central Japan through the Kanmon Straits, which divide the southern island of Kyushu and the main island of Honshu, constantly had to contend with the daredevil pirates of the Seto Inland Sea. The pirates' fortunes were up and down over the centuries, but they have existed since the Nara Period, or the eighth century. Up until the early Edo Period, or the seventeenth century, the pirating tradition was passed on from genera-tion to generation. In a famous chapter of Japanese history, the Yoshino Period, these Seto pirates really came into their own, playing a major role in the sixty years of conflict between the Northern and Southern dynasties, during the 1300s.

One particular band of pirates, known as the Iyo, were based around the Seto islands from the Iyo coastline to Hiuchi-nada and Bingo-nada. As the current Gokumon Island was their northern stronghold, the story goes that they were the ones who named it Kitamon, or North Gate. And somewhere over the years, that name changed to Gokumon—Hell's Gate.

However, there exists another theory, one not based on historical fact. It is rumoured that sometime in the early days of the Edo Period, a giant man by the name of Goemon, six feet seven inches tall, lived on the island. This rumour spread around the whole of Japan, and the island where he was spotted became Goemon Island, a name which eventually evolved into Gokumon Island.

I haven't been able to ascertain which of the stories—the Kitamon or the Goemon—is correct, but there is a general consensus as to how the sinister-sounding corruption of its name to Hell's Gate came about.

This is how the story goes…

During the Edo Era, from the seventeenth to the nineteenth century, the island was ruled by the feudal lord of the Chugoku region of Japan. It was an isolated island of granite, thick with red pine trees, and inhabited only by a few fishermen, descendants of the pirates of the past. The feudal lord decided to make the island a place of exile. From that time on, for many years, all the criminals in his territory who had their death sentence commuted were imprisoned on this island, and it became known by the inauspicious moniker Gokumon, which can be read as Prison Gate as well as Hell's Gate.

And so, through those almost three hundred years of the Edo Era, how many unfortunate souls were exiled on Gokumon Island? Were there some who were eventually pardoned and allowed to return to their home towns? For sure there were many, banished here for life, who died and were buried on the island. A good many of these had intermarried with the fisherfolk, descendants of the Iyo pirates, and started a new bloodline. There were still others who had children with the daughters of fishermen and, after receiving a pardon, left the island, abandoning their children.

By the Meiji Era of the late nineteenth century, exile was no longer used as a punishment, but the people already living on the island were closed-minded and insular to an extreme. They rarely agreed to marry with people from any other place. Thus, each and every one of the barely 300 households on Gokumon Island, and their (just) over 1,000 inhabitants, had both pirate and prisoner blood running in their veins.

It was a man by the name of K—, once a schoolteacher on one of the neighbouring islands, who told me of the laborious process that had to be undertaken if ever there was a crime committed on any of these Seto Inland islands.

"The island I used to work on had a population of about a thousand. They've been intermarrying for two or three—in the worst cases, for five or six—generations. So the whole island is like one large extended family. What kind of authority can a police officer from another part of the country have in a place like that? If there's a crime committed, the whole island closes ranks and the police are powerless. If there's a quarrel among the islanders, for example, a complaint that some property's gone missing, or money's been stolen, and the police are called in to investigate, without fail the moment they close in on a suspect, the parties in question immediately come to their own arrangement. And the story changes completely: 'Oh no, it wasn't stolen after all! I'd completely forgotten that I'd shoved it in the back of a cupboard.' In some ways this makes life easy, but at other times it's a complete pain in the neck."

If the ordinary islands of the inland sea were that way, then how could it not be also in an extraordinary place like Gokumon Island, with its descendants of pirates and prisoners? The people were already ostracized by the inhabitants of surrounding islands, and their hostility to any outsider was uncommonly strong. If a crime were committed on Gokumon Island, one can only imagine how hopeless was the lot of the police.

And then there was a crime... And what a terrible crime it was too, a hideous nightmare of a case, unearthly and insidious, a systematically plotted serial-murder case, truly befitting a place named Hell's Gate. It really was a bizarre, and frankly impossible-seeming, string of murders.

That said, it's important to note that Gokumon Island is not a remote island in the middle of a vast, empty ocean. It is located in Japan's Seto Inland Sea. Although it's a fair distance from the rest of the islands, it does have working electricity and its own post office. And there's a daily ferry to and from Kasaoka on the mainland.

It was the middle of September 1946, about a year after the end of the Second World War. A thirty-five-tonne ferry, the *White Dragon*, had just left Konoshima Port in Kasaoka, headed for the islands. It was packed to the brim with passengers. A good half in those days were fairly well-to-do citizens, and they were on a trip from the mainland to Shiraishi Island for a special fish dinner. The other half of the passengers were island folk who had been over to the mainland to stock up on necessities. They were mostly fishermen or their wives. All of the islands in the Seto Inland Sea were blessed with bountiful fish, but they were severely lacking in suitable land for cultivating rice, so residents were in the habit of taking fish to the mainland to exchange for rice.

The body of the ship with its filthy, worn tatami matting was crammed with these people and their baggage. The stink of sweat and fish along with paint and gasoline and exhaust fumes—any single one of these smells would be unpleasant by itself, but when mixed together in a teeming ship, it was enough to make anyone vomit. However, these fishermen and farming folk were strong both in spirit and stomach. Without a care in the world, they sat there talking in shrill tones, laughing and generally enjoying themselves.

At the far edge of the stern section, there was an odd-looking passenger. The man was dressed in a traditional serge *hakama* skirt. On his head was a shapeless, crumpled felt hat. These days even peasant farmers would wear Western clothes, or at least an approximation of Western

13

clothing, at home. Off on a trip, the world and his wife would certainly be dressed Western-style. Right now, on this ship there was only one other man in traditional Japanese clothing, and he was a Buddhist priest. In those days, to persist in wearing traditional Japanese dress took some stubbornness, but this passenger didn't look stubborn. He had a very ordinary sort of face. He was of slight build, and overall was rather undistinguished-looking. His complexion had the darkness of the southern Japanese, but it didn't give him any semblance of being strong or robust. He looked to be around thirty-five years old.

Apparently oblivious to all the hubbub around him, the man leaned against the window, staring absently out over the ocean. The Seto Inland Sea was a deep emerald green, with picturesque islands dotted here and there, but the man seemed unmoved by such beautiful scenery. In fact, he looked more sleepy than anything else.

As the ferry passed from Kasaoka to Shiraishi Island and then on to Kitagi Island, many passengers alighted, but few boarded. Then, finally, three hours after departing Konoshima Port, right after making a stop at Manabe Island, only three passengers remained in the once cacophonous interior of the ferry.

It was then that something happened to change the expression on the face of the sleepy man.

"Oh, hello, Reverend Father, I didn't notice you there. I didn't realize you'd been away from Senkoji Temple! Where have you come from?"

At the sound of this voice, the sleepy man was suddenly wide awake. He turned around to see the speaker was a fisherman-type, around forty-five years old. He was wearing what appeared to be second-hand army khakis. But it wasn't this speaker who had caught the man's attention—it was the man addressed as the Reverend Father of Senkoji Temple.

The priest appeared to be about sixty—well, perhaps closer to seventy—but he was tall and well built, giving him the appearance of a much younger man in the prime of his life. His eyes, nose and mouth, all the features of his large face, added to the impression of an imposing character. His big, bright eyes were filled with warmth, but at the same time they had a sharpness about them that suggested they could chill a person to the bone. Over his white robes he wore a traditional smock-like travelling coat and a simple hood around his round face.

The priest's eyes crinkled into a gentle smile.

"Hey, Takezo, I didn't know you were on this ferry."

He spoke in a leisurely manner.

"Anyway, where have you come from?"

It was the second time the man called Takezo had asked the question.

"I went to Kure to get our temple bell," said the priest.

"Temple bell? Oh, the one that was confiscated during the war. Is it still in one piece?"

"Yes, it turns out it was never melted down. It survived the war."

"And you went to pick it up… But where is it right now?"

"Ha ha. I may look strong but I'd never manage to get that bell back by myself. I just went to do the paperwork. I'm going to have to get some of the young lads from the island to go and pick it up."

"I see. I'd be happy to go along and help with that. Anyway, congratulations on getting it back."

"Yes, it's returning to its rightful home," said the priest with a smile.

Takezo moved in a little closer.

"When you mentioned returning to a rightful home, it reminded me—Hitoshi-san is supposed to be coming home soon."

"Hitoshi-san?"

The priest looked sharply at Takezo.

"How do you know that? Was there news from his regiment?"

"No, not from the army. Well, not directly. I ran into someone who was in the same regiment as him… when was it? The day before yesterday, or maybe it was three days ago. This man turned up unexpectedly on the island, said he'd been entrusted by Hitoshi-san to let his family know that he'd survived the war. That he hadn't been injured, that he'd be coming home on the next ship, or maybe the one after that. Sanae-san was overjoyed to hear it. She made the visitor food and sent him away with a bunch of gifts."

"Hmm. And so he left again?"

"Yes, he stayed just one night. He left with a whole load of stuff… So do you think this means that Chimata-san is also alive?"

The priest closed his eyes.

"Right. There'll be no problem if the main family line is safe."

There was strong emotion in his voice.

That was when the strange man in the hakama and felt hat sidled up to him.

"If you don't mind me asking, you're not Ryonen-san the priest, from Gokumon Island, are you?"

The priest's eyes popped wide open, and he stared at the man's face.

"Yes, I'm Ryonen. And you?"

The man opened his suitcase and pulled out an envelope. Breaking the seal, he took out a folded piece of paper and handed it to the priest. It seemed to be a page torn from a notebook. The priest looked puzzled.

"The bearer, Kosuke Kindaichi..." he read aloud, but then stopped and looked up at the man's face.

"This is Chimata-san's writing!"

The man in the serge hakama nodded with enthusiasm.

"And you are Kosuke Kindaichi?"

The man nodded again.

"This is addressed to me, the village mayor and the doctor. Will you permit me to open it?"

"Go ahead."

The priest unfolded the paper and scanned the faint pencil writing. After he'd finished reading, he folded the paper again.

"Give me the envelope. I'll keep this safe."

He placed the torn paper back in the envelope that Kosuke Kindaichi had passed to him, and then put it away in a large wallet he pulled from his breast pocket. Then he looked the stranger up and down.

"So, what exactly does this letter mean? That you need somewhere nice and quiet to recuperate? And Gokumon

Island is the perfect location? Chimata-san has entrusted your care to Mayor Araki, Doctor Murase and myself?"

The stranger nodded.

"I hope it's not too much trouble to you. I've brought a little rice with me, but—"

"No, no. Don't worry about that at all. However poor we islanders may be, we can always find enough to feed one extra mouth. And if you're on business relating to the heir of the chief family of the island, everyone will be sure to treat you kindly. Please enjoy your stay… Only there's one thing, Kindaichi-san."

"Yes?"

"What has happened to the head… I mean, Chimata Kito. Why hasn't he returned home yet?"

"K-Kito-san…"

The stranger had begun to stammer slightly.

Takezo took the opportunity to cut into the conversation.

"Please don't tell us he died in the war!"

"Well, not exactly. He didn't die in action. After it had ended, he— Well, he was still alive in August of this year. It was on board a ship that was bringing us soldiers back to Japan…"

"He passed away on the ship?"

The stranger in the serge clothing nodded.

"There'll be an official communiqué, but I've come here to inform everyone at Kito-san's request."

"What terrible luck!" lamented Takezo loudly, both hands on his head.

All three men went quiet and stared into the distance. The priest was the first to break the silence.

"A death in the main family line is very beneficial to the branch family, that's for sure!" he said in a tone of disgust.

The engines of the *White Dragon* droned on and the ferry left behind it a foamy white trail on the surface of the sea. The emerald-green water of the Seto Inland Sea was calm and clear, but the swell of the waves suggested that a storm was approaching. Occasionally in the distance, there was the boom of something exploding.

CHAPTER 1

The Three Gorgons

Kosuke Kindaichi. Reader, if you happen to have picked up the mystery *The Honjin Murders*, you will already be familiar with him. It was back in 1937 that he solved a mysterious murder that had been committed at the home of an old Honjin-owning family in a farming village in Okayama Prefecture. At the time he was a young man of around twenty-five.

What had he been doing since then? Well—nothing. Just like every other young man in Japan, he was drafted by the army and forced to join the war. The best years of his life became a kind of void.

For the first two years, he was in China. After that he was shunted around between different islands to the south, ending up in Wewak, New Guinea.

Kosuke Kindaichi's division suffered a crushing defeat in their final battle, and took to their heels. The survivors met up with other divisions and regrouped. That was when Kosuke met Chimata Kito, four years his junior. Chimata had finished school in 1940 and immediately been posted to continental Asia. He'd followed approximately the same route as Kosuke and, like him, ended up in New Guinea.

Northern Japan-born Kosuke Kindaichi and Chimata Kito from the Seto Inland Sea got along famously. They did everything together. Chimata had caught a severe kind of malaria, which had a tendency to recur, and whenever it did, Kosuke was always by his side, tending to him.

There hadn't been a battle in New Guinea after 1943. The American army paid no heed to the little battalion that had been left there, and was making great strides elsewhere. Kosuke and Chimata's unit, ignored by the enemy, no longer had contact with their main army either. There was no hope for them, and they were left to spend gloomy days, hanging around doing nothing.

Their comrades-in-arms were struck down one by one by fever and malnutrition. On this particular front line, if someone died, no replacement came: they just become short one more man. As they fell, one after the other, the few who were left were stricken with despair. Their uniform and boots were tattered and worn; they sat around like a bunch of helpless statues.

And then the war ended.

Kosuke Kindaichi always found it strange—the total elation shown by his friend Chimata Kito.

"I'm going home alive!" he yelled with utter joy, as if some sort of heavy burden had fallen from his shoulders, or he'd been released from a dark, locked room. It was an extreme, a bizarre, kind of euphoria.

Of course, anyone would be delighted that a war was over, just as anyone would feel horror at the prospect of dying like a bug. But there was no one who seemed to fear dying the way that Chimata Kito did. Each time he suffered a bout of malaria, he would tremble at the shadow of death in the same way a small child is afraid of the dark. He was a tall, powerfully built man, generally of a strong disposition. When it came to anything else, he showed a level of bravery far above all other men, so this extreme fear of death was completely out of character. His fear was so strong it had become an obsession. It was quite eerie, Kosuke thought.

But then, Chimata Kito died after all—ironically, on board a ship headed home, not five days before he would have been able to set foot in his native land. And now here was Kosuke Kindaichi on his way to give his friend's family the news of his death.

Kosuke recalled how, shortly before setting out, he had visited the home of his benefactor, Ginzo Kubo (please refer to *The Honjin Murders*). Ginzo had offered the following advice:

"Ko-san, don't forget you are only visiting Gokumon Island to deliver news of your comrade's death. If you have any other purpose at all for your visit, if there's something else on your mind, I urge you not to go. Listen, Ko-san, Gokumon Island is a dreadful place. Why are you going somewhere like that, Kosuke?"

Ginzo knew Kosuke Kindaichi better than anyone else. He looked at his young friend's face with concern and tried to read his thoughts—

The Buddhist priest's voice abruptly cut off Kosuke's reminiscences.

"It's a case of

"Summer grass—no trace of mighty soldiers' dreams."

"Sorry? Did you say something?" Kosuke asked. He thought he had heard the priest quote a haiku.

The priest was standing at the window, looking out into the distance at the blue of the ocean.

"That noise."

"Noise?"

Just as Kosuke repeated the priest's word, he heard the sound in the distance: a boom as if something was exploding.

"Oh, that! It sounds as if they're setting off unexploded underwater mines."

"The more distant sounds are the mines," replied the priest. "The closer sounds are from that island over there. They're knocking down the military installations. As if toppling what is left of 'mighty soldiers' dreams'. Doesn't it remind you of that haiku? I'd like the great Basho to be able to see all this."

It was a very bizarre situation in which to bring up Basho. Kosuke stared in surprise at the priest, who turned from the window to look at him.

"This area isn't even the worst. If you head west—because we're close to Kure, the islands are full of big craters. They look like beehives. There was even one island that was secretly making poison gas. Now they have no idea how to deal with all the gas that's left there. On our island they built an air defence base with anti-aircraft guns. About fifty soldiers turned up and started digging up the mountain. They made holes all over the place. That's all very well, but when the war ended, they didn't make any effort to tidy up after themselves. They just upped and left. There's no way to clean it up properly. The poem goes, 'Destroy a country, but its mountains and rivers remain', but it's more like 'Destroy

23

a country and completely mangle its mountains and rivers beyond recognition'… Look—there it is."

Kosuke Kindaichi saw it then from the window of the *White Dragon*. Until the end of time he would never forget his first sight of Gokumon Island. To the west, the autumn sky was clear and bright, bathed in late-afternoon sunshine. But the gloomy sky over Gokumon Island all the way to the east hung heavy like molten lead. The island itself loomed out of the sea, just at that moment shimmering as it caught the light from the western sun.

Before the geological depression had formed what eventually would become the Seto Inland Sea, all these islands were the peaks of mountains. This meant that there was very little level ground on any of them. It was common for cliffs to rise straight up from the very shorelines, and Gokumon Island was one of the most extreme examples. Its tallest mountain peak wasn't all that high, but the overall effect was of an island springing from the ocean, its cliffs rising hundreds of feet into the air all around. And these cliffs were topped with further hills, thickly covered in red pine trees. White plaster-walled houses, glowing in the evening sun, were dotted on the hill slopes under a glowering grey sky that seemed ready to attack at any moment. Kosuke felt a cold tingle run down his spine at this ominous sight.

"See up there on that high point? That's my temple. Then just below that, the grand house with the white walls? That's the place you're on your way to visit—the Kito family home."

The priest gestured as he spoke, but right at that moment the ferry turned around the edge of a cliff, and the temple and white house were instantly blocked from view. After they passed by the rock face, a rather flat and calm bay appeared before them. Scattered here and there on the gently undulating land were the small huts of local fisherman.

From the far side of the bay, a smaller boat came towards them. This was the welcome boat from the ferry company. As I already mentioned, there was a scarcity of flat land on these islands, and really no space for a thirty-five-tonne ship to dock. Consequently, each island had a shipping company branch office, which would dispatch smaller barges to meet the ferries, and transport the passengers onto the island.

The smaller boat reached the ferry just as it dropped anchor. The captain of the barge addressed the priest.

"Welcome home, Reverend Father. Oh, you're here too, Takezo-san? Hey, Yoshimoto, take this luggage to Shimura on Shiraishi Island, will you? And say hello to Miyo-chan for me? Ha ha ha."

As soon as the three passengers were aboard, he swung the barge around. With a phut, phut sound it blew rings of steam into the air, and gently set off back towards the shore.

"Reverend Father, is this gentleman going to be staying with you?"

"Ah, no. He's the guest of the Kito family. He'll be staying on the island awhile. Let's make him welcome."

"Of course. And er... if I may ask... How did the business with the bell go?"

"The temple bell? Yes, I got permission to get it. In two or three days' time, I want to send some of the young men to go and pick it up. I hope you won't mind helping to transport it. It's such a heavy object, it's going to require quite an effort."

"With pleasure. But what a pain. They shouldn't ever have asked you to donate it in the first place."

"Hmm, can't be helped. Since we lost the war, everything's been a mess."

"So true... Well, here we are."

Just as the boat arrived at the quay, the rain clouds that had been hanging over Gokumon Island started to release a few drops on the arriving travellers.

"You're lucky," said the barge captain. "Any later and you would have been soaked to the skin."

"Truly. It looks as if we're in for a real downpour."

Right out of the harbour, the road curved steeply uphill.

"Takezo?" the priest said.

"Yes, sir?"

"If you wouldn't mind, could you run on ahead to the Kito residence and let them know that I'm bringing a guest with me."

"Yes, of course."

"Oh, and then perhaps you'd drop by the village mayor and Murase-san's places and ask them to go up to the main house? Let them know it's a request from me?"

"Got it."

Takezo set off at a trot up the hill, and the other two hurried behind him. Everyone they passed along the way bowed their heads respectfully to the priest. Then they stopped and turned to stare after Kosuke Kindaichi.

Dear reader, if you ever visited this island, in no time you would understand that the influence of priests is the most powerful thing of all. For the fishermen who only ever had an inch of plank between them and a watery grave, their faith was absolute, and it was entirely reasonable to them that the man who reigned over that faith had the power of life and death over them. On an island like this, the mayor was a lesser authority than the priest. Even the head teachers of the local primary school were hired and fired at the whim of this man.

After the two passed through the fishing village, the road grew abruptly steeper. As they followed its zigzagging course up the mountain, Kosuke caught sight of a large mansion up above. Viewed from beneath, it looked like a small castle. The granite walls of the mountain soared up like ramparts and were topped with white plaster walls and a massive *nagayamon* gateway. Beyond, the tiled roofs of several buildings were clearly visible. This was the house of the main line of the Kito family, owners of the biggest fishing fleet, and Gokumon Island's most powerful family.

As soon as Kosuke Kindaichi and the priest passed through the main gate, a man rushed up to greet them. He wore an old, faded bowler hat. The wide sleeves of his cape-like overcoat flapped as if he were some kind of bat, and his feet in their white *tabi* socks and sandals kicked up the gravel as he scurried towards them.

"Oh, Ryonen-san, Takezo's messenger just alerted me..."

"Koan-san, let's wait to talk inside, shall we?"

The man wore steel-rimmed spectacles and had a scruffy goatee. He looked as if he'd pulled on his clothes in a hurry—under his cape he wore a *haori* jacket and hakama. He was around fifty-five years old, and Kosuke Kindaichi understood from the priest's words that this was Gokumon Island's Chinese herbal medicine specialist, Doctor Koan Murase.

On the other side of the long, tunnel-like entrance gate was another impressive entranceway, this time to the main house. Hearing their approaching footsteps, a woman came running out to kneel before a large folding screen, place her hands on the ground and bow in welcome. Kosuke Kindaichi's eyes grew wide. He had never in his wildest dreams imagined that in this fisherman's home on this godforsaken island there could live a woman of such amazing beauty.

She appeared to be in her early twenties, her hair falling in abundant waves down to her shoulders. She was dressed in Western clothes—a plain brown jacket and skirt, her only adornment a simple red ribbon at the neck of her white blouse.

"Welcome!"

She looked up at her guests with the most charming pair of eyes. There were dimples in her cheeks which only added to the warmth of her smile.

"Sanae-san, I've brought you a guest," said the priest. "Are the girls at home?"

"Yes, they're inside."

"Good. All right then, Kindaichi-san, Koan-san, let's go in and wait for the mayor. He should be along soon."

Without any more ado, the priest stepped up as if it were his own house and made his way inside. The young woman looked a little dubiously at Kosuke, but then meeting his eye, she blushed and hurried to overtake the priest.

"Ryonen-san, what's this all about?" asked Koan-san. "You asked me to alert the family quickly, so I rushed here without knowing why. But please tell me who our visitor is."

"Didn't Takezo tell you?"

"No, nothing. I was just told to hurry."

"Never mind, let's just go inside and then talk," replied the priest. "Hey, Sanae-san, I just heard from Takezo that Hitoshi-san is alive and well."

"Yes, I'm pleased to say that he is."

"That's good news. At least— Oh, here's the mayor."

Makihei Araki, the village mayor, was about the same age as Koan the doctor, but whereas Koan was as tall and slender as a Japanese crane, Araki was short and stocky. He was not exactly fat; more sort of wide and flat. He also looked as if he'd pulled on his old, worn morning coat in a hurry.

"Ryonen-san, what's so urgent?"

As you'd expect of a village mayor type, his tone was confident and relaxed.

"We were waiting for you. Right, let's go on back."

The moment the mayor took off his shoes and stepped up into the house, there was a thunderclap like a tray of cups being overturned, and the rain began to fall in torrents.

"Oh my. That's a devil of a rainstorm," muttered the doctor, twisting his scrawny goatee.

The rain fell on the path they had just taken, turning the mansion garden white as if covered with icicles.

The guests were quickly shown through to a spacious room, about ten tatami mats in size.

"Sanae-san, this'll be fine. Could you go and ask the girls to come here as soon as possible? No doubt it'll take them a while to get their make-up on though, ha ha. Right then, everyone please take a seat. It's really dark in here, isn't it? Koan-san, how about turning on the light?"

With the lights on, Kosuke's eye was caught by two photographs in the *tokonoma* display alcove. Both were of young men in army uniform. One was clearly Chimata Kito, who had died with him on the ship home from New Guinea. Which meant the other one must have been his relative Hitoshi, whom the priest had just mentioned to Sanae. His features were very similar to Sanae's, and Kosuke supposed they must be brother and sister.

The priest took a seat.

"Right then..." he said, looking at the faces of the doctor and the mayor. "This is why I summoned you here today. This gentleman, Kindaichi-san, was Chimata's comrade-in-arms."

The goateed Koan-san stared at Kosuke in surprise. The mayor pursed his lips. Neither man spoke.

"And he's brought us a letter from Chimata-san."

Koan and the mayor turned their attention to the paper in the priest's hand.

"So... what's happened to Chimata-san?"

"I'm afraid he's dead. Passed away on the repatriation ship."

Koan's shoulders suddenly seemed to collapse. His goatee trembled. The mayor groaned and twisted his face into a frown. Kosuke Kindaichi would never forget this moment of strained silence between the three men in the room. There was an ominous fear that seemed to stab him to the bone. The dread welled up in their eyes.

Outside, the rain still hurtled down like a waterfall. Then they heard voices.

"Sanae-chan, where's this visitor?..."

The rather rough, vulgar female voice came from some-where close by, and was followed by the sound of a *shoji* partition door sliding open.

"What? There's nobody here."

"Look over there. They'll all be in the ten-mat room."

"Yukie-chan, who's this visitor anyway?"

"I bet it's Ukai-san."

"Don't be silly. If it was Ukai-san he wouldn't come in through the front way. He'd slip around the back to meet secretly."

"Meet who?"

"You know perfectly well he comes to see me."

"Shut up. It's me he comes to see."

"*Oneesan*, just a minute. Does my *obi* look okay?"

"Looks okay to me. The bow looks good."

"I dunno—it feels weird. Tsukiyo, fix it for me?"

"Hana-chan, I already told you it looks fine. If you waste any more time, the visitors will all have left when we get there. Hey, Yukie-chan, what are you up to? You can't go on ahead by yourself! That's sneaky!"

The general kerfuffle, racket of raucous voices and footsteps grew steadily closer, until finally there were shadows visible through the paper shoji doors. All of a sudden, the girls seemed to be in the midst of some kind of secretive conversation. The odd phrase could be heard, such as "I don't know, I've never seen him" and "He's not very good-looking". Kosuke could hear the girls giggling, and he couldn't help turning bright red in the face.

The priest gave an awkward laugh.

"Come on, girls, don't just stand there whispering to each other. Hurry up and greet our guest properly."

"Oh no, you can hear us?"

The door finally slid open, and one at a time, cackling with laughter, wearing long-sleeved kimonos in the style of young apprentice geisha, their obi belts tied high at their backs, three young women coquettishly entered the room. They knelt at the threshold and bowed their heads, causing the artificial flowers pinned in their hair to bob and sway like ghostly apparitions.

Kosuke gulped and stared, despite himself.

"Kindaichi-san," said the priest, "these are Chimata-san's younger sisters: Tsukiyo, Yukie and Hanako. All born a year apart. Eighteen, seventeen, sixteen."

They'd been given classically elegant Japanese names, named in turn for the moon, snow and flowers. But looking at these three beautiful, but somehow very oddly precocious girls, Kosuke Kindaichi felt a wave of foreboding wash over him. For the first time he realized how difficult his mission was going to be...

In the oppressive heat of that cramped and overflowing repatriation ship, Chimata Kito had lain dying like a rotting fish. At the very end, gasping for breath, he had repeated the same words over and over.

"I don't want to die. I... I... don't want to die. I have to get home. My three sisters will be murdered. But... but... I'm done for. Kindaichi-san, please... please go to Gokumon Island in my place. You know that letter of introduction I gave you?... Kindaichi-san, I didn't mention it until now, but I've known for a long time who you were... The Honjin murder case… I read about it in the newspaper… Gokumon Island… please go there. In my place. My three sisters… My cousin… my cousin—"

And with that Chimata Kito had taken his last ever breath. In the stinking, seething heat of that repatriation vessel.

DEATH OF THE PATRIARCH

"You're staying at Senkoji Temple, are you, sir?" the barber asked Kosuke. "You should be comfortable there. But I suppose it's also a little inconvenient."

"Not really. I'm used to inconvenience. And to tell the truth, I don't have anywhere else to go right now."

"Ha ha ha. Isn't that the truth? The other day I went to Osaka. The city is awful. These days a city is no place to live."

"And where are you from originally?" Kosuke said. "I can tell you weren't born on the island."

"Me? I'm something of a wanderer. I've been all over this country. I suppose the place I stayed the longest must have been Yokohama. I feel kind of a bond with the people in the east of the country. You must be from that way too, sir."

"No, I'm just like you," replied Kosuke. "A wanderer. I ended up wandering all the way to New Guinea."

"Well, that was because of the war," said the barber with a laugh. "You didn't have any choice in the matter. But you're from Tokyo originally, are you?"

"Well, before I was enlisted, I was living in Tokyo. But when I returned, I found my place completely burned to the ground, so I've decided to spend some time travelling from island to island."

"That's quite the life of leisure you're leading. Tell me, do you have any injuries or ailments? Just looking at you, you seem in good health."

"No, nothing particularly wrong with me at all. Of course, my spirit is completely burned out."

"No doubt. You've been forced to fight in a ridiculous war. Please make the most of your time at the temple. Don't worry about it. You're the guest of the top fishing boss on the island... You want me to give you a parting?"

"No, no. It's fine as it is. But if you could just take a little off the ends."

"Well, there's no accounting for taste. You've got quite a head of hair here. Do you ever manage to get a comb through these locks?"

"No, not really. But lately I've put a lot of effort into getting it this way. It broke my heart when the army shaved it all off. It didn't suit me at all. I looked like a shorn sheep."

"Ha ha. At least with all this hair you don't need to worry about catching a head cold."

The only barber on the whole of the island was this man named Seiko, who had spent some time in Yokohama, and was very proud of his Edo dialect. However, rather like Kosuke Kindaichi's own Tokyo dialect, it wasn't genuine, and seemed rather affected.

What was Kosuke Kindaichi really thinking as he peered at his reflection in the worn, old mirror with its peeling mercury coating? Well, the real reason he was there was to get all the island gossip from Seiko.

It was ten days since Kosuke Kindaichi had arrived on the island, and he'd been in an awkward situation the whole time. Because of the letter he had brought from Chimata Kito, he wasn't treated rudely by anyone, but all the same, it was obviously only surface politeness. Beneath the hospitality, it seemed that everyone was wearing a suit of armour. He understood that when an outsider ventured onto an island like this one, they would always be treated with suspicion, but with regard to himself, Kosuke felt there was an extra level of vigilance.

The news that Chimata Kito was dead had run like wildfire through the island community, and seemed to have stirred things up. Everyone seemed strangely on edge, their expressions unsettled. In the same way that experienced fishermen could smell the rainstorm coming from beyond black clouds way off on the horizon, people seemed to tremble in the shadow of some terrible fate.

Why was this? Why had the death of Chimata Kito stirred up such a panic on the island? What had put everyone on their guard? Kosuke was sure it was connected to Chimata's dying words: "Please go to Gokumon Island in my place… save my sisters… my three sisters will be murdered… my cousin… my cousin…"

The haircut finished, the barber had moved on to Kosuke's face.

"So is the Kito family rich?" Kosuke asked, his face screwed up a little against the roughness of the barber's touch. However, he was careful to keep his voice perfectly calm.

"Well, they are the boss of most of the fishermen on the island. And not just this island. They're the top fishing family among all the islands round these parts."

35

"Does a fishing boss really make so much money?" asked Kosuke.

"Buckets."

Seiko proceeded to explain to Kosuke all about it. It seemed there were three ranks of fishermen. The lowest were the ones who didn't own their own boat or net. They had nothing at all to their name. These folks were the equivalent of poor tenant farmers in the agricultural world. This class of fishermen were the most common. Next level up were the men who owned a boat and net, but both very small-scale: just a small trawl net that two or three people could throw, and a boat that was smaller than a trawler. This group were the equivalent of landed farmers. Finally, above these two groups and in control of all the rest, were the fishing chiefs—like the big landowners of the agricultural world. But these men were much more than just landowners.

"I used to live in a farming community. The landowners were a pretty shady lot in general. The difference between landowners and tenant farmers differs from place to place. But in most villages the rice crop gets divided forty/sixty: forty to the landowner and sixty to the farmers. In other words, the landowner just siphons off a forty per cent share of everything for himself, without lifting a finger. Anyway, often tenant farmers grow their own secret off-season crop, and keep all the profit from that for themselves, which helps a lot. But nothing's that easy in a fishing community—no hiding anything from the big boss."

It seemed the fishing bosses owned boats, nets and fishing rights. And this permitted them to do nothing at all.

They just took the whole of everyone's catch. And then paid the fishermen a daily wage.

"I see," said Kosuke. "It's just like the relationship in the city between capitalists and labourers."

"Yes, well, I suppose… When there's a big catch the men get a bonus. Even when the catch is poor, they still get paid the fixed wage. But whichever happens, the whole catch goes straight to the boss. For the fishermen to be able to work they have to have the boss's boats and nets. They're really grateful for that. Talking of nets… There are so many kinds. Some for catching sea bream, the kind that go around lobster pots, sardine nets… Those sardine nets—round here you don't catch sardines like you find up in the Kanto region, they're these tiny things called *iriko*—anyway, all of those kinds of large-scale nets are owned by the boss. And then they need two or three large-scale fishing boats. So the start-up cost is pretty high.

"And all the time there is that sense hanging over them that there's no more than an inch of plank between them and a watery grave—it's their favourite saying—so fishermen always live in the moment. They drink, gamble and buy women, all at the speed of light, and ask for advances in their wages from the boss to do it. That's the relationship between a fishing chief and the men in a fishing village. The bonds of feudalism are even stronger than between landowners and tenant farmers in a farming village.

"This means that the fishing chief has to work extremely hard. The people he's dealing with aren't your regular country folk. They're rough fishing folk. He has to look after their interests but at the same time it's taboo to spoil or pamper them. Anyway, the most important thing is to maintain authority over them. Kaemon Kito, who passed away last year, was an expert at all that."

The conversation had finally moved on to the Kito family, and Kosuke had begun to get nervous, but he betrayed none of it in his words.

"This Kaemon-san, was he Chimata's father?" he asked casually.

"No, his grandfather. He died last year at the age of seventy-eight, but he was extremely healthy before then. He was a little fellow, but full of spirit. He showed no sign of illness at all, but I think it was the shock of losing the war that did him in. Died very suddenly."

"So he passed away after the war had ended? And what happened to Chimata's parents?"

That was the matter that intrigued Kosuke the most. On his first day he'd met the three sisters, Tsukiyo, Yukie and Hanako, along with the young woman, Sanae, and then later a woman of around fifty with a tired-looking face had turned up at dinner. He'd found it strange that there didn't seem to be any other male presence at all in this grand estate. As he showed Kosuke to his room at Senkoji Temple, the priest had said to him: "You could stay back there at the house, but the household's all women."

"It seems that Chimata's mother died right after giving birth to him," Seiko the barber explained. "His father took a new wife, but she also died quite a while back."

"So, those three girls are his half-sisters?"

"Yes, that's right."

"And what about Chimata's father?"

"Yosamatsu? Yes, well, he's still alive. Alive, but severely ill. He can't appear in public."

"Ill? What is wrong with him?"

"What exactly— Well, I don't want to say this very loudly but, well... he's gone mad."

Kosuke's eyes opened wide in surprise.

"He's mad? Is he in some kind of facility?"

"No. He's not hospitalized. He's there in that house. They've locked him up in a kind of caged cell they made specially for him. It's been a long time now. I dare say ten years. I can't even properly recall his face any more."

Hearing that suddenly brought back a memory for Kosuke. When he'd been a guest in that Kito sitting room, he had heard a weird noise. It had been just like the howl given by some kind of beast: wild and frantic. It had given him quite a scare.

"So does this madness make him act violently?"

"No, he's usually very quiet. He does have a tendency to be a bit of a handful sometimes. Incidentally, it's a strange thing, but you know there's a young woman there by the name of Sanae? She's the niece of the lunatic. Anyway, she just has to say one or two words to him and he calms down completely. On the other hand, if any of those three daughters of his go anywhere near him, he goes completely wild. It's terrible."

"Hmm... that's odd."

"It's not really all that odd. Those three girls... well, I'd say they're even odder. They treat their own father as if he was some sort of tiger or lion in a zoo. They play with him as if he's a toy, an object for their amusement. When he's sleeping, they get a ruler and poke him through the bars of his cell, they throw paper pellets at him, and then they all screech with laughter. It just makes you shudder to hear the stories. They're the most peculiar girls."

Kosuke Kindaichi had already observed for himself how peculiar the three sisters were. They'd been more concerned with their hairstyles and the way their obis were tied than by their own brother's death. During the priest's solemn speech, they were giggling together, tugging at each other's kimono sleeves, nudging each other with their elbows. This behaviour appeared all the more inappropriate and abnormal coming as it did from three young women as outwardly beautiful as they were. Watching it had turned his stomach.

What awful women, Kosuke thought. They were like the three monsters of Greek myth known as gorgons: beautiful young girls whose beauty had competed with that of Minerva so she had turned their hair to snakes, and given them the wings and sharp claws of an eagle.

"By the way, the woman called Sanae, you said she's a cousin of Chimata's?" Kosuke asked.

"Yes, that's right. There's Sanae and her older brother, Hitoshi. He was sent to Burma, but luckily they've had news that he's coming home unharmed."

"Yes, I heard the same thing. One of his comrades came to give the news. So do Hitoshi and Sanae have parents living?"

"Sanae-san's parents?…"

The barber's tone changed. He now spoke with what almost seemed a parody of someone passing on gossip.

"Sanae-san's parents died a long time ago. I've been here for twelve or thirteen years now, and both Hitoshi-san and

Sanae-san were already being cared for by the head family. They say their father was drowned at sea."

"So that household currently consists of a patriarch who has gone mad, his three daughters, Sanae… and then there's another woman, about fifty. Who's she?"

"Oh, that's Okatsu. She was the tea-drinking buddy of Kaemon-san until he passed away last year. Well, to be honest, she was his mistress. Now her looks have faded, but back when I came to the island, she was quite the refined lady, in her mid-thirties."

"I see. And so, the occupants of that house are the mad head of the family, the three sisters, Sanae and Okatsu. And Okatsu-san is taking care of everyone?"

"Ha! That woman? She's not the sort to take care of anyone. She's always kind and pleasant, but that's of no use to anyone. The old family patriarch was careful about who he chose to have an affair with. If you take a mistress with a strong character, there are going to be all kinds of quarrels and clashes. Kaemon-san was canny like that."

"I see. In that case, who on earth is managing that huge house and the family business?"

"Sanae-san is."

"Sanae-san? But she's still only—"

"I know. Everyone admires her. She's an impressive young woman. She can't be much more than twenty-two—twenty-three perhaps—but she's so mature for her years. She's tough enough to deal with those rough fishermen. But she's also got the support of Takezo, the *shiotsukuri*."

"Oh yes. Takezo-san was on the ferry with me coming over here. What does a shiotsukuri do?"

Seiko the barber explained that the job of a shiotsukuri, or tide master, was to watch and calculate the tide. In the military world it would be the equivalent of the commander of a regiment.

"The movement of the whole fishing fleet depends on the directions of the tide master. If he doesn't know his stuff, then they can't even cast the nets. It's a difficult job; there's some kind of secret formula for getting it right. A fishing boss's whole reputation can rest on whether he has a good tide master or not. He's the most important person to the boss. Takezo-san is the best in these parts. He has always worked for the head Kito family, and that has left the branch family unable to get a proper toehold in the business."

"There's a branch family?"

"Right. The main Kito line and the branch line—they're the two fishing bosses on this island. Formerly there was also the house of Tomoeya, but about four or five years ago the Tomoeya chief went bankrupt. The head Kito house and branch Kito house used to be closely related, but over the years they fell out with each other, and because of this, Kaemon-san was troubled to his final days."

"I see," said Kosuke.

"On top of that, that all-important son and heir to the family name is a lunatic, and both of his beloved grandsons had gone off to war. He didn't know if he would ever see them alive again. So there we had the great man, on his deathbed, and he was unable to die in peace—still filled with a bitterness which he could never rid himself of."

"Ha ha, you're very well informed."

"Hm. And so anyway this master of the branch family—his name is Gihei-san. He's married to Oshiho-san."

"Oh, that Oshiho-san!"

"Have you met her?"

"Yes, the morning after I arrived on the island, she came to pray at Senkoji Temple."

"Yes, that's her all right. Not the devout type though. She must have heard rumours about Chimata-san's death and come to find you to check if it was true."

"Now that you mention it, she did ask me a lot of rather prying questions about Chimata's dying words. But she is a relative of his after all. And I have to say, I couldn't help noticing how beautiful she is."

"She certainly is. She's the daughter of the ex-fishing boss we were talking about just now. Tomoeya's daughter. Rumour has it Chimata-san was madly in love with her, planned to make her his wife. Although there's another theory that has Hitoshi-san in love with her too, but it doesn't matter which of them is true. There was no way that Kaemon-san was going to allow either of his grandsons to marry a woman from a bankrupt family like that. As soon as she realized there was no hope, she quickly turned to the main family's mortal enemies—the Kito branch family. Gihei-san, the head of the branch family, is sixty-something this year, and Oshiho-san is only twenty-seven, or -eight maybe. Leastways, she's not thirty yet. Goes without saying she's his second wife. Gihei-san didn't have any children with his first wife, so he had adopted his first wife's nephew to be his heir. But last year Oshiho-san had a baby, and she kicked the adopted son out of the house. Oh, face of an angel, heart of a devil that one! And her husband is totally bewitched by that face of hers."

"I get it. I get it. Er, could you go a little more lightly please? You're scraping a little hard."

"Really? Does that hurt?"

"Not that much, but could you lather up the soap a bit more? By the way, who is Ukai-san?"

"Ukai-san?"

The barber suddenly stopped shaving and stared at Kosuke.

"You seem to be well informed yourself, sir."

"No, no. Not at all."

Kosuke was panicking a little inside, but the barber didn't seem particularly suspicious.

"That man, Ukai, he's another real piece of work— Oh, welcome!"

At the abrupt change in tone, Kosuke opened his eyes. Someone was standing in the shop doorway.

"I'll soon be finished!" continued the barber. "I don't have any reservations after this customer, so come in and have a smoke while you're waiting."

Then very deliberately he added:

"It's really been a while since I saw you, Ukai-san. Have you not been well? You're looking a bit pale. Has the mistress of the branch family been paying you a little too much attention? Ha ha ha. I'm just joking…"

Kosuke sat up too quickly and through the mirror his eyes met those of the young man standing behind him.

Shozo Ukai. He soon learned his full name, but for now, the face he saw was the perfect image of one of those beautiful young boys so popular in romantic novels.

THE APPROACHING FOOTSTEPS

As he trudged up the steadily steepening road, the view of the sea below gradually expanded before his eyes. Now that October was here, Kosuke Kindaichi felt that the sea was a different colour. There hadn't been any typhoons that year, and the rainfall had been relatively light. The sea seemed clearer and more transparent than ever, the colour of liquid indigo, like a print by the famous *ukiyo-e* artist Hiroshige. The tide drew serpentine stripes across the water, among which the Seto Islands were arranged like *go* stones on a board.

When Kosuke was a student, he'd read Ogai Mori's translation of Hans Christian Andersen's *The Improvisatore*, and he'd been spellbound by the descriptions of the Italian sea. Lately, surrounded constantly by the Seto Inland Sea, he couldn't help thinking the view was even more beautiful than the ones described in Mori's writing. Only here there was no woman like Annunziata. And a handsome youth like Antonio?…

Kosuke was suddenly reminded of the young man he'd just seen reflected in the peeling mirror, like some kind of apparition, his beauty almost too perfect.

Ukai had his hair cropped short. His perfect hairline was a frame for his smooth, white, boyish complexion. His fair skin had a sheen to it like glossy silk. His pupils were almost transparent black, and deep within them there was a sense of something untrustworthy. Meeting their gaze in the mirror, Kosuke had also glimpsed in those eyes something vulnerable. It was the kind of look that appealed to a woman's protective instincts.

Kosuke sighed, then resumed his sluggish trudge up the hill, deep in thought. He couldn't get the image of the youth out of his mind. He had been wearing a matching striped-cloth haori overcoat and kimono, his purple tie-dyed obi loosely wrapped around his middle. The style was that of a *kabuki* actor, but without the frivolous edge. Perhaps it was because the youth in question was actually a little ashamed of his appearance: his serious gaze held neither malice nor contempt, but when he saw Kosuke watching him, he had turned not just red, but the deep crimson of extreme embarrassment. Which is why Kosuke had concluded that the youth didn't really enjoy looking like a kabuki actor. And so, if it wasn't Ukai himself who had chosen to dress that way... Kosuke recalled the last thing Seiko the barber had said about the mistress of the branch family. Yes, that kind of made sense now...

There have been too many surprises since I came to this island, Kosuke thought. He began to count them on his fingers. First of all, there's Sanae-san; then, the three Gorgon sisters. Next, there was Oshiho-san, who came up to visit the temple—she had the attractiveness of a mature woman. Kosuke was up to three fingers. The fourth was that handsome youth he'd met today. He couldn't help wondering what surprise was awaiting the final finger of his left hand. And just as he was thinking this, Chimata's dying words echoed in his mind, sending a shiver down the length of his spine.

"The island... go to Gokumon Island... my sisters will be murdered... my cousin... my cousin..."

That suffocating repatriation ship, the unbearable heat

46

and stench. Chimata's emaciated face, the anguish, the delirium, the weight of that final appeal…

Kosuke shuddered as if to shake off bad dreams. In the bay below him, the ferry was chugging in. It was the same *White Dragon* that he had arrived on. Three or four small boats began to make their way from the bay towards the ship, and reached it in no time. There were some loud vocal exchanges between someone on the ferry and the occupants of the barges, but not clear enough for Kosuke to make out any words. Then something big and heavy was lifted off the ferry. Kosuke immediately recognized the cargo.

It was a large bell.

"The temple bell has finally come home," he said to himself.

He looked along the quayside, but the figure of the priest was nowhere to be seen. He turned and set off again on his slow slog up the hill. To tell the truth, he was on the wrong road. If he intended to return directly to the temple, he should have turned left out of the barber's shop. But he'd taken a right, and was now headed up to the branch Kito house.

The head Kito house and that of the branch family sat facing one another across a deep valley. The two separate roads leading up from the village circled the valley, rising and falling on their way past the houses until eventually they converged high on the far side. At that point there was a winding path that led directly uphill and ended at the foot of the steep stone steps leading up to Senkoji Temple.

Was Oshiho-san home today? Kosuke wondered as he approached the branch family house. He purposely slowed his pace as he passed in front of it, but that ploy didn't work out for him. However, he was able to peer into the grounds of the residence.

The granite base, the panelling on the white-plastered walls, the nagayamon gateway were all identical to those of the main family house, but it was clear that everything was on a much smaller scale. The roofs visible over the wall featured a family crest, but nothing as grand as at the head Kito house. And there were fewer storehouses and other buildings.

Passing by the branch house, the road swung sharply to the right. A little further along it curved back to the left, but right at this bend the land formed a protruding plateau. From here you could get a great view over the sea. The islanders had named this spot "Tengu's Nose", after the long-nosed creature of Japanese mythology. Right now, there was a solitary policeman standing on the plateau, looking out through a pair of binoculars over the sea.

Hearing Kosuke approach, he turned, the binoculars still up to his eyes. A smile broke out on his unshaven face.

The island just had a police substation, manned by a single police officer. He was in charge of matters on both land and sea. He had a motorboat, from which he observed the fishing waters, watched over the fishing season, checked fishing permits and the like. In this region, the island police were much busier with maritime affairs than with anything on the land. Gokumon Island's police officer was Sergeant Shimizu. Around forty-five years of age, he was too laid back to bother staying clean-shaven, a good-natured type. He and Kosuke Kindaichi were already the best of pals.

"Something going on at sea?" Kosuke asked.

A set of white teeth appeared from within the stubble.

"Yes, there've been pirates sighted in the vicinity. I got a phone call to keep my eyes peeled."

"Pirates?"

Kosuke was amazed. Then he laughed. While he'd been staying with his benefactor, Ginzo Kubo, he'd read in the newspaper about pirates turning up in the Seto Inland Sea.

"Well, well. The times seem to be regressing somewhat," noted Kosuke.

"History repeats itself. Ha ha. But this lot are a much grander operation than previous generations. More than a dozen in each band, and all armed with pistols—doubtless soldiers back from the war."

"Ouch, that hits home a bit. You know I'm one of those too, don't you?"

Apparently, Sergeant Shimizu had decided to forget about the pirates for now. He sat on the ground and pulled some hand-rolled cigarettes out of his pocket. He offered the pack to Kosuke.

"Hey, do you want one?"

"No thanks. I've got my own... Well, if you're sure? All right then, just one."

Kosuke and Shimizu sat down on Tengu's Nose.

"You out for a stroll? No, it looks like you've just been for a haircut. Was it crowded? If it's not too bad I might drop in myself."

"Go for it. There was just Ukai-san there. I'm sure he must be just about done by now."

49

"Ukai!" Shimizu looked at Kosuke in surprise. "You acquainted with that character, are you?"

"No, I just met him for the first time. It was just that the barber called him Ukai, so I thought that was his name."

Shimizu sat there silently smoking his cigarette. Perhaps the grimace on his face was from the smoke getting in his eye.

"Yeah, he really is beautiful that one," Kosuke continued. "That's one good-looking boy…"

Shimizu's grimace grew more severe with every word that Kosuke spoke.

"Is he from the island?" asked Kosuke.

Shimizu finished his cigarette, carefully crushed the stub under his boot, and then turned back to Kosuke.

"Kindaichi-san, I have a weird hunch," he said. "I'm afraid you're going to laugh when I tell you, but it's a kind of feeling in my bones. I think something's going to happen, here on Gokumon Island. Something very terrible. I can't help feeling it. For example, take that Ukai. You just called him a beautiful boy. It's undeniable that he's beautiful, but is he technically a boy? He must be twenty-three or -four by now. Of course, he's not from this island. I heard he's from Tajima and that his father's a primary school headmaster, but I don't know whether that's true. What is more interesting is the reason why someone from Tajima came here to Gokumon Island. It was for the war. The war brought him here."

Shimizu turned to indicate the mountain that towered behind Senkoji Temple.

"Have you climbed that mountain yet? If you haven't, you should give it a try once. Long ago, on the summit of

50

that peak there used to be a pirate fortress. They had a lookout post up there. Bits of it are still there. Anyway, in a repeat of history, during the war it was used again as a lookout point and a fortress. For aircraft surveillance and anti-aircraft guns. They filled the mountain with holes and a whole swarm of soldiers turned up. Shozo Ukai was one of those soldiers."

Kosuke Kindaichi was instantly curious. He looked at Shimizu as if urging him to continue. The police officer cleared his throat.

"That's right. Even a youth like that was a soldier. But with that small frame, that puny body, they could hardly send him to the front line. Even dressed in khakis that's a pretty pathetic-looking soldier... Anyway, those troops up at the lookout were always coming down the mountain to the village to commandeer all kinds of stuff. And because it was soldiers asking, the villagers did their best to accommodate them. They used to ask for all kinds of outrageous things. At first it was all right, but in the closing stages of the war, the soldiers got more and more shameless with their demands. I suppose the feeling of despair at how badly the war was going probably had a lot to do with it. It became less like requisition and more like looting. And the villagers decided not to put up with it any more. They're rough fisherfolk, and some of them were furious. Anyway, the soldiers up the mountain caught wind of this change in mood, and decided to switch tactics. Whenever they wanted something from the village, they'd send that Shozo Ukai to get it."

"Of course!"

Cheerfully, Kosuke began to scratch his head. Instantly, the hair that the barber had so carefully flattened returned to its familiar bird's-nest form.

"So what you're saying is that he's a charmer, a seducer? Someone who tried to curry favour with all the women?"

"Exactly. Exactly. And by the way, the main targets of the army's requisitioning of goods were the two Kito house-holds. Or at least it was those two places that Shozo Ukai used to be in and out of all the time. Back then, Kaemon, the head of the main Kito house, was still living. He was a tough character, so even if he was up against a soldier, he wouldn't give in to unreasonable demands. He used to refuse point-blank. And then behind his back Ukai would cosy up to those three sisters."

"I see," said Kosuke. "The commanding officer's tactics were successful then."

"Absolutely they were. After a while, the girls couldn't wait for Ukai's next visit, and used to go looking for him on the mountain. The rumours were rife in the village that all three of the sisters had—how can I say—relations with Ukai. Some said that there were strict rules about that sort of thing in the army and such a crazy thing couldn't have happened, but others said that Ukai's commanding officer actually ordered him to do such inexcusable things to those three girls. I have no idea of the truth of the matter. However, what is beyond a doubt is that, in the closing days of the war, the three girls took not only goods and materials, but also quite a sum of money from the house and carried it all up that mountain. They also say that when the commanding officer was suddenly demobilized, he disappeared with everything in his possession, but that could well be a lie."

"What you're saying is that Ukai-san was used as an instrument by his superiors... But wasn't he also demobilized?"

"Of course he was demobilized. He went home to Tajima. It was a huge relief to Kaemon-san, I can tell you. But not a month later he was back again. It seems at home there was a stepmother whom he couldn't bear, and he returned to stay at the branch family house. It was soon afterwards that Kaemon-san suffered a stroke."

Shimizu broke off there. Kosuke waited, looking down over the sea below. A heavy feeling was weighing on his chest. He felt too weary to speak. Shimizu took up the story again.

"The late Kaemon-san was just like the great Daimyo Hideyoshi Toyotomi. There wasn't a single inhabitant of the island who dared to defy him. That is, except Oshiho-san of the branch family... It seems to be true that Ukai had a stepmother. That she bullied him, making it impossible to live there—well, that might be true too. But even if it was, there is absolutely no reason for him to come here and ask the branch family for help. Also, I don't really believe that the youth is quite as shameless as all that. I believe that long before he was demobilized, he must have come to some kind of agreement with Oshiho. Either that, or she sent him a letter summoning him back here. Whichever is the case, there's no question that the whole thing is Oshiho's scheme. The way he's all dressed up like some kabuki actor, and how he just spends his time idly wandering around, it all makes me suspicious about Oshiho's motives. She's just like the commanding officer here before—using Ukai for her own machinations. She has him manipulate Tsukiyo, Yukie and Hanako—the three sisters—in order to throw the head Kito house into disarray. That's what that woman is up to. Kaemon-san knew it. He knew it, but he couldn't complain about her behaviour. He may have been the great lord around here, but he couldn't forbid someone to take in and care for another person. And he couldn't just issue a command and expect someone like Oshiho to listen. You know when it came to the invasion of Korea, even the great Toyotomi Hideyoshi himself realized the impossibility of succeeding; similarly, Kaemon-san knew that some things could not be influenced, and that included the mind of Oshiho-san. This was the cause of the stroke he suffered. He suffered as many hardships as the Shura Buddha."

Evening shadows were falling on the sea. The wind too had turned chilly. But it wasn't the brisk evening breeze that was causing Shimizu and Kosuke to shiver as they did.

The true nature of those unearthly black clouds that seemed always to engulf Gokumon Island—Kosuke Kindaichi was gradually beginning to understand. Just in the way someone suffering a nervous breakdown hears a constant ringing in their ears, he had begun to hear the sound of approaching footsteps reverberating in his head; a sound that was ominous, like the waves crashing against the rocks, like the rumble of distant thunder...

He and Sergeant Shimizu parted ways, and Kosuke headed back to the temple. In the ten-tatami mat room, Ryonen the priest, Mayor Araki and Doctor Koan Murase were sitting in a triangle. There was a heavy silence in the room. Hearing Kosuke approach, the priest addressed him in a rather dejected voice.

"Ah, Kindaichi-san, the official communiqué arrived."

He nodded at the mayor, who continued.

"We didn't doubt your word, but until we got the official notice, we were still clinging to a sliver of hope…"

"But this has put everything beyond a doubt," added Koan, his goatee trembling. "Even though public mourning is banned, we'd better hold the funeral as soon as possible."

Kosuke's ears echoed once again with those ominous approaching footsteps.

THE ELEGANT BEAUTY

Senkoji Temple was halfway up the mountain—well, more like about three-quarters. The east part of the island was all mountain, which rose steeply up behind the temple to the peak of Mount Suribachi, Gokumon Island's highest point. In other words, the temple was on the west slope of the mountain. If you stood within its premises, you had a practically perfect bird's-eye view of the flatter land with its village below, meaning the village was entirely on the island's west side too.

This solitary island had always needed to be on its guard against pirate attacks. In fact, whichever island in these parts you visited, you would find the same thing: they were all designed to be able to mount a defence instantly. The homes were packed together in one area, back to back. Gokumon Island was no exception.

If you stood at the top of the stone steps of Senkoji Temple, the first thing that would catch your eye was the head Kito residence to your right. Viewed from above, this property was a maze of roof tiles. The tiling ran in waves, making the interior of the grounds a complex, seemingly illogical pattern of construction. And yet, it was still a massive, substantial structure.

"That's because the late Kaemon-san was really into building," the priest, Ryonen, had explained to Kosuke. "He kept having more and more added on until it became as complicated and intricate an estate as it is now."

The priest pointed out each structure as he spoke.

"That is the main building; that's the annex house. Over there's the wife's quarters, and those are the storehouses. That one's for fish, that other one for nets…"

All of the buildings seemed to overlap, piled up in layers along the line of the slope down towards the valley.

"Over on the left at the back, up on the highest point, the little building with the shingled roof… What's that?" Kosuke asked.

"Ah, that's— Well, that's the prayer house."

"What exactly is a prayer—?"

"A prayer house is a prayer house. We'll talk about it some other time."

Kosuke turned and scrutinized the priest's face. This man, who could normally talk of anything with ease, had seemed to lose his nerve all of a sudden.

This prayer house was set slightly away from the rest of the buildings, on high ground under the cover of a massive pine tree. From the darkening of the shingles on the roof, it appeared to be a very old building. It was probably a small shrine housing the guardian god of the residence, Kosuke decided.

And then to the left, across the main valley and itself backing onto a further valley, was the Kito branch family residence. Even viewed from above, it was clearly inferior to the head family's. It wasn't just that the house itself was less substantial-looking. With its lack of outbuildings, it didn't hold a candle to the other compound. These two estates, standing across from each other on opposing sides of the valley, suggested very clearly that they were also opposed to each other in spirit. One time the priest had pointed them out and said,

"Back-to-back with Lord Kiso—so cold."

He had the habit of suddenly coming out with the most unexpected haiku at the oddest of times.

As I have mentioned before, the separate roads running uphill by the Kito residences eventually converged at the far side of the valley. From there, a single path would once again twist and wind its way up the mountain towards Senkoji Temple. After several of these bends and curves, you came to a tiny shrine. If you peeped in through the latticed door, there was a small wooden-floored space the equivalent of two tatami mats in size. At the far end was a plain wooden platform upon which there was an odd-looking figure something like a *karako* doll—a boy doll dressed in Chinese-style clothing. According to the wooden

57

sign hanging above the lattice, this was a *jigamisama*, or a god of the harvest.

Gokumon Island also had a farming population. They didn't grow rice, but cultivated several types of potato and other vegetables. None of the fishermen would ever pick up a hoe, but many of the womenfolk would work in the field. That was why it was necessary to honour the local harvest god.

After passing by the little shrine, and continuing for several more bends, the path eventually straightened out. Ahead in the distance were the steps of Senkoji Temple. At their foot was the usual engraved marker stone warning people not to bring strong-smelling food or alcohol into the temple grounds: *No garlic or wine permitted on the premises.*

There were about fifty steps in total, then at the top, carved into the mountainside, stood Senkoji Temple. If you entered through the main temple gate, the grounds were surprisingly expansive. First of all, to the right, the south side, were the priests' quarters. Hanging in the entranceway was a type of metal gong for visitors to strike to announce their presence. To the left of the priests' quarters—or, in other words, straight ahead from the entrance gate—was the main temple building, whose left, the north side, connected to a long, narrow Zen meditation hall. Senkoji belonged to the Soto school of Zen Buddhism, and since the olden days, some of the most famous itinerant monks had come here to practise Zazen. But recent hard times had meant no one was undertaking these journeys any more, and the meditation hall had fallen into disuse.

In front of the raised passageway that connected the meditation hall with the main temple building stood a magnificent old flowering plum tree. This tree was the pride of Senkoji, reaching well above the roof of the passageway, and its south-facing branches were as high as thirty feet. Its trunk was almost too thick to wrap one's arms around. There was a low fence around it, and a sign next to the base of the trunk with faded lettering, blurred and apparently washed away by rain. Kosuke couldn't make out a single character.

At this time there were three men living in the temple grounds. One of them was Kosuke Kindaichi himself; the other two were the priest, Ryonen, and a young *tenzo*, or apprentice priest, by the name of Ryotaku. The apprentice was apparently the person in charge of the kitchen. In a large temple there would also be a *shika* and a *chiyoku*, and people with all sorts of jobs with complicated-sounding titles. But at a temple like Senkoji, the apprentice also took care of the bathhouse and looked after any visitors.

Ryotaku, the apprentice, was a skinny youth of about twenty-five, with deeply tanned skin, who was almost disturbingly quiet. His deep-set eyes seemed to glare out of his bronzed face, so that Kosuke spent the early part of his stay feeling somewhat intimidated by the young man. He feared that the young apprentice was hostile to his presence at the temple. However, this turned out to be his own misinterpretation. As the days passed, he gradually recognized that this was a kind and attentive young man. His taciturnity wasn't born of any kind of hostility, but rather his natural bashfulness. The way that Ryotaku served the priest, Ryonen, was like a son's relationship with an affectionate father.

Ryonen planned to hand over the temple to Ryotaku one day. He had applied to the head temple in Tsurumi for permission to do so, and it seemed it had been granted. There was soon to be an official ceremony. In the Soto school of Zen Buddhism, the lineage was passed on to the next generation while the old priest was still living. The temple was passed on to a disciple. Incidentally, the current priest, Ryonen, was the eighty-first generation of head priests of this temple, which meant that Ryotaku would become the eighty-second.

"Really, with my shallow knowledge of Buddhist teachings, I don't deserve to receive the gift of a temple," the young man would lament bitterly. "I don't know why the Reverend Father is so anxious to pass it to me while he's still in such good health."

"Kindaichi-san! Kindaichi-san!"

Ryotaku the apprentice was calling from the priests' quarters.

"Oh, are you ready?"

Kosuke got sluggishly to his feet, and left the study. When he got to the priest's chamber, he found Ryotaku already dressed in his monk's surplice over his scarlet robes, thoroughly prepared for the wake they were about to preside over, although Ryonen-san, still only in his white robe, was fastening the hooks on his tabi socks.

"Kindaichi-san, I wonder if you could possibly run a quick errand for me?" said the priest.

"Of course. I'm happy to go wherever you want."

"I need you to take a message to the branch family. I really don't want relations between the families to get any worse… I've heard that Gihei-san has taken to his bed with the gout, but Oshiho-san will do just as well. Could you ask her to attend tonight's wake for Chimata-san?"

"Got it. No problem at all."

"And then you could go straight from there to the head Kito family house. Ryotaku and I will be setting out for it shortly. Hey, Ryotaku, could you go get Kindaichi-san one of the paper lanterns?"

"Don't worry. I don't need a lantern," said Kosuke. "It's not even 6.30 p.m. yet. It's still light outside."

"No, by the time you've been over to the branch house and head back to the main house, it'll be dark. The mountain roads are treacherous at night."

"Oh, in that case I'll take a lantern."

It had been years since Kosuke had walked with an old-fashioned lantern hanging from a stick, and to be honest he found it a little ridiculous, but because the priest was so concerned for his safety, he felt he couldn't decline. He set out from the temple carrying the lantern, and as the priest had warned him, twilight soon began to close in.

The date was 5th October, and it had been three days since the Kito household had received the official communiqué informing them of Chimata's death. The formal funeral was going to be held the next day and tonight would be the funeral wake. The whole thing had been arranged by the priest, Mayor Makihei Araki and Doctor Koan Murase. For his part, Kosuke Kindaichi had finally understood why the letter he'd carried from Chimata Kito had been addressed to those three men. They were the three elders of the island, and from the point of view of the head Kito household, they were its three administrators. Since the death of the patri-arch, Kaemon, these three had worked together to manage the affairs of the household.

Kosuke had just descended the temple steps and made his way about halfway down the winding path when he ran into a man on his way up.

"Ah, you're the guest up at the temple. Have you seen the priest?" asked the man.

He was around forty-five years old, short, but with a body that looked as if it had been reinforced with steel. He was wearing a cotton kimono decorated with a family crest, but no hakama beneath it. Kosuke felt he had seen the man somewhere before, but in the moment, he couldn't recall where. From his appearance, he guessed the man must be from the head Kito house, sent to meet the guests.

"Are you here to accompany us? Thank you. The priest is getting things ready right now. He'll be right along."

"And what about you?"

"I'm heading to the other Kito-san's place."

"The branch family?" The man looked puzzled. "What business do you have with them?"

"The priest asked me to inform them about tonight's wake."

"Ryonen-san asked you?"

For a moment, the man looked even more dubious, but then he appeared to change his mind.

"Thank you for doing that. Well then, we'll see you in a little while."

And with that, the man turned on his heel and headed briskly up the hill. Watching him leave, Kosuke finally recalled where he'd seen him before. He was the man he'd met on the ferry on the way to Gokumon Island: the man the barber had said was the best tide master in these parts—Takezo.

Oh, it was him! If so, Kosuke thought, he really should have greeted him properly. It was just that he looked so different from before—practically unrecognizable in the failing light.

Kosuke reached the bottom of the winding path and turned left. His heart was beginning to race. It was about two weeks since landing on the island, and he had been visiting the head Kito family residence fairly often, but today would be the first time for him to set foot in the branch family home.

Sergeant Shimizu, the island's police officer, had only just yesterday issued these words of warning:

"When you come to an island like this one, you must be very careful about talking with the fishermen. Every fishing village is the same. If there are two fishing chiefs, then there will be two different factions; three bosses and there are three factions. They clash swords with each other. But on this island it's worse than usual. The fishing chiefs are sworn enemies, and accordingly, the feuding between the fisherfolk themselves is particularly bad. Whichever side you favour, you'll just get mixed up in their quarrels. I never touch any of that, never get involved, keep complete neutrality."

After a short pause, he had continued:

"Now that Chimata-san of the head family is dead, the mayor and Doctor Koan are seriously worried. If anything were now to happen to Chimata's cousin, Hitoshi-san, then everything would go to the branch family. And then Gihei-san and Oshiho-san would get their revenge. The doctor and the mayor were always under the control of Kaemon-san. But now, Gihei-san has been manoeuvring to get the village mayor dismissed. He's managed to win over the deputy mayor, and there's talk of him luring a fully certified medical doctor over from the mainland. It seems that with the repatriation of all those doctors who went to war, there's a surplus of good doctors in the cities lately."

Kosuke asked about the priest's situation. The sergeant's tone grew more confident.

"He's safe," replied Shimizu rather vehemently. "The priest is safe. His rank is higher than a fishing chief. It doesn't matter how many chiefs there are or how much they fight, the priest who leads the faith of the islanders will always be more important, and more powerful than a fishing boss. He's friends with the mayor and the doctor, but his faith will always win. Ryonen is the almighty power here on the island. But the other two men... well, if they don't manage to get into Gihei and Oshiho's good books, then things aren't going to go well for them."

Right at that moment Kosuke was heading towards this very residence, and it felt somewhat like setting foot in enemy territory. Or was it?... Surely they wouldn't have anything against him. After all, he had no particular connection to either of the Kito family households. And yet, he began to think again about Chimata's dying words... At which point there was a sound like the roar of the sea, like the growl of distant thunder, like wind ripping through the upper branches of a pine tree—a rumbling noise that resounded in his ears.

"Huh? T'master's havin' a lie-down. And who might you be?"

"I'm currently staying at Senkoji Temple. My name's Kosuke Kindaichi. I was asked to deliver a message from the priest."

"I see. Would you mind waitin' a moment? I'll let t' lady of t' house know you're here."

It was rather strange. Kosuke was reminded of the day he arrived on Gokumon Island. At the entranceway to the head Kito residence when Sanae had knelt and bowed to Kosuke, he had been rather taken aback. However, surprised as he'd been, the politeness of the greeting had been perfectly in keeping with Sanae's character. On the contrary, the young woman greeting him now was far from the type to perform such a respectful bow. Not only did she speak in the broad local dialect, but she also had some kind of unfortunate speech impediment. When she referred to Oshiho as "t' lady of t' house", there was something comical about it. "His wife" would have been fine.

"Welcome!"

Kosuke was startled by the sound of Oshiho's greeting. This woman certainly knew how to creep up silently like a cat. When he turned around, she was already standing at the partition screen in an attractively contrived pose.

Oshiho-san was truly beautiful. It was an elegant beauty. And the beauty was not confined to her face; her figure was also perfect beyond compare. The curves of her body were softly rounded. It was clear to Kosuke that she was not from the southern part of Japan. She must have been from Akita or Niigata. She was a classic fair-skinned beauty—the type of woman who had grown up in the north and then spent time in the city adding a layer of polish to her manners. The first time Kosuke had met her at Senkoji Temple, he had been stunned by the sight of her. Now, here in the rather dim light of the old-fashioned *genkan* entranceway, seeing her standing with such grace, he felt almost bewitched, and it made him uneasy.

Oshiho's hair wasn't done up in a traditional roll, nor, he could see, was she wearing the under-piece for a wig. Her hairstyle was one that was completely new to Kosuke. In addition, her kimono and obi were also unfamiliar to him. They appeared to be made of something most exquisite. She looked exactly like the cover illustration of a book on post-war kimono fashions.

"Welcome," she said once again, slipping out from the shadow of the screen. She lifted a hand to her hair, and sank gracefully to her knees.

"Welcome," she said for the third time. There was amusement in her eyes.

"Are you the priest's messenger?" she asked with a delicate inclination of her head.

Kosuke realized that she was slightly drunk. He gulped and, in his usual stammering manner, repeated the priest's message as fast as he could. But his stammer made him all the more flustered, and he began to scratch at his tousled head. It seemed that the war had done nothing to cure him of this lifelong habit.

"I see," said Oshiho, her big, beautiful eyes shining. Then she smiled.

"Word of this matter already came yesterday from the main house. However, because my husband is indisposed, I am afraid I won't be able to leave his side. He's rather difficult, you see…"

And yet, Oshiho was drunk…

"And I believe I already responded yesterday, to say that if my husband happened to feel better, I would go and pay my respects. I wonder if Ryonen-san received my message?"

"Oh, is th-that right? Then I'm sure he must have forgotten. I'm s-so s-sorry."

"No, not at all. I'm sorry. But how thoughtless of the Reverend Father."

"Excuse me?"

"It's unforgivable of him to make use of you in this way."

"Oh, d-don't worry. I'm just here on the island doing nothing special anyway."

"Kindaichi-san?"

"Yes?"

"Are you going up to the main house after this?"

"Yes. Is there something I can do for you?"

"No, no. But I shouldn't keep you any longer. Please do come by for a visit again sometime. You're often dropping in at the main house, aren't you?"

"That's right. I like borrowing Chimata-san's books."

"We don't have any books here, but we can certainly keep you company. Please come by any time. This branch of the Kito family aren't demons or snakes you know."

"Oh… no! I— Well, I'd better be going."

67

"Really? Well, please give my regards to the priest."

As he exited the branch family's residence via the nagay-amon gate, Kosuke's armpits were soaked in sweat. As he had turned to leave, he'd heard male laughter coming from inside the house, and it had needled him a little. Of course, it was probably coincidental timing—they hadn't been laughing at him. And yet, he was unable to shake off an unpleasant feeling. It was drunken laughter, and this meant that whether Gihei was suffering from gout or not, he was still well enough to have a drinking partner. He was probably drinking too...

On Kosuke's return, as he reached the foot of the winding path up to the temple, he ran into a group of three walkers coming down. The apprentice priest, Ryotaku, was in the lead, carrying a lantern. Behind him came Ryonen the priest and Takezo, deep in conversation.

"Oh, Kindaichi-san! Sorry about that. It seems a message had already been sent from the branch house to the main house."

"Yes, that's right. Oshiho-san says that her husband is indisposed, so she's unable to get away."

"I see. Well, never mind. Never mind."

When they arrived at the Kito residence, they found Okatsu, the ex-mistress of the late Kaemon-san, loitering by the main gate, looking anxiously around.

"Okatsu-san, what's the matter?" said Takezo. "What are you doing out here?"

"Oh, Takezo-san, I can't find Hana-chan."

"Hanako? I saw her wandering around earlier."

"Yes, but then she suddenly disappeared... Oh, Reverend Father, welcome. Please come in."

"Okatsu-san, is Hanako missing?"

"No, well—I mean she was right here a moment ago. Anyway, please do go in."

Leaving Okatsu and Takezo at the gate, the other three went in through the genkan entrance hall of the main building. They could hear a radio somewhere inside the house. Waiting impatiently for her brother's return, Sanae was listening to the daily news bulletin on the demobilization and repatriation of the Japanese army.

CHAPTER 2

Like a Grotesque Serpent

The characters for "wake" in Japanese mean "all through the night"—but even in the most rural areas no one takes this literally any more. They usually begin around nine or ten in the evening, or even as late as eleven. The Kito family's wake was to begin after ten, but even by that time Hanako hadn't returned. People were getting anxious.

"Okatsu-san, you helped the girls get dressed, didn't you?" said the mayor, clearly worried. "Was Hanako still at home then?"

"Yes, yes. She was here. She was the first one I helped to get dressed. Next was Tsukiyo-chan, and then Yukie-chan. Girls, that's right, isn't it?"

Tsukiyo and Yukie nodded. The two of them were never still for a moment. They were fiddling with their sleeves, pulling at their necklines, adjusting their hair ornaments and constantly nudging each other, necks bent, and giggling. They lifted their heads just long enough to respond to Okatsu's question, then went right back to whispering.

"Tsukiyo? Yukie? Have you any idea where Hanako went after that?"

The priest's eyebrows were knitted together.

"Huh? Dunno. She's always running around all over the place. She drives me crazy."

"Yeah, she's so annoying."

The priest turned back to the older woman.

"Okatsu-san, about what time was it?"

"I don't rightly know. For sure it was the evening…"

Okatsu inclined her head to one side as if thinking.

"Oh, that's right! While I was helping her get dressed, Sanae-san turned on the radio in the other room. I could hear the music at the start of the news broadcast. Then she turned it right off again."

"So that means it was around 6.15 p.m.," said Kosuke. "And at that time Hanako was still here with you?"

The mayor was getting more agitated by the second.

"Right, we know that she was here until that time at least…" he said.

But to be honest, that didn't tell them anything at all.

"Sanae-san, you don't remember anything, do you?"

In her simple black mourning dress, Sanae was a total contrast to Tsukiyo and Yukie. She opened her eyes wide and tilted her head with its perfectly rounded cheek to one side. The angle served to show off her impressively long eyelashes. Her naturally wavy, shoulder-length hair was extremely fetching.

"I'm sorry, I don't really remember… I know that Auntie was in the next room helping the girls dress. I'm sure that Hana-chan was there at that time. I'm afraid after that I wanted to listen to the radio, so I went into the sitting room to turn it on. But the news had only just started so I turned it off again and went back into the next room…

That's right! I'm sure that Hana-chan wasn't there any more."

This meant that Hanako had gone missing around 6.15 p.m. Now it was 10.30, and they had good reason to be worried.

"Look, there's no point in sitting around here talking about it. Let's get out there and search for her. You know very well where we should be looking."

The voice came from down the far end of the room. It seemed that the tide master, Takezo, couldn't keep quiet any longer. Kosuke had already spotted that ever since the beginning of this conversation he'd been restless and fidgety.

"By that, I take it you mean that you've got some idea of where she might be?"

"Well, I'm not sure, but I wondered if we should check the branch family's house?"

Everyone exchanged startled looks. And Koan the doctor, who until this moment had been nodding off in his seat, suddenly let out a tremendous shout.

"That lover boy from the branch family place was heading up to the temple earlier this evening!"

"What? Koan-san, is that true?" said the mayor. "Hey, Koan-san? Koan-san, don't fall asleep again, all right? Did you really see Ukai-san going into the temple?"

Koan was completely drunk at this point, which was his usual habit, but when Takezo shook him, his eyes popped wide open.

"Yes, I'm pretty sure. I was on my way here and saw him heading up the winding path. But it was getting dark by then, so I can't be absolutely sure."

Sloppily wiping the dribble from his goatee, his body swaying unsteadily, Koan spat out these words along with a gust of liquor-reeking breath like a whale expelling seawater. Then he immediately slumped to the floor. He apparently didn't care how crumpled his haori coat and hakama skirt would become.

"Damn it, he really shouldn't have drunk himself into this state," said Takezo.

"Never mind. Nothing we can do about that now," said the priest. "He's always this way. But, Araki-san, we still have to do something about Hanako."

"Okatsu-san, do you know if Hanako was planning to meet that man Ukai today?" asked the mayor with a frown.

"Well, I don't know... Tsukiyo-chan, Yukie-chan, did you hear anything about this?"

"I don't know anything. Ukai-san and Hana-chan? No way! Right, Yukie-chan?" Tsukiyo's expression clearly said that the idea was ridiculous.

"We don't know," Yukie pouted. "Hana-chan's always telling lies. She's probably just asleep in one of the rooms in the house somewhere."

"Okatsu-san, could you check the house one more time?" said the mayor.

"I looked everywhere already— Well, I suppose it won't hurt to check again."

Okatsu-san... Her real name was Katsuno, but no one ever called her that. They just called her by her nickname. If you observed carefully, you could see that she used to be very beautiful, but now she seemed to have lost all confidence and self-respect. Her eyes always seemed to be holding back tears, and she was as timid as a mouse. Perhaps almost twenty years of cohabiting with Kaemon and his boundless energy had sapped her completely of any physical or mental strength.

Okatsu got to her feet. Sanae followed suit.

"I'll help you," she said, and the two women left the room.

"If she's not in the house, then we'd better split up and search outside. Takezo-san, will you go up to the branch house?"

"I would like to volunteer. It's just—"

"Is something wrong?"

"I don't get along with the lady of the house."

"Then, Ryotaku, would you go please? Takezo-san, would you be able to do it if Ryotaku went with you?"

"Ah yes, if Ryotaku's there—"

"I'll go down and search the village," said the mayor.

"It'd be great if we could get Koan-san to wake up, but I'm afraid in this state he'll be useless."

All of sudden there was a loud shriek from within the house. It sounded like Sanae's voice. Everyone jumped to their feet, but when it was followed by the sound of stamping feet and the growling of some kind of beast, everyone relaxed.

"Ah, the patient seems to be in quite a rage tonight," muttered the priest.

"Yes, he's been crazy since this morning. He's in such a mood!" said Tsukiyo.

"Right," said Yukie. "If we go anywhere near him, he bares his teeth at us like some kind of monkey. I hate it when he's all crazy like that."

This was when Kosuke finally understood. The barber had told him that Chimata's father, Yosamatsu, had gone mad and been in long-term confinement in a barred room. It seemed the lunatic was raging. As he listened to the man howling like a wolf and rattling the bars of his cage, Kosuke couldn't help feeling the heavy darkness that must weigh on this family, and his heart felt a chill as deep as midwinter.

Okatsu came back, then Sanae a little while after, her eyes wide with fear.

"Sanae-san, the patient sounds pretty bad today," remarked the priest.

"What?" Sanae's voice was faint. She was shockingly pale and her eyes were full of fear. "Oh… yes. He's been rather wild lately… Auntie, did you find Hana-chan?"

It turned out that Hanako was nowhere to be found. Everyone now flew into action, with the priest giving directions.

"Right, Araki-san, you go down to the village to look for her. Takezo and Ryotaku will head to the branch family place, find that man Ukai and ask him if he's seen Hanako. I'm going back to the temple to search for her. I can't believe she'd be at the temple at this time of night though…"

"Ryonen-san, is there anything I can do?" asked Kosuke.

"Yes, Kindaichi-san, please come with me— Oh…"

The priest's gaze fell on the doctor, Koan.

"Actually, would you mind taking Koan-san home? It's a little dangerous for him to go alone."

"Got it."

The tasks allocated, everyone got to their feet. It was around 11.00 p.m. at this point. Outside, the wind had got up, and the sky was pitch-black and overcast. They went out of the front gate, where the mayor separated from the

75

others and headed downhill. The others began to climb up, and when they reached the top of an incline, Kosuke headed off to the left towards Doctor Koan's house.

"Thank you. I'll leave him in your hands," said the priest.

Takezo, who had been supporting the drunken man on his shoulder, passed him over to Kosuke.

"Kindaichi-san, take care not to fall."

"I'll be okay."

The house was about a hundred yards away. Although he was blind drunk, Koan hadn't completely lost consciousness, and he was determined to try and walk on his own feet, so he wasn't too much of a burden. They staggered together along the pitch-black path. If the lantern were to get blown out, they could easily have fallen right off the edge. The lantern in his right hand, supporting Koan on his left shoulder, and struggling against a headwind, Kosuke somehow got them both to Koan's house.

"Oh dear, sir. Oh dear, dear."

Koan was widowed and lived with his elderly house-keeper. She seemed to be rather dramatically surprised by the arrival of her employer in such a state. Kosuke brushed off her profuse thanks and left right away. The wind was growing steadily stronger and, now that he was alone, the sound of the waves below was loud in his ears. It was so unrelentingly dark that it was as if someone had spilled a bottle of black ink across the sky. The power of the wind on his back seemed to push him along and he scurried down the road.

Was something wrong? Or rather, had something bad happened? In this dark, in this wind... a young girl like

Hanako, it was unimaginable that she'd be out playing around on a night like this. Something was wrong. Something had happened.

With this strong premonition, Kosuke soon arrived at the spot where he'd parted from the others. As he continued towards the east, he saw glimmers of light from the lanterns across the other side of the valley. He guessed it was Takezo and the apprentice priest, Ryotaku, on their way back from the branch Kito house.

Kosuke soon came to the base of the winding mountain path up to the temple. He waited and eventually, as he'd expected, Takezo and Ryotaku turned up.

"How did it go? Did they know anything?"

"No, they said they had no idea."

"Was Ukai-san there?"

"They said he was already asleep. We wanted them to wake him up so we could talk to him, but she was completely unwelcoming. We were turned away."

"Was it the lady of the house who came to the door?"

"No, it was a maid—I'm afraid I'm the enemy as far as that family is concerned," Takezo said with a grimace.

Kosuke had learned from the barber that Oshiho had tried to lure the famous tide master away to join the branch family fishing fleet. Loyal to the head Kito family, Takezo had turned her down point-blank. This had severely angered both Gihei-san and his wife.

"Where are you going to look next?"

"Hmm. Well, we can't just leave all the women alone at the house," said Takezo. "It's tough on Sanae-san having to take care of them all."

He shivered uneasily.

Ryotaku had been standing silently holding his lantern, but he suddenly spoke up.

"Oh, the Reverend Father is still on his way up to the temple."

About halfway up the winding path was the tiny circle of light from a single lantern, bobbing along as if suspended in mid-air. Seeing this, Takezo made a decision.

"Let's go and ask the priest what he thinks we should do next."

"Good idea. I'll go with you," said Kosuke.

The three men headed side by side up the winding path. The owner of the lantern in the distance appeared to notice them as he raised the lantern up high in the air and waved it in greeting. Kosuke waved his own lantern in reply, and the other light began once again to move. Unconsciously they all quickened their pace as if to chase the light ahead. The wind, gusting off the sea, battered the branches of the red pine trees. Whenever the road curved so they were facing west, the men could barely lift their heads to look ahead.

One bend, a second bend, a third… The lantern light ahead of them was at times visible, at others hidden. As they passed the little shrine to the harvest god, the light ahead was about to reach the temple steps. The priest was a rather old man, and that long flight must be quite a challenge for him. The silhouette of the priest slowly climbing the steps came in and out of view. Just as the three younger men got to the bottom of the steps, the bobbing light disappeared for a moment, then as they started up it reappeared at the top.

"Ryotaku! Ryotaku!"

It was the priest's voice, calling in an urgent tone.

"Yes?"

The young apprentice called back from the steps, but the priest didn't offer any response. He just disappeared through the temple gate.

"I wonder what's the matter with the Reverend Father?" said Ryotaku. "He seems in an awful hurry."

Kosuke had another strong sense of foreboding. He set off ahead of his two companions and began to run up the temple steps. Perhaps the feeling was contagious, for Ryotaku and Takezo bounded after him.

The priest reappeared at the top of the steps, waving his lantern.

"Ryotaku! Ryotaku!"

He seemed more agitated than ever. His voice had gone up in pitch and had begun to tremble.

"Yes, Reverend Father, what's the matter?"

"Is Kindaichi-san with you?"

"Yes, Kindaichi-san and Takezo-san are both here with me."

"Oh, Takezo too? Oh, Takezo, I'm glad you're here. It's horrible! It's horrible!"

The priest turned and ran back through the temple gate. The three men barely paused to exchange looks before tearing off after him. Kosuke was the first through the gate, and immediately spotted the lantern glow moving back and forward in front of the Zen meditation hall.

"What's the matter, Ryonen-san?"

"Oh, Kindaichi-san. Look! See for yourself!"

His voice was shrill as he raised the lantern for Kosuke to see. At that moment, Ryotaku and Takezo also arrived on the

79

scene and both let out screams of terror. Kosuke somehow managed not to scream, but he was just as horrified as the rest of them. For a moment he was frozen to the spot, as if his feet had been nailed down.

This narrator has previously described how in front of the connecting passage between the meditation hall and the main temple building was a magnificent old flowering plum, the pride of Senkoji Temple.

It was autumn, so of course there was no blossom on the tree, and most of the leaves had withered and fallen, but from its southern branches hung the most awful sight that anyone could encounter in this lifetime.

Hanako had been bound at the knees by her own obi belt, one end of it still around her waist, the other coiled around the branch like a colourful python. In other words, Hanako herself resembled a grotesque serpent, hanging head down from the branches of the plum tree. Her eyes were open, wide open. The flames of the lanterns were reflected in those eyes, and they seemed to glitter as if mocking everyone for their fear.

A bitter gust of wind blew in from the sea, and the forest around the temple was filled with murmurs. All of a sudden, the rasping cry of a bird pierced the darkness. At once, Hanako's upside-down corpse began to sway, and the black strands of her hair, loosened from their coil, squirmed on the ground like black rat snakes. The priest hastily pulled his prayer beads from his pocket and began to chant.

"I put my trust in you, Shakamuni Buddha, I put my trust in you, Shakamuni Buddha."

Then he expelled his breath in a deep sigh along with some mumbled words—words that would stick in Kosuke's head for a long time to come.

To Kosuke's ear, it sounded like:

"Out of reason, but it can't be helped."

THE PREPOSITION PROBLEM

"Out of reason, but it can't be helped."

What on earth could that mean? Did Ryonen-san know the identity of the killer? Was it someone who had lost his reason? Startled, Kosuke searched the priest's face for an explanation, but he stood wordlessly rolling the prayer beads between his fingers.

Takezo and Ryotaku were utterly dumbfounded, staring at the upside-down python before them. The wind was growing stronger and stronger, and the forest of red pines that surrounded the temple began to make a hideous commotion. The black coils of hair squirmed even more wildly.

Kosuke finally came to his senses, and, simultaneously, his sense of professionalism kicked in. Or rather, his natural instinct to enquire and pry raised its head.

Holding up his lantern, he carefully examined the position of the body and the way the obi had been attached to the tree branch. After he was satisfied that he had checked it thoroughly, he turned to Takezo.

"Takezo-san, I'm sorry to ask you, but could you go and fetch Doctor Koan? He's probably sobered up a bit by now."

"Huh? Yes, no problem."

Takezo rubbed at his eyes, as if just waking up from a bad dream. He turned to the priest.

"Reverend Father?"

However, the priest was in a very peculiar state. He was standing facing the Zen meditation hall, but did not seem to hear Takezo's voice at all. He was in a daze.

"Reverend Father? Reverend Father?"

Ryonen suddenly dropped his priest's staff and it fell to the ground with a thud. He scrambled to pick up it up.

"Wh-what is it, Takezo?" he said, his voice shaking.

"I'm going to do as Kindaichi-san requested, and run over to fetch Koan-san," said Takezo.

"Yes, hmm. Of course. Well, if you don't mind…"

The priest gulped and repeated the same chant twice over.

Takezo watched him as if trying to work something out in his head.

"What about the family? Shouldn't somebody go and inform them?"

"The family… Well… Yes, you'd better call in there too. Maybe for now you should just let them know that Hanako has been found. Don't say anything about her being murdered. Kindaichi-san?"

"Yes?"

Kosuke watched the priest's expression.

"Hanako was murdered, wasn't she?"

"It seems so. It certainly doesn't look like suicide," Kosuke said, hastily stifling the inappropriate laugh that was about to burst out. He began awkwardly to scratch his head.

"Ah yes… well, Takezo, please don't mention it to the

family anyway," said the priest. "They're all women. I don't want to scare them too much."

"Understood. I'll go as fast as I can."

"Just a minute… Can you also let the mayor know? Get him to come up here?… Kindaichi-san, what about the police? Should we inform Sergeant Shimizu?"

"I don't think he'll be home," said Kosuke.

"Why not?"

"He said he'd been called to Kasaoka Police Headquarters. Just after noon he took a motorboat over to the mainland. But… Takezo-san?"

"Yes?"

"Drop by the police station just in case. If you find Shimizu-san is back, get him to come up here."

"Got it. I'm on my way."

The wind was really blowing up a storm now. The pine tree branches made cracking, crashing noises. In that gale, Takezo sped off, looking like a *yajirobe* balancing doll, the arms of his kimono out to each side. As he disappeared, large drops of water began to fall from above. The wind had finally brought the rain with it.

"Damn it!"

Kosuke looked up at the dark sky and clicked his tongue in annoyance.

"What is it?" asked the priest.

"The rain—"

"Rain? Yes. Looks like we're in for a real downpour. Oh, I see. If it rains—"

"If it keeps on raining until morning, it'll wash away all the footprints."

"Oh, footprints!"

The priest began to breathe more heavily as if he had suddenly realized something.

"I completely forgot. Kindaichi-san, could you come here a moment? I need to show you something. Ryotaku, could you come too?"

Up until then, the apprentice priest had been a statue. Now he finally opened his mouth.

"Reverend Father, the body… Should we leave it like this?"

His voice was more timid than ever.

"Ah, what do you think, Kindaichi-san?" said the priest. "Do you think we could take her down now?"

"I think we should leave her there for now. Sergeant Shimizu might be back on the island."

"Well, all right then. Ryotaku, leave Hanako there for now and come with us."

They left the gruesome plum tree and walked over to the front entrance of the priests' quarters. The rain suddenly fell in a torrent. It was as if a bow had loosed a hail of arrows.

"Damn it!"

Kosuke glared up at the sky.

"Ah yes," said the priest, running to shelter under the eaves of the building. "Most unfortunate about the rain. Anyway, Kindaichi-san? You recall that I got back here just before the rest of you? I was about to enter the building by this front entrance, but then I remembered that I'd locked it from the inside. And so… if you'd come this way… Be careful where you step…"

They followed the side of the building under the eaves until they reached the back door, which faced the edge of the steep mountain. The door was slightly ajar, the interior in darkness.

"The front entrance was locked so I came round here to the back. And, well, I found this..."

The priest lifted his lantern.

"What is that?"

"Someone has wrenched off the padlock."

Kosuke and Ryotaku both gasped. The broken padlock was hanging from the ring in the lintel of the door.

"Ryotaku, it was you who locked this door. It wasn't like this when you—"

"Reverend Father, of course not. I closed the door and fastened the padlock as usual."

"So the person who opened this door—" Kosuke began.

"I got out the key to open it and found it in this state with the padlock broken off," explained the priest. "I was surprised and opened the door to check inside. And this is what I saw."

He held up his lantern so it lit the interior through the gap of the open door. There, all over the packed dirt floor of the entranceway, were large muddy footprints.

Ryotaku gulped.

"Reverend Father, do you think there was a burglar?"

"I think so. Look, those footprints are still wet. That's what shocked me and why I ran out to call you."

"So that's why you came running out."

"Yes, I went to call you all up here, but then I wondered about the rest of the grounds. I took my lantern to search them, and that's when I saw—"

The priest broke off and swallowed.

"—Hanako's body."

"So, Ryonen-san, that means that you didn't have a chance to check inside yet," Kosuke asked.

"Of course not. I was too preoccupied."

"So, let's go in and investigate."

"Right, Ryotaku, you go in first and turn on the lights," said the priest.

"Please—no!" begged the apprentice.

"What's the matter with you? Ha ha. You're shaking. Are you such a coward?" the priest teased him.

"But the intruder must still be inside."

"No, look," said Kosuke, pointing to the ground. "These footprints are facing inwards, and then there are more there going out again. But I'll go in first."

"No, no. I'll go."

Reassured by Kosuke's discovery, Ryotaku went through the door and turned on the electric light in the kitchen. But as soon as the room became bright, he let out a shout.

"What is it?" called the priest, alarmed.

"Reverend Father, it looks as if the intruder came right in with his muddy shoes still on. Look at all these footprints everywhere."

"Ugh, look at this mess. Now, does anything seem to be missing?"

"I'm just checking now."

"Ryonen-san, could you lend me your lantern?" Kosuke said.

Kosuke had given his own lantern to Takezo. Now he took the priest's and examined the outer perimeter of the door. Right behind them was the base of a steep cliff. Most days the sun never came out on the island, so the ground was always very damp. In this moist earth there were clear footprints scattered around. From his own military experience, Kosuke knew that these were made by army boots. The prints went into the building, then came back out again. However, over by the path where the ground was harder, it was impossible to make out any prints at all. And then there was the rain on top of everything...

"Damn it!"

Glaring at the rain that now fell in sheets, Kosuke clicked his tongue once again. He turned around and returned to the back door of the priests' quarters. Neither of the other two men was in the kitchen any more.

"Ryonen-san! Ryotaku-san!" he called out.

"In here!"

Ryotaku's voice was coming from Ryonen's private chambers. Kosuke made his way through and found Ryotaku by himself, checking inside the closets.

"Did you find anything missing?"

"Not yet."

"And the priest?"

"He's gone to check the main hall."

Just then they heard the priest calling from that direction.

"Ryotaku! Could you bring me a light?"

Luckily, the candle in Kosuke's lantern had not gone out yet. He and Ryotaku rushed over to the brightly lit main building. Kosuke opened the south-facing latticed shutters to find the priest leaning over the balcony balustrade looking down.

"Ryonen-san, did something happen?"

"I'm not sure. Lend me your lantern a moment."

The priest held the lantern out over the balustrade, and the offertory box below became clearly visible. Next to it were five or six cigarette butts along with several spent matches.

Kosuke turned to the apprentice.

"Ryotaku-san, do you clean down there?"

"Every morning. And I'm certain that none of the worshippers at this temple would smoke a cigarette in that area."

"So the intruder dropped them there. Before he snuck into the temple, he sat at the foot of this staircase and smoked a few cigarettes."

Luckily the eaves of the temple hung far out at this spot, so that the cigarette butts and matches hadn't been soaked by the rain. Kosuke went down the stairs and got a sheet of paper out of his breast pocket and collected all of them. Then a grin spread across his face and he began to scratch at his mop of hair.

"Ryonen-san, look at this. These cigarette butts contain a huge clue. See? They're hand-rolled and the smoker used a page from a dictionary."

"Ah yes. Looks like an English dictionary."

"It is. *The Concise English–Japanese Dictionary*. The smoker didn't have any rolling papers, so he used whatever was to hand. Ryonen-san, who on this island is likely to own an English dictionary?"

"Let's see… Well, the Kito family for a start. Both Chimata and Hitoshi went to school, so they probably owned English dictionaries."

"And is there anyone in that family who smokes?"

The priest gave a sharp intake of breath. His eyes grew wide, and he had to grasp hold of one of the ornamental knobs on the temple balustrade in order to stop his big thick hands from shaking.

"Ryonen-san, wh-what's wrong?"

Alarmed at how heavy the priest's breathing was, Kosuke had begun to stammer.

"Ah yes… well… no, it couldn't possibly be…" the priest continued.

"Wh-what's the matter? Is there somebody at that house who smokes?"

"Ah yes. I once saw the girl Sanae rolling a cigarette. Now I remember that she was using a piece of paper with lettering all over it, just like this one. And when I asked her who was going to smoke it—"

"You asked her who the cigarette was for?"

"Sanae replied that it was for her uncle."

Kosuke let out a gasp. The piece of paper in his hand trembled.

"And by Sanae's uncle, you mean the man who is locked up in the caged room?"

"That's right. The patient. And I remember what I said to Sanae at the time. I said it was fine to give a cigarette to a lunatic, but not to let him have the matches. And Sanae said that she'd be extra careful."

Right then, there was a frightful racket above their heads as a rat ran across the temple roof. All three men jumped. The wind was still howling and the rain was now coming down horizontally. Hanako's sodden corpse swung back and forth. Waterfalls poured from the ends of her dark hair.

Through chattering teeth, Ryotaku began to chant.

"Ryonen-san, are you really suggesting that the person who came here tonight was the man who is locked in a cell? The head of the Kito family?"

"Ridiculous! Of course I'm not suggesting anything of the sort. You were the one asking about the cigarettes—"

Watching the priest's face very carefully, Kosuke continued.

"But you did say something very strange just now."

"Me?... When?"

"When we first saw Hanako's body."

"When I showed you the body? I did? I said something?"

"You did. I couldn't quite make it out, but it sounded something like 'Out of reason, but it can't be helped.'"

"'Out of reason, but it can't be helped'? Did I say that?"

"Yes, I'm quite sure that you did. I thought it was weird. 'Out of reason' refers to the head of the Kito house, I suppose, and I wondered why you mentioned him. Ryonen-san, do you think that Yosamatsu-san had something to do with this case?"

"'Out of reason, but it can't be helped.' Did I really say those words? Out of reason, but it can't be helped... Out of reason, but it can't be helped..."

All of a sudden, the priest's eyes bulged, and he fixed Kosuke with the intensest of glares. His broad shoulders heaved, and the corners of his mouth began to convulse. Then in the next instant, he raised both hands to cover his face, and staggered backwards.

"Ryonen-san!" Kosuke's heart began to pound. "Have you remembered something?"

His face still in his hands, the priest stayed silent, as his shoulders continued to heave. After a few moments, he lowered his hands, but he continued to avoid Kosuke's gaze.

"Kindaichi-san," he said in a low voice. "You misunderstood. It is indeed possible that I said that phrase, but it had absolutely nothing to do with the head of the Kito household."

"So... so... Ryonen-san, what did those words mean? Who or what is out of reason?"

"I can't tell you. It's... it's such a terrible thing."

The priest gave one more intense shudder, then finally managed to inhale a deep breath. Then, in a flat, discouraged tone he began to speak.

"Kindaichi-san, in our world there are some things so dreadful, so terrifying that you would scarcely believe they existed. They are things that common sense and accepted practice would dictate are impossible, but they do exist. Out of reason... that's right. It's a mad state of affairs. But right now... I cannot tell you. There may come a day when I'll be able to speak to you frankly, but that time is not now. Please don't ask me any more. Do you understand? There's no point in questioning me... Oh!"

And with that he grabbed the handrail and set off down the stairs.

"It looks like Koan-san's here," he called back to the others. "I can see lanterns approaching. Come on, we'd better search the meditation hall while we're waiting for him. It's the perfect opportunity."

As mentioned before, the meditation hall and the main temple building were connected by a passageway. The meditation hall was a long, narrow building, about eighteen feet wide and forty feet long, and was built so that its main windows faced east, or away towards the mountain. If you came along the raised passageway from the main temple building to the south of the meditation hall, opened the little wooden door and walked along its central aisle, on both left and right sides there was a line of single tatami mats. On each of these mats, one person could sit in the Zazen cross-legged position. There were ten mats on the left and ten on the right. But right after the fifth mat, there was an aisle that intersected the main aisle at a right angle. Just at the cross-point between the two aisles, in other words, right in the centre of the meditation hall, there was a statue of Buddha. It was Yakushi Nyorai—the healing Buddha. Halfway along the meditation hall's west side was its main entrance. Beyond that was the temple garden, which contained the now-gruesome plum tree. Lattice windows ran along the wall on either side of the entrance door.

After the priest had searched the whole meditation hall from top to bottom, he examined that main entrance door, which faced west onto the garden. It was securely bolted from the inside.

"Hm, well, nothing out of place here. Ryotaku, was there anything missing from the living quarters?"

"I'm afraid I haven't finished searching properly, but right now there doesn't seem to be anything at all out of place."

"Hm. Strange kind of burglar. Maybe our temple is so impoverished that there was nothing here worth stealing.

Well, I think Koan-san will be arriving any minute. Let's go outside to wait for him."

Kosuke was deep in thought. Something was nagging at his mind. It was a problem of grammar.

The priest had offered so many excuses. But it was all clever sophistry. The person who was "out of reason" was obviously Yosamatsu, the head of the Kito family. Of course, it didn't matter whether it was about Yosamatsu or not—this killer had to have lost all reason. However, what was nagging at Kosuke's mind was the prepositional phrase "out of". Surely it would have been more natural to say "beyond reason" or even "lost all reason"? But this wasn't what he had heard. It had been "Out of reason, but it can't be helped".

Why had the priest put it like that?

TONIGHT'S BROADCAST

In the pouring rain, Doctor Koan Murase and Mayor Makihei Araki came running, their umbrellas turned inside out by the wind. Takezo was with them too; he must have called in at home, as he had changed out of his formal kimono. All three were completely soaked, and Koan's goatee was dripping with water.

They met the priest at the main temple gate.

"Ryonen-san!"

The muscles in Koan's cheek twitched as if he were trying say more; his prominent Adam's apple bobbed up and down, but he was unable to produce another word.

Mayor Araki for his part, stood with his lips pressed tightly together, staring at the priest's face. For a moment, an eerie hush fell over the three men; finally it was the priest who made a move.

"Thanks for coming. So, first of all, you'd better come and see Hanako."

Takezo had given them the gist of what had happened, so as soon as the priest gestured in that direction, they set off towards the plum tree: Koan a little wobbly on his feet, and the mayor with steady strides.

Just as the priest was about to follow, Takezo stopped him.

"Reverend Father?"

"Oh, Takezo. Thank you. How were they up at the house?"

"Tsukiyo-san and Yukie-san were already asleep, but Sanae-san was there looking terribly worried—"

"She's a bright girl, that one. She's probably worked out what's happened."

"I think so. She tried to come with me, but I stopped her. I asked Okatsu-san to look after her."

"And what about Sergeant Shimizu?" asked Kosuke.

"He doesn't seem to be back yet."

"Really? Well, thank you for checking."

The doctor and the mayor were standing by the plum tree, transfixed. Despite being a medical professional, Koan was trembling with fear; Mayor Araki was staring at the corpse, expressionless, but as the priest approached, he turned to address him.

"Ryonen-san, how much longer must we leave her hanging here like this? Shouldn't we take her down?"

"Hm, well, Kindaichi-san said we ought to leave her

like this until the police sergeant has had a chance to see the crime scene, so we didn't touch her until now. But we really can't leave her like this until the morning. Now that you and Koan-san have seen it, it should be all right. Hey, Kindaichi-san, can we take her down?"

"I suppose so. Let me help."

"No, no. Takezo-san, you do it."

"No, no. Please let me. Where should we take her?"

"I think you'd better put her in the main building for now. Ryotaku, go and spread out some straw matting or something in the main hall."

Takezo and Kosuke soon managed between them to release the body from the tree, and carry it to the main building.

"Right, Koan-san, it's up to you now," said Kosuke. "Please examine her as carefully as you can."

Koan was still a doctor. He had watched Hanako being taken down from the tree and lain down in the main hall, and was no longer shaking at the sight. With a practised hand he began to examine the body.

"Koan-san, what's the cause of death?" asked Kosuke.

"She was strangled. Look here on her neck. There are marks from a towel or something similar. And yet…"

He lifted Hanako's body slightly.

"Before that, it looks as if she received an extremely strong blow to the head. There's a laceration here on the back. She hardly bled at all, but I think it was probably enough to knock her out."

"So you're saying someone hit her over the head, and when she was unconscious they strangled her?" Kosuke asked, as if for confirmation.

"Yes, it looks like that's what the malefactor did," said Koan, using a rather dated expression. "Whacking someone over the head and knocking them out was too unreliable, so they strangled her too for good measure… And they used a large cotton handkerchief or towel—probably a traditional cotton *tenugui*."

"And how long ago do you think she was killed?"

"Well, I'll need to do some further examination to be sure, but I'd say five or six hours ago, more or less. What time is it now?"

Kosuke checked his wristwatch. It was exactly 12.30 a.m.

"So that means that she was killed today… no, I mean yesterday… she was killed last night between 6.30 and 7.30 p.m."

That was exactly the time that Kosuke himself had figured. This old-fashioned doctor was surprisingly accurate, and Kosuke looked at the old man with the goatee with a new-found respect.

Kosuke of course was no doctor, but he possessed quite a bit of medical knowledge. Thanks to his benefactor, Ginzo Kubo, Kosuke had attended a university in America. While he was there, he had taken a part-time job at a hospital as an apprentice nurse. He'd taken the job partly out of guilt at relying entirely on the money that Ginzo provided him, but at the same time, he'd kept in mind that in later years the experience might be useful to him in his unusual chosen profession.

And then of course he had the experience of several years on the front line as a soldier. In summary, Kosuke had seen more than his fair share of death. Death from bombs and guns, death from disease. Kosuke had always observed the bodies of the victims, and had not forgotten a single one. He had a good sense of how rigor mortis worked. In the case of Hanako, his estimate had been the same as the doctor's.

In other words, Hanako Kito had been killed between 6.30 and 7.30 on the evening of 5th October. This was an indisputable fact, but when had Hanako arrived at the temple? Kosuke attempted to put the events of the evening in order in his head.

The last time Hanako had been seen alive was right when the news had been starting on the radio—or around 6.15 p.m. She must have slipped out of the house and come straight to Senkoji Temple.

It so happened that Kosuke had left the temple at 6.25 p.m. He had checked his watch when the priest had offered him a lantern, so he was sure about the time. He'd set off down the mountain, and had met Takezo on the way, roughly halfway down the winding path. That must have been about 6.28 p.m. Then Kosuke had left Takezo and gone on to the Kito branch family house.

He'd been delayed at the house for a few minutes, but when he got back to the foot of the winding path, he'd met the priest, the apprentice and Takezo coming down from the direction of the temple. Then the four of them had gone on together to the head Kito house, where Sanae was listening to the repatriation news on the radio. More accurately, it was just coming to an end as Kosuke and the others had entered the house. In those days, the evening radio programme schedule was as follows:

6.15 p.m.: Main News

6.30 p.m.: Weather Report, preview of the evening's
programmes

6.35 p.m.: Repatriation News

6.45 p.m.: *Come On! Come On!*—an English language
learning programme

Kosuke was pleased at the unexpected accuracy with which
he was able to track his own movements. Now, by going over
this schedule in detail, he was able to make the following
deductions:

Between leaving Senkoji Temple at 6.25 p.m. and arriving
at 6.45 p.m. at the Kito house with the other three men, he
had been on the route that everyone would take between
the houses and temple. But there was one small gap. He
couldn't be sure of the time that the priest, Ryotaku and
Takezo had left the temple. It was possible that it was after
the time that Kosuke had turned off the winding path onto
the road to the branch family house. If that were the case,
it left a window of time when no one would have been on
the winding path up to the temple.

However, that was irrelevant. Even if Hanako had set off
up the winding path to the temple at the exact moment that
Kosuke had turned off it and onto the road to the branch
house, it would have taken a young woman about ten minutes to climb the path to the temple, and the priest's party
must have left the temple somewhere around that time—
otherwise they wouldn't have met Kosuke at the foot of the
winding path on his way back from the branch house. And
obviously, if they had set out from the temple within those

ten minutes, they would have run into Hanako on her way up. In other words, Hanako couldn't have been going up to the temple at that time.

Kosuke needed to work out when Hanako could have gone up to Senkoji Temple. If she'd left home at exactly 6.15 p.m., there was a ten-minute gap before Kosuke left the temple at 6.25 p.m. If Hanako had arrived at the temple within those ten minutes (and it wasn't entirely impossible if she had hurried), then surely someone would have noticed her? The study in which Kosuke was staying faced the back of the temple grounds so he wouldn't have seen her, but the temple gates were fully visible from the sitting room of the priests' quarters. Moreover, it was possible to see out over the winding path below. At that time, the sliding shoji blinds on the windows were wide open. Kosuke was sure that either the priest or Ryotaku would have spotted Hanako coming through the gate.

Kosuke suspected that when Hanako had left the Kito house around 6.15 p.m., she hadn't gone straight to Senkoji Temple. She must have stopped by somewhere else, waited until she was sure everyone had left the temple and then climbed up the hill. But that hypothesis threw up a couple of important questions:

1. Where had Hanako stopped off?
2. More importantly, why had Hanako gone to Senkoji Temple in the first place?

It turned out that the answer to the second question wasn't difficult to find.

In order to ascertain whether there were any more injuries to Hanako's body, the doctor had opened the front of her kimono. Tucked inside was a letter. It had been concealed deep inside her under-kimono, and consequently survived the downpour. It was barely wet at all.

"There's a letter!" cried the mayor, as he peered over the doctor's shoulder.

"What? Huh. What a ridiculously fancy envelope!" said the priest, taking the letter and holding it up to the electric light. "Kindaichi-san, my eyes aren't very good. Could you read it for me?"

Kosuke took the envelope from the priest. It was the kind of patterned envelope that a schoolgirl would use. It was addressed "To Tsukiyo-sama". On the back, "From you-know-who".

"What's this? To Tsukiyo-sama? This was a letter for her older sister Tsukiyo?"

"That's strange," said the mayor. "Why would Hanako-san have a letter addressed to her sister?"

"Hmm, well. Let's take a look inside for now," said the priest. "I'm pretty sure I know who this you-know-who is. And it's definitely been dictated by the mistress of the branch family. That's the kind of thing that woman would write."

Kosuke opened the envelope and read the letter aloud.

Tsukiyo-sama,

Meet me in Senkoji Temple grounds at 7 tonight. The temple should be deserted at that time. We'll be free to talk without prying eyes.

—You-Know-Who

As he read, Kosuke's skin began to crawl. He was hit by a feeling that was difficult to explain—a mixture of discomfort and amusement. The writing style was straight out of an Edo Era love story.

"Ukai-san for sure," said the mayor.

"It seems so, but from the phrasing, I am sure that Oshiho-san dictated it to him. There's no one besides that woman who would write those hideous phrases," said the priest.

"Is there anyone here who would recognize Ukai's handwriting?" Kosuke asked.

There wasn't.

"Even though no one knows his handwriting, there's no doubt that he wrote it. He used that letter to lure Hanako to this temple."

"But, Ryonen-san, this letter was addressed to Tsukiyo-san," Kosuke pointed out.

"That's by the by. There was a letter for Tsukiyo, and for whatever reason Hanako got her hands on it. And instead of delivering it to her sister, as she should have done, she slipped out and came here herself. And yes, yes, I remember now, Koan-san—didn't you say you'd seen that lover boy heading towards the temple earlier in the evening? What time was that?"

"I don't know… I don't check the time very often. On my way to the main house, at one of the bends in the road, I looked in this direction and caught a glimpse of that boy turning onto the winding path."

Doctor Koan had arrived at the Kito house shortly after Kosuke and the others, so Kosuke estimated this must have been around 6.50 p.m. Which meant that right after Kosuke had visited the branch family house, Shozo Ukai had slipped out and followed him.

The tide master, Takezo, joined the conversation.

"So, Ryonen-san, you believe that he lured Hanako up here, and then, and then… he murdered her?"

"Ukai?… Murdered Hanako?…" said Koan, as if weighing it up in his mind.

The priest and the mayor exchanged glances. That Ukai had lured Hanako to the temple, no one had any doubt. But as to the matter of murdering the girl… it seemed that nobody was willing to express an opinion.

Kosuke really didn't know much about Ukai, but from the one time he had met him, his impression was of some sort of mannequin. He really didn't see the young man as the kind of crazed killer who would have committed a murder like this. He knew you should never judge people by their appearances, but still…

"Ryonen-san, is Ukai-san a smoker?"

"A smoker?"

The priest frowned.

"I haven't seen him smoking. But why do you ask?"

"It was those cigarette butts we found earlier. I wondered if Ukai-san was the one who had dropped them there. I thought it was possible that he could have got those particular rolled-up cigarettes from Tsukiyo or Yukie or Hanako."

"No, he doesn't smoke."

It was Takezo who spoke.

"I remember offering him a cigarette once, and he turned it down, saying he didn't smoke. However, Reverend Father?…"

Clearly irritated, Takezo rocked forward onto his knees and smacked his fist into the tatami.

"Somebody killed Hanako, but why did they leave her hanging there in a place like this? And worse, upside down?... Whoever killed Hana-chan, why did they do it in that brutal manner?"

And there was the crux of the matter. Detective Kosuke Kindaichi had been pondering the exact same question. Was it simply the murderer showing off? Just like some novelists, trying to find a fresh story, think up the most excessively theatrical settings, had this murderer, just on a whim, painted this ghastly spectacle out of flesh and blood?

No, no, no.

Kosuke Kindaichi didn't believe anything of the sort. He was convinced that the fact that Hanako's corpse had been hung upside down on the tree held some kind of profound significance. It was crazy, utterly insane. But the whole of Gokumon Island itself had something crazy about it. The island's peculiar ways must have had some profound effect on both the murderer's motive and method.

Takezo's words had jolted them from a bad dream. Previously frozen to the spot, now an icy shudder ran between all of the men.

At that moment a yell came from the direction of the priests' quarters.

"Reverend Father!"

It was Ryotaku's voice.

"Reverend Father, Reverend Father, I know what it was that the burglar stole. Reverend Father, the burglar took—"

Still yelling, Ryotaku came hurtling out of the priests' quarters towards the main building, a triumphant look on his face. He was brandishing a wooden tub-shaped container that usually held cooked rice.

"Reverend Father, this container was still half full of rice. And now, as you can see, it's completely empty!"

The burglar had stolen half a pot of rice.

CHAPTER 3

The Haiku Folding Screen

Dawn brought with it a thick layer of fog. It had continued to pour with rain up until the moment that day broke, but then it seemed as if the remainder of the rain had simply turned to mist and wrapped Gokumon Island in its damp folds. Senkoji Temple, sunk deeply in the dark grey fog, was blurry like a lingering dream in the eye of someone awakening from sleep.

Kosuke Kindaichi had dozed off around dawn, but now he awakened to the sound of chanting coming from the main temple building. It was still dark in the study where he was sleeping, but the chill morning light that filtered in through the gap in the *amado* rain shutters lingered in the corners of the room. Kosuke rolled onto his stomach and looked at the watch he'd placed by his pillow. It was already past eight. It seemed the priest was also starting his morning late.

Still lying on his belly, Kosuke reached for his pack of cigarettes and lit one. As he puffed on it he vaguely heard the sounds of the religious service; the ring of the gong was particularly chilling, like being soaked up to the neck in icy water.

He began to think over the events of last night, trying to grasp the elements of reality beneath the garish staging of the murder. But his tired mind found it hard to focus, staggering around like a blindfolded child in a game of tag.

He decided to give up thinking, and tried to get up from his futon, but his listless body seemed to prefer to stay enfolded in the perfect warmth of the bedcovers. And now, the rhythmic sounding of the gong was beginning to lull him pleasantly back into the state of sleep. It sounded like "lie, lie" and tempted him to do just that. For a while Kosuke surrendered his body to that sweet sensation. Then he lit another cigarette and as he lazily smoked it, he ran his eyes over the double-leafed *byobu* folding screen by the head of his futon.

A couple of evenings before, the priest had brought in this screen especially for Kosuke, and placed it by his bed, explaining that the nights got cold on Gokumon Island and it would block the draught. It was a prettily decorated screen, the kind you might use as part of the traditional *ohinasama* doll display. Its base paper was made from what looked like recycled wood-block printing paper from the leaves of an old haiku poetry collection. It appeared to be covered with verses, but the calligraphy was so stylized that Kosuke could barely make out anything more than one or two *hiragana* characters. Anyway, on top of the base paper, there were three *shikishi*—thick square cardboard cards for writing poetry. Two of these were stuck on the right leaf of the screen, and one on the left. On each card, there was a simple sketch of either a monk or the master of a tea ceremony—it was impossible to make out which. On the two right-hand cards, it was a personage wearing a kind of cloth scarf tied on his head and a black haori-style jacket. From the three deep wrinkles drawn on his forehead, he appeared to be an old man. The two cards showed him in different postures, but it seemed quite likely that they were the same person. And then, on the left-hand card, was the image of an extremely bad-mannered character. He was dressed in a similar haori jacket to the other two sketches, but in his case it was hanging open, almost down to his navel. He sat cross-legged with his hairy legs on full display. He wasn't wearing a hat, and his round, shaved head reminded Kosuke of the mythical sea monster *umibouzu*. Above each of these portraits was what seemed to be a haiku, but they had been quite carelessly scribbled, and were even more difficult to decipher than the verses on the base paper. There was really no need for him to try to read anything as unintelligible as this, but whenever he was being idle, Kosuke always developed a feeling of irritation deep in the pit of his stomach that threatened to erupt; so, in order to stifle that feeling, he applied himself to reading the folding screen.

First, the haiku on the top right… The five characters in the top line, and the five in the bottom were both apparently written in hiragana… This much Kosuke could discern, but those characters were the problem. For a good while he stared at the top line and the bottom line in turn, but the poet's peculiar lettering squirmed like the traces left by worms in the mud, and the whole thing looked like complete nonsense. Kosuke gave up, and turned his attention to the name of the poet. Bizarrely, there seemed to be two different signatures. If he looked really, really carefully, underneath one of these names he could just about make out the character "*utsusu*", copied. At this moment he realized that these poetry cards weren't something that the artists had written themselves: some other person had copied the original poets' writing. It so happened that by looking even more closely it was possible to make out this other person's name on the other two cards, and similarly "copied" appeared under the name in each case. In other words, all three of these poems had been written out by the same person. Next, Kosuke looked for the most legible version out of the three. He finally succeeded in making out the name Gokumon.

"I see…"

Kosuke gave a satisfied grunt.

This "Gokumon" was clearly an alias that someone had used, one that referred to the name of Gokumon Island. Which also meant that the writer was a resident of the island. Kosuke had worked all of this out, and yet of course he still understood nothing of the content.

Next, he turned his attention to trying to decipher the names of the original poets. They were each made up of three hiragana characters. After studying them for a while, Kosuke concluded that the two names on the cards on the right were the same. In other words, the two portraits of the master with the headscarf and the haori were indeed the same person. But the man's name… after a lot of brain-racking, Kosuke finally came to the conclusion that it read "Okina", which meant "the master".

"What the?… It's Basho!"

With apologies to the venerable master, Basho Matsuo, it has to be said that Kosuke Kindaichi's tone at this point was one of total disgust. However, this was not to say that

Kosuke felt any disrespect at all towards this veritable God of Haiku. It was simply that after all the time, energy and hard work he'd put into the task, the name he'd finally been able to decipher was the most popular haiku poet who had ever lived. Who wouldn't feel deflated after that?

On the other hand, given that these were haiku by Basho, there was now a chance of deciphering them. It was very possible they were famous haiku that he already knew.

Right away, Kosuke was able to check if there were any other instances of the hiragana syllables "O" or "Ki" or "Na" from the name "Okina" in the top and bottom lines. There were, and after examining the writing down to the minutest detail, he finally came to the conclusion that this must be the haiku:

How tragic—beneath the helmet, a hidden cricket.

It felt like a huge weight had been lifted from his shoulders. After deciphering that haiku on one of the right-hand cards, it was surprisingly easy to work out the other one.

In the same lodge sleep courtesans—moon and bush clover.

These were both poems that had appeared in Basho's famous collection *Oku no Hosomichi* (*The Narrow Road to the Deep North*); consequently, Kosuke had studied both of them in junior high school.

Now that he had figured out the two haiku on the right, it was time to tackle the one on the left. Going by the portrait of the poet, it was not by Basho. The master would never have been this slovenly in his appearance. Moreover, the name under the haiku was definitely not Okina, or Basho, or any other derivation of the master's name at all. However, given that the two haiku on the right were by Basho, then it followed that the one on the left was also by some other well-known master poet of the past. Surely, no one would dream of displaying a verse by some common, run-of-the-mill, talentless poet alongside the work of the ultimate master of haiku? Kosuke began to rack his brain for the names of other well-known haiku poets, and eventually came up with Basho's famous disciple Takarai Kikaku.

"Of course, that says 'Kikaku'. Why have they made the lettering so damn complicated?"

Kosuke snorted with annoyance. All that he could remember about Kikaku was that he was infamous for some incident on a bridge with a character called Gengo Otaka. Unfortunately, Kosuke was not familiar with his work at all. He realized he had a challenging task before him to work out this haiku.

"Right, what were some of the haiku of his that were popular?... Yes, yes,

"Year's end—water's flow and the fickleness of fate.

"Hmm, no, it's definitely not that one."

Kosuke proceeded to rummage through all the drawers of his memory, until he had dragged out a version of two or three haiku belonging to Kikaku.

"Autumn moon—across the tatami stretch shadows of pine.

"And then there's the one that goes

"Evening cool—a shooting star over Musashi Plain.

"No, it's neither of those. Oh—hold on—wasn't there one about pampas grass at Ise Shrine?… Hmm… no, it doesn't matter anyway, it's definitely not that one either…"

How on earth was he supposed to read this?

He was finally able to make out a couple of hiragana characters but that was all. Nothing but a bunch of prepositions… He had no clue what kanji characters could possibly fill in the blanks.

It was at this point that he heard a voice calling his name. It came from the direction of the priests' quarters.

"Kindaichi-san! Kindaichi-san!"

All at once, his obsession with the haiku on the folding screen vanished like morning mist.

"Kindaichi-san, are you still sleeping?"

The voice belonged to the island's police officer, Shimizu. Kosuke leapt out of bed. He realized he'd missed the friendly bearded face.

"Just a m-minute. I'll be right th-there."

The morning prayer readings were still underway, but drawing to an end, as indicated by the sound of the bowl gong being struck slowly, sending a chilling feeling through the air. Kosuke hurriedly pulled on his clothes, sticking his nightwear in the nearest closet. Opening the amado rain shutters, he noticed the thick fog for the first time. The surprise caused him to sneeze three times in succession.

Barefoot, he entered the chilly kitchen to Shimizu's broad smile. However, the policeman quickly assumed a more serious expression, and with a clearing of the throat, hurriedly composed himself.

"Morning!" said Kosuke. "Sorry, I seem to have slept late."

"Understandable. You must have been exhausted by the shock of last night."

By the look of Shimizu's bleary eyes, he hadn't had much sleep either.

"And in that terrible rain too... Did you get back just now?"

"Yes, things didn't go so well out there. It was like being thrown suddenly onto the set of some film."

"Why's that?"

"We were pursuing a pirate ship—exchanging fire: bang, bang, guns going off all over. Couldn't you hear it from here?"

"No, I didn't hear a thing. So it happened close to here?"

"No, no. Over by Manabe Island. It was terrible. It looked like there were about seven or eight gangsters on the ship. They were desperate, like a cornered rat trying to bite a cat. The shots came flying. And we didn't exactly hold back either. Both sides shooting like crazy at each other. It was a bigger battle than the Dannoura."

It was a blatant exaggeration, comparing it to a major twelfth-century sea battle.

"That sounds terrible," said Kosuke. "And did you capture the pirates?"

"They managed to get away. Unfortunately, one of their bullets hit our engine and we broke down. And off they sailed on the foam-capped waves on their merry way. Their ship was around fifteen tonnes, but it could get up a lot of speed."

"I'm really sorry to hear that. When you say 'we', it wasn't just you by yourself then?"

"No, no. We were using police HQ's ship so there were a bunch of us on board. This was the same gang that had destroyed the storehouse at Mizushima and stolen textiles and other valuable goods. We were lying in wait for them. Oh yes, by the way, I came across a fellow who knows you."

"Who knows *me*?"

Kosuke was a little taken aback. From the flow of the conversation, it sounded rather as if Shimizu was suggesting he was related to the pirate band. Shimizu composed his face once again, fixed his eyes rather suspiciously on Kosuke's face and cleared his throat. When he spoke next, his tone had changed completely.

"Kindaichi-san, I don't know why, but I've grown fond of you. So I'm going to give you a tip-off in secret… If there is anything shady or crooked about you, I'd suggest you run away from here right now."

"Wh-wh-what did you say?"

At Shimizu's unexpected show of kindness, Kosuke had completely lost his nerve.

"Wh-who was it told you I was shady?"

"Someone who says they know you. This person asked me if anything strange had happened on Gokumon Island, and I said that there was nothing out of the ordinary here. And then I said that a drifter by the name of Kosuke Kindaichi— Well… ah…"

"Don't worry, I don't mind being called a drifter. And so you told him about the suspicious drifter by the name of Kosuke Kindaichi?"

"Right. And he was amazed by that information. He said, 'Kosuke Kindaichi is there on the island?' And he asked if this Kosuke Kindaichi looked like this or that, and his description of you was spot on, Kindaichi-san. So I said, 'Yes, that's him,' and this person was even more surprised. He said, 'Oh no, there's no reason for that man to visit an insignificant out-of-the-way place such as Gokumon Island. He must have some sort of specific purpose.' He told me to watch out. To keep an eye on you. And that if he had a moment, he was going to pay a visit and check things out for himself."

Kosuke was more than surprised to hear of this conversation—he was astounded. He stared at Shimizu.

"Shimizu-san, th-this person you're talking about. Wh-who on earth was it?"

Shimizu immediately put on his official face again. With the most dignified expression he could muster, he stared right back at Kosuke.

"His name is Isokawa. Inspector Isokawa—a veteran of the Okayama Prefectural Police headquarters. A very capable detective by all accounts."

Kosuke immediately began to scratch his head, a look of joy on his face. He scratched so hard that dandruff flew in clouds around him. Shimizu was forced to take a good few steps backwards to get out of the line of fire.

"You do know Inspector Isokawa then?"

"Y-yes, I know him. I know him. H-how is he? Is he in good health?"

"Yes, he seems well. Lots of people lost their jobs in the police force thanks to the war, but it seems he's all right."

"And he s-says he might visit Gokumon Island?"

"Kindaichi-san?"

The policeman was looking at Kosuke even more suspiciously.

"What's wrong? Are you crying?"

"Oh no, no. Ha ha."

Kosuke quickly wiped his eye with a finger.

Dear reader, if you have read *The Honjin Murders*, I am sure you will understand why Kosuke Kindaichi shed a tear right then, and I am certain you will sympathize with his plight. The mysterious locked-room murder that took place in a small farming community in Okayama Prefecture was the debut case of Kosuke Kindaichi, Private Detective. Solving the murder case alongside him was Okayama Police Inspector Isokawa. However, this was not the only reason for Kosuke's tears. Between the Honjin murder case and this current one, there had been a war on a global scale, and many men had been posted overseas and never returned. A good number of people remaining in Japan had had their houses burned to the ground, and been scattered all over the country, and there was often no way to ascertain whether they had survived the war. And now, here on this remote island, an island that Kosuke himself barely had any connection to, he had suddenly heard news of an old friend. It was completely unexpected and moving, and now he was feeling sentimental.

Shimizu looked searchingly at Kosuke's face.

"So you don't need to run away?"

"Far from it. Karma will always get me. Ha ha."

Kosuke laughed. Shimizu snorted dubiously.

"Look, Kindaichi-san, as soon as I heard this morning about the events of last night from Takezo, I was determined to lock you up. Then there was my talk with Inspector Isokawa. You've definitely had some dealings with the police in the past. And from the way the inspector talked about you, you're obviously quite a well-known character."

"Of course. You're quite right." Kosuke stifled a giggle. "But the fact that you haven't put me in handcuffs yet—does that mean that you've changed your mind?"

"That's right. I thought it over, and there is one thing that doesn't make sense. But I have come to a conclusion about you that is quite the opposite of what you claim. And if my theory turns out to be right, then I'm going to be forced to throw you in jail."

"What do you mean, the opposite?"

Once again, Kosuke looked at Shimizu in surprise. What was it in the expression on this amicable policeman's face?

Shimizu screwed up his eyes and blinked nervously several times.

"You say you were a comrade of Chimata-san of the Kito family. And that you came here to the island at his request?"

"Th-that's right."

"Well, that's my problem. If, in fact you were instead the comrade of Hitoshi-san, cousin of Chimata, and you had come to the island at his request, that would fit my way of thinking perfectly. I'd have to lock you up immediately."

Kosuke couldn't believe his ears. He fixed Shimizu with a gaze that could have bored a hole through his face.

"Shimizu-san, what on earth are you saying? Why if I was a friend of Hitoshi's would you have to put me in shackles?"

"Don't you get it? Chimata-san, the heir to the Kito name, is dead. There was an official letter, so there is no doubt whatsoever of that. And now that Chimata-san is dead, the whole of the Kito family estate belongs to his cousin, Hitoshi-san. But hold on a minute! There are still the three sisters: Tsukiyo, Yukie and Hanako. To sort out the matter they need to be killed off first..."

A cold tingle ran down Kosuke's spine. Hackles raised, he glared at Shimizu's unshaven face. Then he began to speak in a strained voice.

"Understood. So let me summarize what you're telling me: if I were Hitoshi-san's comrade-in-arms and I had come here to Gokumon Island at his request, then I would be under suspicion of having been employed by him as a kind of assassin?"

"That's right, that's right. That's the direction I was going in. But you—"

"Hold on just a minute! There's a flaw in your logic. First of all, there is no way that Hitoshi in Burma could have any idea of the death of Chimata in New Guinea. Second of all, it's a perilous undertaking to employ a henchman to carry out an assassination. I believe it would be much easier and safer for him to come home and secretly commit the crimes himself."

"No, I don't agree with you. I think this is much the simpler method. Imagine Hitoshi-san came home and suddenly the Kito girls started dying one by one. He'd be the prime suspect. But nobody would suspect him while he's still in Burma. Let's say you were Hitoshi-san's hired assassin, you who have no connection at all with the Kito family: you could commit the crimes without falling under suspicion."

"Bu-but, like I said before, with Hitoshi in Burma and Chimata in New Guinea, there would be no way for him to know that Chimata had died."

"So he was taking his chances that Chimata was dead. He knew perfectly well that Chimata had been dispatched to the front. He decided that in such a devastating war there was a good chance that the heir would have been killed. So he entrusted the job to his good buddy who was coming home first. If Chimata-san was still alive, then never mind, but if he was dead, then he asked you to kill the three sisters before he returned… In fact, now that I think about it, if Chimata-san had been alive, he probably would have asked you to kill him first of all."

To hear these dreadful words from the mouth of such a good-natured person as Sergeant Shimizu made them all the more shocking. Kosuke clenched his teeth, gulped and stood there for while in total bewilderment. Eventually he managed to turn his gaze back to the pupils of the policeman.

"Nevertheless, your hypothesis is incorrect, Shimizu-san. I am not a friend of Hitoshi's; I was Chimata's comrade and friend. Please acknowledge that."

Shimizu sighed and relaxed his shoulders.

"I do acknowledge it. In fact, just now I called into the Kito house, and asked Sanae-san. She said that the note you brought with you was without a doubt in Chimata-san's handwriting. On that point, both she and Okatsu-san were very sure. That's why I'm not going to arrest you after all."

"Well, thank you very much for that. But, Shimizu-san, how did you come to think such terrible things? Is Hitoshi-san really the kind of person who would do something so hideous?"

"I don't know. I really don't know how those suspicions ended up in my mind either. It's all the fault of this cursed Gokumon Island. It's just as I told you before: the inhabitants of this island aren't like other folks—they have this bizarre, different sense of things. Inside that hard shell that they all have around them, they are engulfed in a way of thinking that is unimaginable to mainland Japanese people. And then came the war. They all more or less went crazy. And maybe I've gone crazy too. And probably that's how such terrible thoughts ended up in my head."

Shimizu stroked his neck sadly and stretched it to the left and right.

His way of thinking had been mistaken. He knew Kosuke had never even met this Hitoshi. And that was proof enough for him. However, how could Kosuke just laugh off this unfounded delusion that had been in Shimizu's head? His hypothesis from beginning to end contained an element of horrible truth.

Once again, Kosuke could hear, like the roar of the sea, like the growl of distant thunder, like an ominous rumble, the echo of Chimata's dying words: "Go to Gokumon Island… My three sisters will be murdered… My cousin… My cousin—"

"Ah, Shimizu-san, thanks for coming."

119

The words jolted Kosuke from his thoughts. He turned around to see the priest, Ryonen, and the apprentice, Ryotaku, returning from morning prayers in the main temple building. Both of their faces were puffy from lack of sleep.

"Ryotaku, could you get breakfast ready right away? Kindaichi-san, you must be hungry."

The priest turned to the police officer.

"I'm sorry to have more unexpected trouble for you to deal with. The body is in the main building: I'm sure you want to see it right away. But I'm just going to eat quickly first, so could you wait a minute?"

And with that, the priest turned back to address Kosuke once more.

"Kindaichi-san, you said you'd investigate those foot-prints again when the sun was up. Have you done that yet? I see—you overslept and just got up now? Ha ha. Well, that's to be expected. Nobody got much sleep last night what with all the fuss and that storm to boot.

"All night autumn wind howls—mountains out back.

"That one was written by Sora Kawai, one of Basho's appren-tices who stayed at the temple. Sora is not a great poet, but this haiku really conveys the feel of a night like last night."

Typical of Ryonen, he quoted an old haiku, albeit with a slight twist, and followed it up with a laugh. His voice was sleep-deprived, but still pleasant.

WAIT AND HE WILL COME

As I've said before, the inhabitants of Gokumon Island had strong connections to the temple. The first night that Kosuke Kindaichi stayed at Senkoji, he was woken before dawn the next morning by the sound of footsteps, the praying voices of pious men and women, the rattling of the rope on the temple gong. He'd wondered what festival it was that day, but later had realized that this was an everyday situation on the island. Before going out fishing, before setting off for work, if they didn't pay a visit to the temple first, the islanders would feel unsettled all day. However, this was less of a strong religious faith, and more part of a regular daily routine such as washing your face or brushing your teeth.

This morning, however, Sergeant Shimizu seemed to have the situation under control, and not a single visitor had stepped through the temple gates. Inside the grounds, still enveloped in a thick layer of fog, there was not a soul to be seen. Even though Kosuke Kindaichi had inadvertently overslept, he was relieved to see that no one had trodden all over the crime scene.

"Kindaichi-san, go and get something to eat for now. We were all up late last night and you must be really hungry. Shimizu-san, can we offer you a cup of tea? You can finish your job afterwards."

"Thanks."

Breakfast at the temple was a simple affair. Steamed rice with barley, miso soup and a couple of slices of pickled daikon radish. Sergeant Shimizu couldn't be bothered to take off his shoes, so he just sat down on the entrance step, and slurped at the cup of tea that the apprentice priest, Ryotaku, brought him.

"By the way, Ryonen-san," he said, apparently remembering something, "is it true what I just heard from Takezo, that last night the burglar made off with all your cooked rice?"

"Yes, he did. Completely cleaned out the pot."

"About how much was left in the pot, Ryotaku-san?"

"I suppose about three portions. I'd forgotten that we were going to eat at the wake up at the Kito house last night, and accidentally cooked the usual amount of rice for the evening meal."

"I see. So he wolfed down a tonne of food. Ryonen-san, do you think murdering someone works up an appetite?"

Shimizu was utterly serious. Kosuke almost spat out his tea, and had to put his cup down quickly before he choked.

"*Gochisosama*—thank you for breakfast," he said, jumping to his feet. "Well, I think it's time to go and investigate the footprints of this killer with the huge appetite."

As previously mentioned, right outside the back door of the priests' quarters the edge of the mountain rose steeply, and consequently the ground was always wet. However, thanks to the overhanging eaves, the torrential rain of the previous night hadn't washed away the footprints.

"Oh, those military boot prints? If I'd known I'd have come in a little more carefully. I see what you mean—they go in through the door and then back out again."

The prints had already been trodden all over by the priest, the apprentice, Kosuke Kindaichi, and now this morning by Sergeant Shimizu, so it was something of a mess, but it was still possible to make out clear prints both entering the back door and leaving again.

"Shimizu-san, are there residents of the island who wear military boots?"

"Ah, plenty. These days there are so many demobilized soldiers returning to the island. And then just the other day they were distributing army boots. Hey, just a minute, Kindaichi-san?"

Shimizu was bending over the footprints, and he had suddenly called out.

"Take a look at this. See that print? There's a little mark in it in the shape of a bat? I wonder if it's the mud that makes it look like that? Or was there some sort of a crack in the sole of his boot that made it?"

"Yes, I see it. This was the right foot. Just a moment…"

Kosuke bent down and tried to find a matching right boot print among the jumbled mess.

"Shimizu-san, I think you're right. The sole of his right boot had a mark in it. See those over there? They're the same."

The boot prints that Kosuke was pointing to, despite being varied in depth, all had a little bat-shaped mark around the toe area.

"So we can conclude that his right boot had a mark on the sole. Whoever is wearing a boot like this one is the killer. Hm. This is the best piece of evidence we could have found."

Sergeant Shimizu sounded extremely pleased with his discovery. But all of a sudden, Kosuke's body snapped upright again. It was a sudden reflex that startled the police officer.

"Kindaichi-san, what is it?"

But the detective didn't appear to have heard him. His eyes were fixed on a spot in distant space. A shadow of doubt crossed Shimizu's face.

"Kindaichi-san? Hey, Kindaichi-san! What's the matter? Don't tell me you know the man who wears this boot!"

"I know him?"

Kosuke turned and looked blankly at Shimizu, but catching the expression of distrust in the policeman's eyes, he quickly shook his head.

"Th-that's absurd. How would that even be possible?"

"And yet, when you looked at those prints, something surprised you."

"That's not it, Shimizu-san. That's not it. The reason I'm surprised right now—no, I think we'd better have this conversation afterwards. Let's search the area first."

Shimizu looked even more suspicious now. Kosuke avoided his eyes, and moved stealthily out of the narrow passage between the door and the cliff. At that moment, he could never have imagined the consequences of leaving a shadow of suspicion in the mind of this good fellow Shimizu. If he had realized, he wouldn't have hesitated to share his discovery with the policeman on the spot.

This is what Kosuke Kindaichi had discovered...

While examining the right boot prints in the earth outside the priests' quarters, he had noticed that there were more footprints heading into the building than out of it. Not only that, among the inward-pointing footprints there were definitely a few that overlapped some of the outward footprints—in other words, had been made after them.

What did this mean? Most of the prints had been made by somebody going into the living quarters and then coming back out. That much was clear, but it appeared that the killer had then turned around and gone back inside again. But then, once he'd gone back in, where had he gone after that? There was no set of footprints coming back out a second time, so what did that mean?...

Kosuke had been puzzling over this when suddenly a scene flashed through his mind. He recalled the night before when they had been standing around the old plum tree, how strange the priest's behaviour had been. He had been standing facing the Zen meditation hall when he seemed to be surprised, and dropped his heavy priest's staff with a loud clatter. As he bent down to pick it up, his hands had been shaking quite violently. Perhaps as he looked into the meditation hall, the priest had caught sight of someone—that someone quite possibly being the killer.

If that was the case, then the behaviour of the priest from that moment onwards had to be viewed with suspicion. After dropping and retrieving his staff, and sending Takezo off to inform others, he had led Kosuke and Ryotaku to the back entrance of the priests' quarters in order to show them the footprints. This had taken them out of sight of the meditation hall, and would have given anyone hiding there the perfect opportunity to escape. Moreover (and at this, the turmoil in Kosuke's chest grew stronger)— moreover, right after that, as Kosuke was examining the footprints in the earth, the priest had gone through the kitchen and his living quarters and ended up alone at the main temple building. What if before going to the main building, he had slipped over to the meditation hall and fastened the latch on the doorway, thereby concealing how the killer had escaped? And then later, in order to demonstrate to Kosuke and Ryotaku that nothing was amiss, perhaps he'd purposely taken them into the meditation hall to look around.

Kosuke was sure of it: the priest knew the identity of the killer. When they had discovered Hanako's body, the comments he had made about being out of reason… yes, the priest knew the killer. No, not only knew him, he'd deliberately allowed him to escape.

As he thought this over, Kosuke began to search painstakingly the central courtyard and garden of the temple. But as he'd expected, there wasn't a single mark even resembling a footprint. The grounds of this temple, which had originally been constructed by cutting into the side of a granite mountain, would get as arid as a whetstone after successive days of dry weather, but after a downpour like last night's, all the earth had washed away. Kosuke paid special attention to the vicinity of the meditation hall, but he couldn't find anything like a footprint there either. Naturally, in the main temple building and the meditation hall there had been no muddy footprints. It meant that the killer must have removed his boots before entering. So he must have been barefoot when he finally escaped from the meditation hall. Even if there hadn't been such torrential rain last night, the tracks of someone who had tiptoed barefoot still might not be visible in the dirt. There was just the one spot, by the offertory box in front of the main temple building where they had found the cigarette butts, where Kosuke could see five or six dried muddy footprints. And all of the right boot prints had the same bat-shaped mark in them.

"Hey, Shimizu-san, the killer was definitely hanging around here for a while. This spot is in a straight line from the temple gate. You can't see the steps themselves but you can see the path beneath. So if he sat on this staircase, he could see who was about to come up the temple steps, and he smoked while he kept watch."

"He smoked? How do you know he was smoking?"

"Because there were cigarette butts on the ground just here. That's right—you didn't know about those."

"There were cigarette butts? What happened to them?"

"We collected them. It was the priest who found them."

"Kindaichi-san?"

Shimizu-san drew himself up to his full height. He made the greatest dramatic effort to look displeased.

"What on earth do you think you are playing at? What do you all take me for? I am the upholder of the law and public order on this island. You have disregarded me, and cut down the corpse without my permission, collected cigarette butts which were clearly evidence. What were you thinking? When there is a crime committed, particularly in the case of a homicide, it is of the utmost importance that the crime scene be left intact. I know that this is procedure of which you are perfectly well aware. Or perhaps it is that you are purposely attempting to hinder my investigation?"

"Now, now, Shimizu-san."

"Don't you 'now, now' me! Right then, show me these cigarette butts. No, don't just show them to me. You need to put them back in the exact same spot you found them."

"B-but that's impossible!"

"What's impossible? How and in exactly what position were these cigarette ends lying? There may have been something of great significance in that. If you can't return them to their original position, then I am going to have to arrest you on the charge of destruction of evidence."

"Wh-why, Shimizu-san? Why would you say something so heartless? Why are you being so tough on me? Aren't we friends?"

"What do you mean? What kind of friends are we exactly? Don't be so disrespectful. You're nothing but a drifter from who-knows-where, and I'm this island's respected officer of the law."

This was a whole new level of overbearing manner that Kosuke had never seen from Shimizu. He was completely flummoxed.

"W-well, y-yes, that's true… Oh, good morning! You arrived at the perfect moment. We were just about to pay you a visit. Well, not strictly speaking 'we'. Sergeant Shimizu here had just announced his intention to do so. Hadn't you, Shimizu-san?"

Kosuke was addressing Oshiho from the branch Kito family, who had just entered through the temple gates. Behind her was the handsome young Shozo Ukai. As far as Kosuke was concerned, their arrival couldn't have been more timely. He still had no idea why Shimizu's attitude had undergone this abrupt change, but he decided to make use of the visitors' arrival to dodge his attack for the time being. He immediately paid Oshiho assiduous attention. He didn't notice that his behaviour only served to raise Shimizu's suspicions even further.

"Oh dear," said Oshiho. "Were the two of you having some sort of quarrel?"

Oshiho had made an extra effort with her make-up this morning. Her face as it appeared from the morning mist was as delicately white as a moonflower. And then the way that she moved! She seemed to have some kind of refined technique to make her figure seem to waft on air. Her whole body brimmed with sensuality.

"Well, er, why no. We weren't quarrelling."

As usual, Kosuke felt himself on the point of stammering, and had begun to scratch his bird's nest of hair. It seemed that the scratching was helping him to get the words out.

"I see. Well, I am very glad to hear that."

Oshiho threw Kosuke a seductive glance, then turned back to Shimizu.

"I came up here because a very strange rumour reached my ears."

Face-to-face with Oshiho, Shimizu's demeanour changed completely. There was no sign of the bravado of his earlier conversation with Kosuke.

"What k-kind of strange rumour?" he stammered.

"Well, strange is strange. I thought I would bring Ukai-san here and find out all about it. Kindaichi-san, where is Ryonen-san?"

"He's right here!"

The priest came trudging over from his quarters to the main temple building.

"Welcome, Oshiho-san. How is Gihei doing? I hope his gout is a little better. Hey, Ryotaku! Get some *zabuton* cushions for everyone to sit on. And you, er... oh yes, Ukai-san, please come over here and sit yourself down. There's nothing to be afraid of. A handsome young man like you, everybody's fond of you, nobody's going to bite you. Ha ha ha. By the way, Oshiho-san?"

Oshiho-san was lost for words at the priest's treatment of Ukai. She looked with astonishment at the priest, who had plonked himself down cross-legged on a zabuton. He didn't waste time, adding:

"I was listening from over there, and you really don't need to hold back. Is there something you need to hear all about, Oshiho-san? Or is there something you need to tell this priest? If there is, please speak freely. Young Hanako there is also listening."

The priest pointed towards the back of the main hall.

When Shozo Ukai heard this, his expression clouded, and he moved into Oshiho's shadow. Her face coloured. As she was so pale, the redness was all the more obvious. For a moment her eyelids were on fire, and her eyes seemed to flash. However, she seemed immediately to regret it. To get too agitated here, in public, would be a defeat from which she could never recover. Oshiho-san was not in the habit of removing her armour in front of others. Politely lowering herself onto the cushion that the apprentice priest, Ryotaku, had offered her, she gave a sickly-sweet laugh.

"Tee-hee. You are such a tease, Ryonen-san."

Her face was quickly returning to its usual hue.

"You make it sound as if I came here to complain about something. But it's just that I am such an unrefined, ill-mannered woman that I have no idea how to speak politely. I came because something unexpected has happened, and

I inadvertently sounded offensive because I was upset. You know what they say: even a worm will turn."

"A worm? You, my dear lady, a worm? Certainly not—you are no worm. You are a much greater creature than that. A snake perhaps."

The priest glanced at Oshiho's reddening cheek.

"Well, never mind about all that," he continued. "What is this upsetting thing that you wanted to talk about, Oshiho-san?"

"Yes, I heard that last night Hana-chan was found murdered in this place, and the whole village is talking about it. People are claiming that, at my instigation, Ukai-san lured Hana-chan here and that he and I killed her together. Isn't that the most outrageous thing you ever heard?"

"I see. Well, that is indeed a terrible thing to say. However, Oshiho-san, don't you think that one might say that there is no smoke without fire? Are you sure that you didn't do something along those lines?"

"Me? I am devastated that even you, Ryonen-san, would cast such aspersions."

"Now, now. Of course I'm not suggesting that you two murdered poor Hanako. But that said, it does seem that she was here because of a letter from Ukai-san asking her to meet him."

"A letter from Ukai-san? Really? Ukai-san, did you ask Hanako to meet you here?"

"Me? Ask Hanako-san? No, I don't remember doing that."

Ukai crinkled his pretty forehead. This was the first time Kosuke had ever heard the young man speak. As he would have predicted, the voice matched his appearance: fragile, beautiful, with just a little bit of a waver. There was something pitiful about it too—you could hear that he was a lost soul.

"Ryonen-san, Ukai-san says he has no recollection of writing such a letter. Are you sure there hasn't been some kind of mistake?"

"No, actually I have expressed myself badly. The person whom Ukai-san asked to meet him here wasn't Hanako. It was her older sister Tsukiyo. I have no idea why Hanako appears to have taken that letter and come here in place of her sister. Ryotaku, would you mind passing me the letter? I suppose it's possible, Ukai-san, that you might recall writing this letter?"

Ukai and Oshiho exchanged glances, then she leaned forward to look.

"Oh, I see! Hana-chan had *this* letter… Well, this one I do remember. Ukai-san, it's clear that you wrote this letter so we had better just say it. I dictated it to Ukai-san, who wrote it down. Is that all right with you? Ukai-san and Tsukiyo-chan are a perfectly suited couple. However, people are always trying to break them up, to tear them apart. I find that truly vexing, and I do everything I can to help their love flourish. All I am trying to do is bring them together."

Oshiho spoke calmly, but behind those gentle words Kosuke sensed this woman's will of steel, along with a darker kind of determination born of ill will.

"No, that's all well and good. It doesn't matter what your intentions were. What we would like to know from you, Ukai-san, is whether you were here last night… Well, it's clear that you did come to the temple. I mean, we have a witness who saw you climbing up the path."

Ukai wavered a moment, but urged on by the look that Oshiho threw him, he took a step towards the priest. Then, assiduously avoiding everyone's eyes, he hesitantly began to speak.

"Yes, I was here. In fact, I thought there might be a misunderstanding about that and that's why I came here today. I sent Tsukiyo that letter, and I expected her to meet me here, so I came up to the temple and waited. I waited thirty minutes, an hour, but she never came. So I gave up and went home. That's all."

"Hmm, I see. And while you were waiting did you happen to see Hanako?"

"No. Not once. I couldn't ever have imagined that Hanako would turn up here."

"What time did you get here?"

"What time?... Hmm, I'm not sure. I left home, and..."

He turned to Kosuke.

"It was right after you left the branch family house, Kindaichi-san. I saw the priest and the others come down the winding path and meet you down at the bottom, and then I watched you all leave for the head Kito house. I waited until I couldn't see you all any more before going up the road towards the temple. And then I can't be sure exactly how long I was waiting up here, but I got home just before the clock struck 8.00 p.m. Maybe I was here until about 7.30."

"Hmm. And if, as Ukai-san says, he didn't see Hanako anywhere, then where on earth was the girl during that time?"

Rubbing his chin thoughtfully, the priest looked at everyone in turn. For a while nobody spoke, until Oshiho pushed herself up onto her knees as if to get up from her zabuton.

"Either way, Ukai-san doesn't know anything of this matter," she said firmly. "There is absolutely no reason for him to kill Hanako-chan. And besides, he doesn't have the courage to do anything like that."

Up until this moment, Kosuke had been watching the jousting between Oshiho and the priest with great amusement. Now he opened his mouth for the first time.

"I have a question for you, Ukai-san. While you were waiting for Tsukiyo-san, did you smoke any cigarettes?"

"Cigarettes? No, I don't smoke."

"Last night, were you wearing Japanese or Western clothing?"

"Japanese. I don't own any Western clothes at all."

"But I think you must own something Western. Shoes, for example? Army boots?"

"Yes, I have some army boots."

"Shimizu-san, I think you should get him to show you those boots later. I don't think they'll be the ones though… Anyway, Ukai-san, I have one more question for you. It's about the letter you sent to Tsukiyo. Do you know how that letter fell into Hanako's hands?"

Ukai hesitated again, and blushed a little. Once again he looked to Oshiho for encouragement.

"When I exchange letters with Tsukiyo-san, we leave them in the trunk of the Aizen laurel tree. Its trunk has a small hollow in it, so we leave the letters inside."

"The Aizen laurel?"

Everyone's eyes grew wide. Grinning, Kosuke scratched his head.

"From the story you mean? Very romantic. But does the Aizen laurel actually exist?"

Ukai turned red again.

"I hadn't even heard of the name Aizen laurel. I've heard people say the tree is actually called a Nozen laurel, but Tsukiyo-san won't listen. She calls it the Aizen Laurel. There's a small thicket in the valley at the foot of the winding path and the tree is in there. Around July it's covered in pretty red blossoms. Tsukiyo-san says if you stand near that tree, it brings you good luck…"

The novel *The Aizen Laurel* by Matsutaro Kawaguchi had been made into a film and caused the female population of Japan to shed many a tear. The song from the film, "If You Wait, He Will Come", was still hugely popular throughout the country. There was no cinema on Gokumon Island, but when the film came to Kasaoka on the mainland, a boat was chartered to take all the girls on the island to see it there. The three daughters of the Kito house were reportedly its most ardent fans. They'd gone so far as to stay at an acquaintance's house in Kasaoka, and went to the cinema to cry over the film every single day of its run.

"I see," Shimizu burst out, as if finally releasing pent-up emotion. "It's a case of 'if you wait, she will come', then? So last night the Aizen laurel had no effect, and no matter how long you waited for Tsukiyo-san, she didn't come. For whatever reason, Hanako grabbed that letter instead. Ukai-san, do you think Hanako had guessed your secret?"

"I think she must have done. Out of those three Kito sisters, Hana-chan is the most persistent."

It was Oshiho who had spoken.

"Anyhow, we don't know for sure why Hanako had that letter—"

Shimizu broke off mid-sentence.

"Here's the mayor."

Mayor Makihei Araki came through the temple gate, with his customary serious expression and pursed mouth. Takezo was right behind him.

The mayor quickly nodded a greeting to the assembled company, and then turned to the policeman.

"I'm sorry, Shimizu-san—such a problem. I've not been able to get through on the phone."

"The phone? What about the phone?" asked the priest.

"Ah yes," Shimizu answered, "when I heard this morning about the murder, I tried to contact police headquarters right away. Unfortunately the phone wasn't working properly and I couldn't get connected. So I asked the mayor here to keep trying. If we can't get through on the phone, I'm thinking we should send somebody, or maybe send a message via the ferry… Whichever we do it's going to take time. Araki-san, is there no chance of getting the phone line fixed soon?"

"If the fault is somewhere under the ocean, it's going to take a while. So as it might be some days before they can send someone from headquarters, what should we do with the body? We can't just keep it here indefinitely. Perhaps we ought to take it up to the main house? Maybe use a door as a stretcher? What do you think?"

"Good idea," said the priest. "Everyone had a good look at the scene of the crime last night, so we're not lacking in witnesses. Depending on Sergeant Shimizu's opinion, I think it might be better to take the body home now."

Shimizu looked extremely perplexed, but after a quick consultation, he finally agreed to having the body of Hanako transported to the head Kito house.

And with this, Gokumon Island's first murder victim was laid on a stretcher, and carried down the mountain from Senkoji Temple.

That very night, the second victim was about to go missing.

BENEATH THE HELMET, A HIDDEN CRICKET

Seiko the barber had once said the following:

"This is what I think—the inhabitants of this island are by nature criminals. They're all descendants of pirates and exiled prisoners. But more than that, I believe the blood of deserter soldiers of the Taira Clan is mixed in there too. I'm talking about that Oshiho-san. Look at her and you can see she hasn't got Chugoku-area blood. I'm thinking that genetics means that mutants like that just happen to appear from time to time. Oshiho can't fight against the blood that runs in her veins. No doubt she's somehow descended from the Taira nobility of hundreds of years ago, and it's suddenly manifesting itself now in her generation. Sanae-san's the same. Compared to Oshiho she looks a lot more like one of the islanders, but she has that kind of pride beyond her youth and a frightening strength about her that's very uncommon. I feel bad saying it, but Sanae-san is some kind of mutant too."

From his wanderings around Japan, Seiko had become

quite knowledgeable on certain topics. He seemed to be well informed about the rules of genetics. Kosuke Kindaichi was always very interested in Seiko's theories, but now, today, he felt even more respect for the man.

Sanae's comportment when the men brought Hanako's body to the house was admirable. Of course, she turned pale at the sight and there was horror in her eyes. But she never lost her composure. On the contrary, she berated Okatsu for throwing a fit unbecoming for a woman of her age; and all the while she was comforting the bawling, shuddering Tsukiyo and Yukie, she was able to give comprehensive directions to Takezo. Watching her, Kosuke remembered the words of Seiko. At that moment Sanae was like a courageous samurai receiving the body of a relative fallen in battle. Even at a time like this, she was able to run her castle. She showed an uncommon ability to keep it all together.

"And so?…"

When finally Hanako's remains were laid out in the family Buddhist chapel, and everyone had assembled in the formal sitting room, Sanae turned to the priest. In her eyes was an infinite amount of bitterness and resentment. The priest gave an awkward cough.

"Ah… Well… an extraordinary happening. I am terribly sorry."

He rubbed his forehead with the palm of a large hand.

"After such a happening, it seems that Chimata-san's funeral will have to be postponed," added Mayor Araki rather clumsily.

Sanae turned to look at him.

"No, that doesn't matter in the least. I'm more concerned with knowing who would do something like this. Who— who would do such a brutal and pitiless thing to Hana-chan?"

No one had an answer to that question. The room slipped into a heavy silence. It was an awkward quiet, and Kosuke couldn't help feeling that someone there carried some kind of ulterior motive concealed in their heart. Finally, Doctor Koan spoke, his goatee quivering:

"If we knew that, then we wouldn't be in this terrible situation."

He dropped his narrow shoulders in defeat.

"No, there has to be a way to know," said Sanae, turning to the doctor. "This is not a huge city like Tokyo or Osaka. There aren't that many people. And we are surrounded by sea. People don't just come and go. And so if someone murdered Hana-chan, it must be an islander. Or rather—"

Sanae broke off and threw a glance in Kosuke's direction.

"—either an inhabitant of this island, or someone who is currently on the island. Surely we can work out who the killer is? Can't we, Ryonen-san?"

"I suppose so."

"Hana-chan had a letter from that man… from that Ukai in her inner kimono, didn't she?"

"Well, yes, she did. It was certainly because of that letter that Hanako slipped away from here and went up to the temple. But I can't imagine that the man had any intention of doing something so terrible. Apart from anything else, he had absolutely no motive to kill her."

"Why not? How do you know? Well then, if we say it wasn't Ukai, then how about one of the people associated with him? How about Gihei-san or Oshiho-san? Those two... those two—"

"Sanae!" cried the priest sharply.

Sanae recoiled a little and stared at him, but then hung her head. The priest continued in a gentler tone.

"We should not speak rashly. Of course it's not unreasonable for you to be upset by all this. And it's human nature in such a state to feel suspicious of everyone. But do not make rash accusations. Those kind of people, if they hear you're accusing them, they might turn it around on you. There is no point in brooding over it: if there is any evidence they're involved, the police will find it. Let the police do their job. Right, Shimizu-san?"

"Ah... yes, yes, quite right. Ryonen-san here is correct. And as long as there is clear proof, it doesn't matter whether it's a fishing boss, or a fishing boss's wife, we won't go easy on them. I'll lock them up. Don't you worry yourself about that."

Shimizu spoke solemnly, pulling at his longer bits of stubble between his finger and thumb, but Sanae didn't seem to have any faith in the policeman. She continued to stare down at the floor, biting her lip. A single teardrop fell onto her lap.

That was when Kosuke's ears pricked up.

"Right, talking of finding clear proof... Before anything else, we have to search for evidence. And regarding that, Sanae-san, there's something I'd like you to look at."

From his inside pocket, Kosuke produced the bag of cigarette stubs, at which Sergeant Shimizu registered his discontent with a snort and a scowl. The priest and Doctor

Koan exchanged glances. The mayor kept staring stoically ahead, his expression unreadable.

Sanae looked puzzled.

"Cigarette butts?…"

"Yes, these cigarettes. I'd like to ask you some questions about them. Did you roll these for the, er, man in the back room… I mean, for the invalid?"

Sanae nodded.

"I ask because these cigarette butts were found in the grounds of Senkoji Temple. In other words, very close to the body of Hanako."

Sanae's eyes opened wide in horror, and she stared at Kosuke for a few moments. Her breathing began to speed up.

"But, but, it's not possible… It must be a mistake. It can't be only our family who owns a dictionary like this one. There must be others who have the same one. These have to be someone else's cigarettes."

"Yes, th-that must be it. It m-must be it, but I'm just going to make sure. When was the last time you rolled cigarettes for your uncle?"

"Yesterday… Yes, it was yesterday evening."

"How many?"

"Twenty cigarettes."

"Really? Could you just go back there and— No, never mind."

Something seemed to have occurred to Kosuke, and he began to scratch his bird's-nest head.

"I'm sorry if th-this is rude, but wh-why don't you take me back there? It's not as if I suspect you of anything. Th-this is an important matter."

Stammering and gulping, Kosuke finally got the full speech out. By the way they stared at Kosuke, it was clear that the priest, the doctor and the mayor were all astonished. Shimizu clicked his tongue to show his disapproval once again.

Sanae was also surprised, and she looked questioningly at Kosuke awhile before speaking.

"Come this way," she said, almost to herself. She got up from her zabuton.

"Sanae-san, will you be all right?" said the mayor nervously. "Are you sure it won't have a harmful effect on the patient?"

"No, I think we'll be fine as long as we're quiet. My uncle seemed to be fast asleep just now."

"All right then, I'll go with you," said the priest, getting slowly to his feet. "Shimizu-san, you come too."

Leaving just the doctor and the mayor behind, they all ventured into the back part of the residence.

Kosuke had frequently spent time in the tatami-matted sitting room, but this was the first time he had set foot in the rest of the house. Just as he had seen when surveying the property from above, the residence was something of a maze. From one passageway to another, he thought they were going downhill but then suddenly they'd be going uphill again, the corridors turning and winding this way and that, as if displaying the full glory of Kaemon's wealth. If he'd been left behind somewhere on the way, Kosuke wondered if he would ever have made it back safely to the sitting room. Eventually they ran out of corridors and came to a covered bridge.

Sanae turned to look at the rest of them.

"Would you mind waiting here a moment? I want to check on my uncle first."

With that she hurried across.

Kosuke leaned against the wooden-slatted side of the bridge and peered out with curiosity. The mist had turned to light rain, and was soaking the garden. In the distance beyond the garden, built on a small hill, there was a building with a shingled roof. It looked to be the building that the priest had pointed out from the mountain above, the place known as the prayer house. Kosuke's gaze moved from that building and down to the ground under the bridge. Suddenly, he started as if he had seen a ghost, but that was the very moment that Sanae returned.

"Follow me. But please try to be quiet. My uncle is fast asleep."

"Yes, we'll be careful."

The priest followed Sanae across the bridge. Shimizu was about to cross too when Kosuke grabbed his elbow and yanked him back in order to whisper something in his ear. Shimizu's reaction was one of surprise, and he immediately bent down to look under the bridge.

"All right. If you don't mind…" said Kosuke, and set out across the bridge alone, leaving Shimizu on the other side. On the far end the passageway made a right-angled bend, right after which was Yosamatsu's cell.

Cell. That word had evoked an image of something dark and gloomy in Kosuke's mind. If this had been what he had expected to find, then he must have been utterly disappointed. Of course there was a grid of sturdy iron bars stuck deep into the floor—undeniably grim in itself—but the room itself was pleasanter than he'd hoped. There was no shortage of ventilation and light, the space was at least ten tatami mats in size, and there was even a decorative tokonoma alcove complete with parallel shelves. In other words, if there hadn't been a metal grille separating the room from the corridor, it would have been an ordinary—no, in fact, a luxurious—living space. What's more, there was a door on one side leading to a bathroom and toilet. This was definitely a first-class version of a cell.

Yosamatsu was lying on a futon behind a byobu folding screen. He had some stubble on his face, but his hair was neatly trimmed. He wasn't dirty either, and seeing him this way, sleeping peacefully, there was no suggestion of his being mad at all. He was on his back, and his profile with its long nose looked very much like Chimata's as he had lain dying in the repatriation ship.

There was a long, narrow pole hanging on the outside of the metal grille. One end of it had a metal attachment in the shape of a fish hook for picking things up. Sanae took it and passed it through the bars of the grille, hooking it though the handle of the tray by Yosamatsu's side. On it were an ashtray and a packet containing cigarettes. Sanae carefully pulled in the pole, sliding the tray to within arm's reach. It seemed this was how she managed things so that there was no need to open the grille. She reached down and took the cigarette packet and without a word handed it to Kosuke. There were six cigarettes in the packet.

"And the ashtray?…" whispered Kosuke.

Sanae took it and handed it to him. Kosuke took out a paper from his kimono pocket and tipped the cigarette butts onto it.

"When did you last empty this ashtray?"

"Yesterday evening. When I gave him the new cigarettes."

"And at that time you gave him twenty cigarettes?"

Sanae nodded. Kosuke scratched his head with glee.

"Take a look at this. There are six cigarettes remaining in the packet, and five stubs in the ashtray, making only eleven total. That means—"

But their whispering must have disturbed the sleeping Yosamatsu, who sat up heavily on his futon.

"Oh, Uncle, are you awake?"

The priest swiftly moved his large frame in front of Kosuke, shielding him from the patient's eyes.

"Yosamatsu-san, how are you feeling?"

Yosamatsu remained in a sitting position on his futon, staring blankly at Sanae and the priest. Going by Chimata's age, this man must have been well past fifty, but he only looked around forty. It was probably from the lack of exercise, but he was quite plump, his shoulders and back rounded in his flannel pyjamas. His crossed legs were swollen in the manner of a beriberi sufferer. And then there was his skin—his complexion dull and lifeless, his eyes without spark. It was now obvious at a glance that this was a man with a mental illness.

Kosuke was slightly disappointed, but then suddenly there were bursts of laughter from a little way away. The voices belonged to Tsukiyo and Yukie. Apparently clowning around somewhere nearby, their voices were convulsed with laughter.

"Oh no, this is bad!" said Sanae. "Ryonen-san, please go and take those two away."

Kosuke soon understood what was bad. As soon as he heard Tsukiyo and Yukie, Yosamatsu's expression changed completely. Into those blank eyes came a beast-like fury, his hair bristled, and his cheeks began to spasm.

"Kindaichi-san, let's go."

The priest grabbed Kosuke's arm and pulled him back to the connecting bridge, where they could hear the sound of the bars of the cell being rattled, accompanied by a howling like a wild beast. In between, Sanae's voice could be heard; it sounded as if she was on the verge of tears. Sergeant Shimizu came over.

"Wh-what's all the fuss about?" he asked the priest. Then he turned to Kosuke and gave him a meaningful nod.

"Oh, the lunatic went on one of his rampages again. When he gets like that there's no one besides Sanae who can handle him. That girl has an amazing talent for making him calm."

The three men made their way back to the main sitting room to find the doctor and the mayor sitting in silence.

"Sounds like the patient's throwing a fit again," said Doctor Koan nervously. The mayor looked as gloomy as ever. Somewhere beyond them they could still hear Tsukiyo and Yukie laughing. The priest frowned.

"He's a problem," he blurted out. "But those girls too. As soon as he hears their voices, it makes him totally crazy. Even though they're father and daughters. It's a weird kind of karma."

"Incidentally, Kindaichi-san, what happened about the cigarettes?" said Shimizu.

"It's as we thought," replied Kosuke, taking out the two packages—one with the six remaining cigarettes and the other with the butts from the ashtray.

"They are the same cigarettes. Look. They've been rolled in one of the D pages from the dictionary. See how the entries go alphabetically? *dumdum, dummy, dump*... Well, one of the butts we picked up at the temple had *dumping, dumpish, dumpling*. So whoever smoked those cigarettes at the temple had definitely taken them from the batch of twenty that Sanae rolled yesterday evening. And then... Shimizu-san, did you examine that footprint?"

The police officer pulled a face.

"Well, it's... it's really odd. It was definitely a print from the same boot... Yes, the footprints we found at the temple are exactly the same."

"What footprint are you talking about?" asked the priest.

"Right. Well, Ryonen-san, you know how earlier Shimizu-san and I were investigating the footprints left behind at the temple? Well, I spotted a similar print—only one, mind you—under the connecting bridge to Yosamatsu's cell. I got Shimizu-san to check it out."

This revelation caused a look of amazement to appear on the faces of both the priest and the doctor, and even the normally poker-faced Mayor Araki.

"And so... so you discovered that it matched the prints you found at the temple?"

Shimizu nodded stiffly. The other three looked at each other in shock, until the priest got to his feet.

"However, Shimizu-san, if that's the case, what does it mean? You're not saying that that lunatic—"

"I have no idea about that," Kosuke broke in. "But I can say that last night whoever left those prints came from this house up to Senkoji Temple."

The priest, Koan and Araki were dumbfounded.

Kosuke and Shimizu soon made their excuses and left the Kito residence. As soon as they'd passed through the gate, Shimizu spoke up.

"Kindaichi-san, would you mind dropping by the station? There's quite a bit I need to discuss with you."

The light drizzle from before had stopped, but as always the clouds hung low over Gokumon Island, threatening to rain again on the two men.

"Yes, of course. The phone lines still aren't working, are they?"

The police station was just down the hill on the edge of the village. This was the busiest part of the island, and was also where the village mayor's office and the barber's shop were located. When they got to the police station, they found that the telephone had been reconnected.

"It's getting dark already!" remarked Kosuke.

"Right. The weather is so bad here that the nights always seem to draw in early. Hey, Otane, we've got a visitor."

Shimizu's wife was known as Otane-san. She was a petite woman, very friendly—a good-natured soul like her husband. However, this evening it seemed she wasn't home.

"Oh dear, she seems to be out. I can't imagine where she's gone..."

Muttering to himself, Shimizu made his way down the narrow corridor that led to the living quarters behind the police box. But a few moments later he started to yell.

"Kindaichi-san! Kindaichi-san! Could you come here a moment?"

"What's wrong?"

The corridor was as dark as a tunnel. Kosuke fumbled his way through and came out in a modest-sized garden. On the far side of this garden was a small but solid-looking building. It was the police station's jail cell.

"Hey, Shimizu-san? Where are you?" Kosuke called out.

"Here! Over here."

Shimizu's voice came from inside the jail building. Thinking nothing of it, Kosuke went to the doorway and stuck his head inside. All of a sudden, he felt a push on his back. Thrown off balance, he stumbled two or three steps forward, only to hear the door slam shut behind him, and a laugh of delight.

"Sh-Shimizu-san, wh-wh-what are you doing?"

"Right, that's better. Sorry, but until someone gets here from headquarters, you're going to have to stay here."

"Sh-Shimizu-san, have you gone mad? Wh-why on earth have you locked me up?"

"Ha ha. I think you'd better ask yourself that question. Everything about you is suspicious. Although you're just some drifter, you go around claiming to be a detective… The cigarette butts, the footprints, none of it rings true to me. Not to worry, it won't be for long. Tomorrow I'll make a call to headquarters and someone's bound to come right away. Just put up with it until then. You've even been given special treatment, see? I've put bedding in there for you. And I'll bring you something to eat. We don't want you to starve to death, do we? Just imagine you're back on that ship. Ha ha ha."

At last Shimizu seemed to have rid himself of the weight that had been on his shoulders. He gave a cheery laugh, and ignoring all of Kosuke's protests, turned around and headed back into the police substation.

"Idiot! Idiot! Shimizu—you're an idiot! You've made a terrible mistake! I'm not what you think. I'm… I'm…"

But it was useless. Shimizu believed Kosuke to be a suspect, and, well, there was no point in trying to reason with him, because he had gone. Kosuke could scream, he could cry, but no one was going to come and save him.

Nevertheless, he stamped his feet in frustration, battered the door with his fists, spewed out as much foul language as he could muster, until eventually he began little by little to see the humour in the situation. Shimizu's weird perception of him began to seem amusing, and eventually he found himself in fits of laughter at the bizarreness of it all. When Shimizu's wife, Otane, brought him his evening meal, he was in a fine mood. She, by contrast, found the prisoner decidedly odd. After he'd eaten his meal, he spread out the specially allocated bedding on the floor of the cell and collapsed onto it. Aided by the lack of sleep the night before, he fell right away into a deep slumber, and was totally oblivious to everything that happened after that.

He was awoken in the morning by the clamorous ring of the telephone.

"Ah, sounds like the phone's working at least," he thought.

He lifted his head to be dazzled by the morning sun shining straight into his cell. For once the weather was beautiful. Kosuke stretched his arms and legs and gave a huge yawn, but was put immediately on the alert by the sound of

Shimizu talking on the phone. He was speaking fast, and it was impossible to make out what he was saying. He hung up, and Kosuke could hear the tread of his policeman's boots approaching. Presently, his face appeared on the other side of the peephole in the door.

"Ho ho, Shimizu-san. You're mean. Just mean. Sneak attacks like that are unfair."

Shimizu screwed up his face and stared at Kosuke awhile as if checking him out. Finally he gave an awkward cough.

"Kindaichi-san, you didn't leave here last night, did you?"

"Did I lea— What?! Ho ho. Stop fooling around, Shimizu-san! Didn't you lock the door yourself? I'm not a ninja, you know."

Kosuke broke off, peering up at Shimizu's face. The police officer looked completely haggard. His unkempt stubble was the same as always, but his eyes were sunken and bloodshot. It was obvious that he hadn't slept the night before.

"Sh-Shimizu-san, d-did something happen?"

Shimizu's face suddenly collapsed like that of a child bursting into tears, and Kosuke heard the clatter of the cell door being unlocked.

"Kindaichi-san, I've done something unforgivable to you. I think I've made a terrible mistake."

"Shimizu-san, it really doesn't matter about that right now. Please tell me what's happened. What is it?"

"Please come with me. If you come, you'll understand."

They left the police station and headed up the road towards the branch Kito house. From the expressions on the faces of the people they passed en route, Kosuke could tell that something very strange had happened once again.

They climbed up, passing by the branch Kito house and arrived at the small plateau known as Tengu's Nose—the place where he had once seen Sergeant Shimizu looking through his binoculars in search of pirate ships.

There was a crowd of people gathered on the plateau, including Ryonen the priest, Mayor Araki and Doctor Koan, who for some reason had his left arm in a sling. Sanae was there too. So were Okatsu, Takezo and Ryotaku the apprentice priest. Standing slightly off to the side was a group of three: Oshiho, Ukai and, standing between them, a man who Kosuke had never seen before, but whom he assumed to be Oshiho's husband and the head of the branch Kito household—Gihei. He was short and stout with salt-and-pepper hair, and heavy eyebrows of pure white, set off by his deeply tanned complexion. He looked rather stern and perhaps even cruel.

As he approached, Kosuke was struck by how everyone was strangely silent. What was it that they were all staring at?

Kosuke finally made it to the plateau, but immediately stopped dead in his tracks. All the people were gathered in a semicircle around a large temple bell, which was standing in an upright position on the ground. It was the same bell that had been returned to Senkoji Temple after the end of the war. It had been dropped off here temporarily on its way to the temple. It would have been a slightly shorter route to take it up past the head Kito residence, but the incline on this side of the valley was a bit less steep. Sticking out from underneath the bell, Kosuke saw something that made his blood run cold. It was the sleeve of a kimono.

"It's Yukie-san," whispered Shimizu, wiping his sweaty brow. "Yukie-san's sleeve."

"You mean— You mean, Yukie-san is under that bell?"

No one had the courage to reply. There was an eerie silence. The sun shone brightly, the sea was still and calm, the soft breeze brushed everyone's cheek. Despite the pleasant weather, Kosuke's body began to shudder and ooze with sweat.

True to form, the priest had a haiku for the occasion. This one he delivered in the tone of voice normally used to recite a requiem.

"How tragic—beneath the helmet, a hidden cricket."

CHAPTER 4

The Mechanics of a Temple Bell

Even though it was the priest's habit to quote a haiku for all situations, this time he had gone too far.

How tragic—beneath the helmet, a hidden cricket.

It truly was an ingenious allusion. However, perfect as it was, it was impossible not to feel discomfort at such an off-colour metaphor.

The priest had probably not intended to poke fun at this dreadful situation in any way. It was just his habit and the words had slipped out. In any situation death should be treated with solemn respect and to poke fun at it was, to put it bluntly, tasteless. The unpleasant reaction that Kosuke felt in his throat was born of a mix of anger and moral disgust.

Now, with the eyes of everyone on him, the priest appeared to be aware of his verbal gaffe. He wiped his brow with the back of one sturdy hand. His face composed, he began to murmur, "I put my trust in you, Shakamuni Buddha, I put my trust in you, Shakamuni Buddha…"

At the sound of the chant, Kosuke, too, was finally able to regain his own composure. He turned to Shimizu.

"If Yukie is under there, we'd better find a way to move the bell as soon as possible."

"We've instructed the young folk to lift it and they're making preparations now. Takezo-san, do you think they're ready yet?"

"Yes, I think they're here."

Takezo had been looking down the hill, apparently signalling to someone.

"Takezo-san, how do you propose to lift the bell?" Kosuke asked.

"There's only one way—to build scaffolding around it and then use a pulley to raise it."

Gokumon Island being a fishing community, they often had to lift heavy objects, so they had all the necessary equipment.

"I see."

Kosuke began to circle the bell, his head bent, examining it in detail. Shimizu followed. The bell had been placed near the very edge of the cliff.

"I say, Kindaichi-san, the malefactor—"

(Once again, the old-fashioned term.)

"—how did he manage to lift such a heavy object? He couldn't possibly have built scaffolding and attached a pulley. He wouldn't have had the time for a start..."

Kosuke finished his 360-degree perusal of the bell.

"Ex-ex-excuse me, everybody. Would you all mind stepping back a little? Yes, yes, like that. Please don't move from that spot."

In the manner of the assistant to a street performer, he moved the crowd back, and began once again to examine the perimeter of the bell. Finally, he seemed to get an idea, and began to scratch at his scalp with utter abandon.

"I see. I see. You want to know how the killer lifted such a heavy bell, do you? Well, it's simply a problem of mechanics. The mechanics of a temple bell... Shimizu-san, please take a look. Right here, just under the bottom rim of the bell, you see this hole that's been dug in the ground? And then that thing there is the remains of a stone pedestal that used to have a statue of Jizo or something. See, it's about a foot... no, maybe about eighteen inches from the hole, quite close to the bell. Then..."

Kosuke pointed at something away from the bell and beyond the pedestal.

"Look over there. You see that sturdy pine tree? That pine tree, this pedestal and the hole dug under the rim of this bell—those three elements are in a straight line. What's more, that pine tree has a thick branch at an absolutely perfect height—the branch there that's pointing downwards. In other words, using these three elements, he was able to construct a mechanism to raise the edge of the bell."

Shimizu was having difficulty comprehending but he still looked in each direction that Kosuke pointed and nodded along.

It was as Kosuke had explained.

In the ground under the rim of the bell, there was a hole about six inches in diameter. Around two feet away from that hole, there were the remains of a stone pedestal. In the past a statue of Ojizosama, the guardian deity of children, had stood there, but at some point the statue itself had been lost and all that remained was the base. It was very old but, although worn away, Kosuke could just make out a lotus flower design. If you drew a straight line from the hole at the bottom of the bell over the stone pedestal, you would eventually reach a large pine tree growing on the cliff side. This pine tree had a thick, sturdy branch growing in the direction of the bell.

"And?…"

Shimizu looked at Kosuke expectantly.

"In conclusion…"

Kosuke began to walk as if counting paces from the pedestal to the tree.

"Five to one… yes, about five to one. That's the ratio of the distance from the hole to the pedestal, and the distance from the pedestal to the pine tree. If you take the former distance as 1, then the latter is 5 times the length. If we apply the law of levers, we can construct the following equation. If Q is the weight of the bell, and P the force required to lift it, then $P = Q/5$. In other words, the force needed to lift the bell is in inverse proportion to the difference between the distances from the hole to the pedestal and the pedestal to the pine tree. By the way, Ryonen-san, do you happen to know the approximate weight of the bell?"

"Let's see…"

The priest screwed his face up.

"I suppose when we donated it they must have weighed it. Ryotaku, do you happen to remember?"

"Reverend Father, I wasn't at the temple back then."

During the war, the apprentice priest had been posted to a munitions factory on Mizushima Island.

"I believe it was 370 pounds. Maybe just a little over."

It was Mayor Araki who cut in. He immediately pursed up his lips again. Next to him, Doctor Koan, with his arm in its sling, stood long-faced.

"About 370 pounds? That's way lighter than I expected. So, one-fifth of 370 pounds... that's about seventy-five pounds. If someone here has the strength to lift that much weight, we can raise the edge of that bell. If we have a sturdy stick or pole of some kind, I will demonstrate how before your very eyes."

"Kindaichi-san, would this do?"

Takezo picked up a long, thick wooden pole from the ground by his feet. Kosuke looked a little taken aback, but after a short pause during which he closely observed Takezo's face, he suddenly snatched the pole from the tide master's hand.

"Takezo-san, where did you find this?"

"It had been dumped over there in those bushes... This is a pole used for tying up the boats in the harbour. Someone must have carried it up here. I found it just now."

"A pole from the harbour? So anyone who wants to use it can do so? And it was discarded just over there in the bushes..."

Kosuke turned to the policeman.

"Shimizu-san! The dimensions of the temple bell were no problem to our killer: they were no impediment to him at all. He didn't even bother to conceal how he lifted up the bell. He just disposed of this pole right by the scene of the crime."

"So you mean that this pole—"

"That's right. That's right. See here? There's a mark on it made by the rim of the bell. And this mark here was made by that stone pedestal. But the proof is in the pudding. Come on, let's give it a try."

Besides Kosuke and Sergeant Shimizu, there were ten onlookers standing in a semicircle on the top of that cliff. In order they were the priest, Ryonen; the apprentice priest, Ryotaku; Mayor Araki; Doctor Koan; Takezo; Sanae; and next to her, Okatsu, who looked as if she were about to faint. And then, a little distance from the rest were Oshiho, Gihei and the handsome Ukai. The sea continued to sparkle down below, and the soft breeze to blow. And yet all eyes were dark. Even Oshiho looked fearful as she stood there, obsessively adjusting her kimono.

Kosuke was his typical overexcited self. As he stuck the end of the pole into the hole under the rim of the bell, the other end of it trembled slightly. Then he adjusted the bell end until it rested on top of the pedestal. The pole now stuck out from the bell at a diagonal, pointing up into the air.

Kosuke looked around.

"Would someone mind pushing down on the far end of this pole? Takezo-san, do you think you could manage that?"

Takezo looked a little reluctant but he stepped up.

"I need to push down on the pole, right?"

"That's it. If you push as close to the end of the pole as possible, that will give you the most leverage. Please apply all your body weight to the pole. Then the pedestal here becomes the fulcrum as the lever is pulled down. And the edge of the bell will slowly tilt and lift upwards."

All of a sudden there was a buzz of voices, as people caught on to what Kosuke had been talking about. He hurried to position himself in front of the bell as Takezo got to work.

"Don't anyone come close—nobody come near, all right? Okay, Takezo-san, that's it, just a little more. Just a little more. That's it… that's it."

Takezo turned bright red in the face as he pushed with all his might on the end of the lever. The veins in his arms and face expanded like earthworms, and he dripped with sweat. He may have been short in stature, but he had honed his body on the sea currents. His muscles bulged and throbbed until he got the end of the lever down to the level of his navel.

"That's it. That's it. Behind you there's that overhanging pine branch. Try to wedge the end of the pole under it, so that when you let go the pole won't spring back up. Yes, that's it. Just right. Now try letting go."

As instructed, Takezo struggled to wedge the end of the pole under the branch. It took a few adjustments, but finally he was able to remove his hands. The branch bounced up and down two or three times, but showed no sign of snapping. The end of the lever stayed firmly in place.

It was a curious mechanism. The bell now leaned about twenty degrees off the vertical, one side of its rim a little more than twenty inches off the ground. It seemed like a one-in-a-thousand chance, but this delicate equilibrium was somehow sustained.

There was a sigh from the assembled crowd. Then a buzz of voices, more of a commotion than before. It was perfectly reasonable under the circumstances. Underneath the raised bell was a kimono dyed so vividly that you could almost smell the colours. From where they stood, they couldn't see much more than the sleeve, but that was enough. The body of Yukie was sitting upright under the bell.

"Ha ha ha ha ha!"

A laugh suddenly rang out, causing everyone to start. All eyes turned on Oshiho. Her laughter was spiteful, malicious, and continued unbroken.

"Oh, it's awful! Just like that play, *Dojoji Temple*. But this is the wrong way around. Ukai-san, isn't it you who should be under that bell? It's supposed to be Anchin hiding under the bell. It's not in the script for Kiyohime to be under there. But—"

Oshiho suddenly seemed to notice something.

"Oh yes, yes—that's it! Yukie-chan's mother was supposed to have been an actress. Her signature piece was being under the bell in *Dojoji Temple*. That's the role that's supposed to have captivated Yosamatsu-san, and got her promoted from mistress to second wife. Ha ha. The sins of the mother have been paid for by the daughter. So then—"

"Oshiho, be quiet!"

The sharp voice of her husband, Gihei, cut her off. But Oshiho was not about to back down.

"But, but, how can you see this and just stand there in silence? What kind of a puzzle is this? If someone wanted to kill Yukie-chan, why didn't they just kill her? What kind of person on what kind of whim decides to create this parody of the *Dojoji Temple* play? It's just like Kaemon-san with all his parodies of other things. It's too much, too much. This is craziness. Everyone's crazy. It's true. It's true. Everyone's completely mad."

"Oshiho, be quiet!" Gihei roared at her. "I am so sorry, everybody. Oshiho here is suffering from hysteria. It's a habit with her. She sounds as if she knows what she's talking about, but it's just because she's too faint-hearted to bear the terror of this discovery. Oshiho, let's go home."

He took her hand.

"No, I don't want to. I want to see more. I want to see the look on Yukie's face when she died."

It was true that Oshiho was hysterical. The excitement in her eyes was not normal. She spoke like a young child. She stamped and pouted and tried to pull her hand out of her husband's grip. She was just like some spoiled brat. Until now, Kosuke had only met the carefully composed version of Oshiho, and this was the most bizarre transformation. She had become something repulsive, abnormal. He couldn't forget what Shimizu had once told him: on Gokumon Island, everyone was crazy.

"Oshiho, what a mess you are. Ukai-san, take her other hand. Shimizu-san, if you have questions for us, please feel free to come by any time. I'm not one to hide or run away. Ukai-san, please keep a firm grip on her hand. She's like some wounded beast when she gets like this. She gets out of control."

"I won't! I won't! I hate you, Ukai-san. Let me go! You— you—"

Oshiho stamped her foot in anger. Her clothes were in disarray, her hair dishevelled, she looked utterly deranged. Gihei and Ukai flanked her, each holding a hand, and dragged her down the hill.

"No! I don't want to! Get off me, Ukai-san! Let me go! Gihei! Please!…"

162

Oshiho's pleas faded further into the distance, and when they finally could no longer be heard, everyone seemed to let out a collective breath. They looked around at each other.

"Ha ha ha," the priest chuckled. Then, as if ridding his mouth of something foul, "Well, that was quite a performance, wasn't it? What a handful she is for Gihei-san to manage."

"Ah yes, well... That's a whole other issue," said Shimizu, with his trademark awkward cough. He turned to Kosuke.

"So, you're saying that the malefactor lifted the bell this way, and pushed Yukie-san's body in through the gap?"

"Sorry? Yes... Right, right."

Kosuke was a little flustered as he responded to Shimizu. In fact, he was deep in thought. It was the beginning of Oshiho's outburst that had caught his attention.

Yukie's mother had been a stage actress. Her speciality had been the trick with the bell in the Noh play *Dojoji Temple*. Yosamatsu had become enamoured of her and taken her as his mistress and then his second wife. This was the first Kosuke had heard of any of this. In fact, now that he thought about it, he had never heard anything about Tsukiyo, Yukie and Hanako's mother. He'd simply heard that she'd died many years ago. Until just now it had never occurred to him that she might have some connection to the murders. And yet, according to Oshiho, the mother of those three girls was an actress. Her trademark performance was the trick of disappearing into the bell in *Dojoji Temple*. Within this piece of information there was a connection in this murder case—this mad, crazed murder case. It might

163

even be the key to solving it… But he would think this over more later. It was too challenging to think about two things at the same time.

"Th-that's right. With the lever against this pine tree, you wouldn't need any help lifting the bell. So even a lone killer could manage it—I mean that he could have performed this stunt without an accomplice."

For a while nobody spoke, then one by one they moved stiffly towards the bell and peered under the rim, looking at the brightly coloured kimono. I'll repeat what I wrote at the start of this scene. The sun shone brightly, the sea was still and calm, the soft breeze brushed everyone's cheek. And yet, the view on that plateau was as dark and malevolent as a scene from hell. It was hideous. Sanae was the first to speak.

"Yukie-san… Was Yukie-san… Was she put under here while she was still alive?"

Apparently, Sanae had a much stronger disposition than Oshiho. The shock that she must have received was incomparable—the wound must have been far, far deeper. But she showed no sign whatsoever of hysteria or wild behaviour. Instead, she stood there shivering, her face drained of blood.

Kosuke turned to Sanae, compassion on his face.

"No, don't worry. She wasn't. Yukie-san was spared the terror of being entombed alive. There are marks on her neck from strangulation."

"But, but… Kindaichi-san?" said Takezo. "Why did the malefactor put her body under the bell? Why didn't he just leave the body where it was after killing her? Why was it necessary to be this brutal? This is just a despicable thing to do."

Kosuke didn't respond right away. He felt himself engulfed by a heavy sense of disbelief. He shook his head slowly from side to side, then finally spoke in a voice devoid of life.

"I have no idea. Why did the killer hang Hanako from the plum tree? Why did he cover Yukie with the bell? I have yet to work it out. If the killer isn't mad, and if it isn't some kind of performance, an attempt to show off—if instead there is some kind of deep meaning to all of it, then finding what that meaning is will also be the key to solving this whole case. But for now, I don't know. I'm completely stumped. For now I can only think that the killer is some kind of lunatic."

He gave a deep sigh and reached up to scratch his unruly head of hair.

At this moment, the young men of the village arrived, each carrying logs or pulleys or nets over their shoulder. Sergeant Shimizu turned to Kosuke.

"Kindaichi-san, I may have done you an unforgivable wrong, or maybe your life's work is to perpetrate a massive fraud on us. But… but anyway, last night you were locked up in the police station cell. And the key was safely in my possession. I am now persuaded that you had nothing at all to do with last night's crime. And yet I don't find I can fully trust you yet. I'm completely confused. Why? Because for one, this case is just too bizarre, and that is partly your fault, Kindaichi-san. Just who are you? All these mechanics of a temple bell, how do you know all this stuff? In the blink of an eye, you can recreate the killer's exact methods. How did you know that, Kindaichi-san? Either you yourself are the perpetrator, or you must be his associate. Come on, Kindaichi-san, tell us plainly right here, right now. Tell us you're not the killer. Tell us you have nothing to do with these murders. If you do, I will believe you and stop feeling so anxious."

The scaffolding was finally constructed, and pulleys used to raise the bell. Yukie's body was retrieved, and Doctor Koan examined it. It was determined that Yukie had been murdered between 6.00 and 7.00 p.m. the previous evening. Cause of death was strangulation, the weapon a cotton tenugui hand towel, or something similar. Yukie's body was then transported by Takezo and some of the young men to the head Kito residence. The priest, Ryonen, and the apprentice, Ryotaku, along with the mayor and the doctor accompanied them. Their job done, the rest of the young men were sent home to the village. The only two left were Kosuke Kindaichi and Sergeant Shimizu.

Shimizu sat down near the cliff edge and began to bite his nails. Two sleepless nights had taken their toll on him and his face looked utterly fatigued. He couldn't rid himself of his suspicion of Kosuke and it was causing him mental agony. Kosuke laid his hand gently on the policeman's shoulder.

"Shimizu-san?" he said gently.

Shimizu looked vaguely in his direction.

"Shimizu-san, please look at me."

The policeman looked Kosuke in the eyes.

"And now please look at that bell."

Shimizu looked at the bell, hanging by its pulleys. It was going to remain like that until someone from police headquarters arrived to inspect it. To the eyes of someone who knew nothing of the murder committed there, the sight of a bell hanging from its scaffolding on this clifftop would have been extremely odd. Shimizu shuddered at the sight.

"I will swear on that bell," said Kosuke. "I had nothing to do with the death of Hanako, nor the murder last night of Yukie. Please look into my eyes and see that I'm not lying to you."

Shimizu looked into Kosuke's eyes for a good long time, until, finally releasing a heavy sigh, he said:

"Kindaichi-san, I've decided to trust you. There doesn't appear to be any kind of falsehood in your eyes… That said, who on earth are you? What's your profession? What is your purpose for being here on Gokumon Island? Why would you come to this confounded place? That's what I don't understand. Why are you on this dreadful remote island?… Oh!"

Shimizu suddenly jumped to his feet and rushed over to the cliff edge. He shaded his eyes with one hand, and looked out to sea. From behind the silhouette of neighbouring Manabe Island, a steam launch came into view. Phut phut, phut phut, blowing faint rings of steam into the air, the launch calmly crossed the surface of the ocean towards Gokumon Island. It was a different boat from the usual ferry, the *White Dragon*.

At the sight of it, all the melancholy seemed to vanish from the policeman's face. He broke out into a smile and turned to Kosuke with weirdly glittering eyes.

"Kindaichi-san, do you recognize that boat? That's the local police launch, and on that boat is the veteran police officer Detective Inspector Isokawa. You say you and he are acquainted. So, are you going to be all right? No need to make your escape? Well, I don't think you'd be able to

167

escape anywhere now. Kindaichi-san, if there's any funny business going on with you, now you're going to get your comeuppance. Ha ha ha."

Shimizu threw back his head and burst into gleeful laughter.

THE MAN WHO LEAPT INTO THE SEA

The police launch put down anchor in the open sea and the welcome boat paddled out to meet it. A curious crowd of islanders gathered on the quay to watch them arrive.

Sergeant Shimizu and Kosuke Kindaichi rushed down the hill as fast as they could and joined the crowd. But as they waited, Shimizu's demeanour became less calm, precisely because Kindaichi was too calm himself.

"Kindaichi-san! Kindaichi-san!"

Shimizu nervously pulled at his moustache.

"In what capacity do you know Inspector Isokawa? Are you going to be all right with him coming here?"

"Yes, well, I'm sure I'll be fine. But, Shimizu-san, is the inspector really arriving here today?"

"I'm pretty sure he'll be here. When I telephoned, they said he was in Kasaoka. Yes, look! That's Inspector Isokawa right there."

Police officers were stepping off the launch into the welcome boat. The third man to board it was definitely Inspector Isokawa.

"Ah yes, that looks like him. He's really aged," remarked Kosuke.

There was deep emotion in his voice.

The so-called Honjin murder case had taken place in a rural farming community in Okayama Prefecture. Kosuke Kindaichi had worked together with Inspector Isokawa on the case. It had been the autumn of 1937. A good nine years had passed since then, and, under normal circumstances, Isokawa should have risen to the rank of police superintendent by now. However, war had intervened and he'd been called up to military service. This had delayed his promotion, and he was still at the rank of inspector. Now he'd been transferred to the prefectural criminal division, and he seemed to be quite happy there in his role as veteran officer. He owed his speedy arrival on Gokumon Island to the fact that he had been visiting Kasaoka because of the pirate problem.

All of the police officers on the welcome boat were dressed in military-style boots, and were heavily armed.

"Why is everyone wearing all that gear?" Kosuke asked Sergeant Shimizu. "Whenever there's a crime on an island, do they always turn up dressed that way?"

"It is strange," Shimizu replied. "First of all, there are too many officers. Surely they don't need that many people to catch a criminal?"

"Ha ha, well, if it's me you're trying to catch, I think you are plenty strong enough by yourself, Shimizu-san. I wouldn't stand a chance against your brute force."

"Hmm, I wonder."

Shimizu regarded Kosuke with a doubtful expression.

The welcome boat moved away from the police launch and made its way slowly towards the quay. Inspector Isokawa must have spotted Kosuke because his deeply suntanned face broke into a wide smile, and he waved a hand. This took Shimizu completely off guard. He turned and stared at Kosuke.

"Kindaichi-san, Kindaichi-san, was the inspector waving at you?"

Shimizu was stunned by the unexpected degree of affection in the inspector's expression. Kosuke grinned.

"It's fine. It's fine. Anyone would have made the same mistake. But, Shimizu-san, last night… you know when you tossed me into that police cell? Well, it's probably best not to mention it to the inspector."

He slapped Shimizu lightly on the shoulder, and then proceeded to push his way through the crowd of islanders down to the jetty. The first person to disembark from the welcome boat was Inspector Isokawa.

"Hello there," said Kosuke.

"Hello!"

"How have you been?"

"Yes, well, not too bad… You haven't changed at all."

"No, no. That's not true. I've been through a fair bit. You've aged a few years yourself though, Inspector."

"I reckon I have. I didn't have any of these white hairs back then."

"But you've also bulked up a bit too. Quite the dignified presence you have now."

"Ha ha. Dignified presence I may have, but these past ten years I've remained an inspector, even though many of my colleagues have made it to superintendent."

"You know, it doesn't matter. It's fine. It's all the fault of the war. There's nothing we can do about it. Let's not grumble."

"Yes, yes. You're right. Sorry to start in on the complaints right away. By the way, Shimizu?"

Shimizu was standing there, looking from one man to the other in wonder. Now that the inspector addressed him, he jumped as if awoken from a dream.

"Sir!" he replied, in the manner of a soldier answering his commander.

"What on earth is going on here? Two young women murdered one after the other?"

Shimizu's mouth opened and closed like a fish's but no sound came out. The honest policeman had realized his mistake regarding Kosuke and was now overcome with shame.

Kosuke swiftly intervened.

"Why don't we discuss that once we get the inspector settled? By the way, Inspector, what are all these men doing here? All armed to the teeth like that?"

There were six police officers in addition to Inspector Isokawa, all with pistols tucked into their belts, which seemed a bit like overkill. Beside them, there was a gentleman in a suit who appeared to be a police medical officer.

"Oh, this lot? Well, even if it hadn't been for the murders here on the island, even if we hadn't got a call from Shimizu here, they would have turned up anyway. You know, your killer might even be the same guy."

"What do you mean, the same guy?" asked Kosuke.

"One of the pirate crew. I'm sure you've heard from Shimizu already—two days ago we were pursuing a pirate gang in waters around here. They gave us the slip back then, but just yesterday one of their crew was captured in Uno. From his confession we learned that while we were chasing

171

their ship, another of the gang thought they were done for, and he jumped overboard. From the spot where he jumped, we think he might have been able to swim as far as this island, or possibly Manabe Island. Kindaichi-san, have you heard any talk around here of anything like that?"

Kosuke was quite stunned by this news. He felt his heart pound faster in his chest. The moment he heard Inspector Isokawa's story, the thought of that mysterious intruder who had stolen rice from Senkoji Temple flashed through his mind.

"Kindaichi-san, have you remembered something?" asked the inspector.

"That's it!" Shimizu interrupted. "Kindaichi-san, that must be him! The burglar who stole all that food..."

"No, j-j-just a minute. Could you both be quiet? I... I've been wr-wrong about this. If... if that was the case, then I n-need to think for a moment."

Kosuke clenched his teeth and began scratching violently at his messy thatch of hair. There was an intense look in his eyes.

Right... That's right... If that's what happened then it would be consistent... First of all, he sneaks into the head Kito house. Then he goes to Yosamatsu's cell and he steals the cigarettes in the way that Sanae showed us yesterday. For a smoker, a cigarette is as vital as food. Without them it's as if he's starving. And then he climbs up to Senkoji Temple, and sits down where he can watch the path up to the temple and smokes five or six cigarettes one after another. After that, he goes into the kitchen and finds the pot of rice...

But—and here it was as if the ship of Kosuke's theory ran into a large submerged rock—if that was the case, what on earth was this man's connection to the murder? Hanako must still have been at the temple when he went up there, so did he kill her? No, no, he'd got the timing wrong... By Kosuke's previous reckoning, when the priest had arrived back at the temple... no, not just the priest—the priest followed closely by Ryotaku, Takezo and himself—when they'd all got back to the temple that night, the rice thief was still there on the temple grounds. Or this was what Kosuke had concluded from the behaviour of the priest that night.

But on the other hand, surely this thief must have left there long before the time that Hanako had been killed? However daring this pirate gang member may have been, there was no way he could have hung out so long and so calmly at the scene of a murder as horrific as that of Hanako... And so, this man must have snuck into the temple earlier. In conclusion, he, Kosuke, must have been deluding himself when he imagined that the priest knew the thief was still hiding in the temple. There must have been a totally different explanation for the priest's behaviour that night. Of course there was. If this pirate was the killer then there was absolutely no reason under the sun for the priest to try to protect him. Although... although... it was certain that the priest knew something. When he'd blurted out, "Out of reason, but it can't be helped." And his behaviour... Damn it, damn it. It was getting more difficult to solve by the minute. Whether this pirate character was the killer or not, what he needed to know was the exact time he was at the temple. And it would also be helpful to work out when he was at the head Kito house. From that he would have an idea what time he went up to the temple...

All these thoughts ran through Kosuke's mind as he stood there, stock-still, holding his breath. He thought about how all this had occurred the night of Chimata's wake. How after Hanako had disappeared, Okatsu and Sanae had gone to search the house one more time. Right after they'd left to do that, there had been a loud shriek from deep inside the residence. That had been Sanae's voice, but right afterwards they had heard the lunatic roaring, so they'd written off Sanae's scream as being related to that. But now he thought about it, that was a little odd. Yosamatsu was very attached to Sanae, and it only took a word from her for him to calm down. Obviously, Sanae was perfectly aware of this, so she surely wouldn't have screamed that way just because he was acting wildly. And yet she had screamed. And not only that—when she had arrived back in the sitting room, she'd been completely pale and wide-eyed, as if something had frightened her. So what had surprised and scared Sanae so much? Had she seen a strange man in the vicinity of the lunatic's cell? Had she even seen him in the act of stealing the cigarettes?

But then...

But then, why didn't she call out for help? Why did she let the man escape? More than that, when she came back to the sitting room, why didn't she even mention having seen him? Why did she let everyone believe that the lunatic had caused her to scream?

The next problem was that of the footprints. There had only been one single boot print with a bat-shaped mark on the sole under the connecting bridge. There must have been some other prints in a damp place or in the shade that ought to have still been visible after the heavy rain, but there had only been that one solitary print. Did that mean that after the man had left, somebody had gone around removing all the boot prints? And had happened to miss that one under the bridge? And was that someone Sanae? In other words, did Sanae know that man? And if so, who could he be?

Kosuke finally turned to Inspector Isokawa.

"Inspector? That man, the one who is supposed to have jumped into the sea, do you happen to know anything about him?"

"No, I'm sorry to say we know absolutely nothing. Even the gang member we picked up in Uno said he didn't know him very well. He says that the man joined the pirate crew very recently. He said his name was Taro Yamada, but there's no way of knowing whether or not that's his real name. He's a sturdily built young man of around thirty. By the deep tan of his skin, the pirate guessed he might have been recently repatriated from somewhere far south. He was dressed in military uniform and army boots, and carried a pistol and a lot of spare bullets. Before he jumped into the sea, he secured the pistol and bullets in a leather bag and tied it on top of his head. He was quite a troublesome character, according to this gang member. So do you suspect that he's on this island, Kindaichi-san?"

"I do. And what's more, I believe he has an important connection to this case. Shimizu-san, if this kind of man had made it to the island, where do you think he would be hiding?"

175

"Hmm, I s'pose he might be on Mount Suribachi."

Shimizu-san was back to his old self.

"Suribachi's that mountain you see over there, behind Senkoji Temple. There are the remains of a pirate fortress up there. During the war they built an air defence observation point and anti-aircraft base on the top of the mountain. It's a complete maze of holes up there now. I'd say it's the perfect hideout. By the way, Inspector, sir?"

Shimizu added, with a little affected cough:

"From what you just told us, I have an idea. There is a local on this island who says that last night he saw someone like the man you describe. Until I heard your story, I thought he might be making it up, but now I'm sure it was this man."

"Wh-who is it who saw him?" said Kosuke in surprise.

"Koan-san. He didn't just see him, he even got into a scuffle with him."

"Oh. I see now. That's why the doctor had his arm in a sling."

"That's right. He got into a scuffle with the man and got pushed over the edge of the road and took a tumble down into the valley. Broke his left arm. Now because it was Koan, I thought he was embarrassed that he'd got drunk again and fallen, and he'd made up a cover story. But now I see that somehow this brute must have snuck onto our island."

The three men, followed by the police officers, had been walking as they talked, and they now arrived in front of the tiny police station. When they looked around, they saw that most of the onlookers from the harbour were trailing behind them like a funeral procession.

Kosuke turned to Inspector Isokawa.

176

"I suppose you'll want to examine the corpses right away," he said. "But I would very much like to hear first from Shimizu-san the sequence of events of last night."

"Oh, really?"

Isokawa looked a little confused, but continued:

"Well then, I'd very much like to hear the story too. By the way, where are the bodies?"

"They were returned to their home. See? Up there? That building that looks like a castle? That's the head Kito family residence."

"Ah, I see. Hey, you!"

Isokawa called over one of the police officers.

"Take the doctor up to that house and have him examine the bodies. Doctor, if you wouldn't mind."

Guided by one of the local police officers, the medical officer set off up the hill towards the Kito residence, and the rest of the group headed into the police station. It's not only people in cities who burn with curiosity to know the latest gossip: here in this remote village too, men and women, young and old, hung around the police station like flies.

It was just about lunchtime, so the police took out the bento boxes they'd brought with them and offered some of their food to Kosuke and Shimizu. Shimizu's wife, Otane, with a woman's tact, quickly spotted the blunder that her husband had made regarding Kosuke, and now she tried to make it up to him by treating him like an honoured guest. Kosuke felt a bit awkward at first, but then he remembered that he hadn't eaten anything that morning...

"I see. That was the sequence of events the night before last, or when the first victim was killed. Now tell me about last night."

Kosuke Kindaichi, though prone to stuttering whenever he got excited, was a very skilled storyteller when calm. He'd given Inspector Isokawa a brief outline of all that he knew of what had happened since his arrival on Gokumon Island. He had left out only one detail—the deathbed request of his war buddy, Chimata Kito. Kosuke felt he wasn't ready to share that yet, and that if he spoke openly about it, there was a possibility that he might cause some kind of trouble to somebody on the island. However, Inspector Isokawa couldn't get rid of the nagging feeling that something was missing from the story.

"About last night's happenings, Inspector—I might not be the right person to tell you the details of that. I slipped up. I was completely exhausted and fell fast asleep early. In the end, I was dead to the world all night and missed everything."

"You? You slept through it?"

The inspector looked at Kosuke suspiciously, but then Shimizu cut in, sounding like the most miserable person who had ever lived.

"No, in fact… about that—it was me who made the worst possible error in judgement. I have to tell the truth—I had no idea what kind of person this Kosuke Kindaichi was."

"What 'kind of person' Kindaichi-san was? You never mentioned anything about this before."

"I know. In fact he was the chief suspect in a serious crime."

"Suspect in a serious crime?... Kindaichi here?"

For a moment the inspector's eyes appeared to pop out of his skull. The next instant he exploded with laughter.

"Ha ha. Shimizu, what the hell are you talking about? This man, Kosuke Kindaichi? Ha ha ha."

Inspector Isokawa proceeded to explain his past relationship with Kosuke.

"So, what on earth did you do to him?" he added.

"Well, I, er... from your tone, Inspector, when we first discussed Kindaichi-san being on the island, I thought he was well known to you for—er—other reasons, and then when I returned to the island and found there had been a serious crime committed... Well, after some careful consideration, to be safe... Well, in fact, last night I locked him up in a jail cell."

If there had been a hole in the ground right now, Shimizu would have crawled into it.

"This man? You put him in jail?"

"Don't worry," Kosuke intervened. "It was a very informative experience for me. Ha ha."

His face turned serious again.

"No, Shimizu-san," he continued, "this was both of our faults. The inspector should have explained more clearly about our relationship. And to be honest I found it amusing that you had started to harbour some doubts about me. I deliberately wound you up. I'd be lying if I claimed I'd said nothing to stoke your suspicions. I really did bring it on myself. More than anything, it was just too embarrassing to admit that I was a famed private detective."

Kosuke laughed.

Inspector Isokawa looked momentarily as if he'd just bitten into a very sour-tasting bug, but Kosuke's laughter was infectious.

"Ha ha. There really is no match for an honest, determined kind of fellow. Never mind. Never mind. As long as my friend, Kindaichi-san, has no problem with it, then there is no need to give it another thought. So, let's get on with hearing your story of the night of the second murder."

"Yes, sir!" said Shimizu, once again replying in the manner of a soldier to his commanding officer. He hurriedly wiped the sweat from his brow with the back of his hand, and in a flustered tone began to explain the events of the previous night. Unfortunately his way of talking was so incoherent to both Isokawa and Kosuke that they had to constantly ask him to repeat or explain many points. Shimizu was completely rattled, partly due to his unfortunate blunder, but also because of his audience: a veteran prefectural-level detective inspector along with a famous private detective. (How could this man be a famous detective? This scruffy-looking man with the unkempt mass of hair?) He just couldn't seem to take his eyes off Kosuke as he gave his account.

The following is a summary of the events of the previous evening, as gleaned from Shimizu's details.

1. After locking Kosuke Kindaichi in the jail cell, Shimizu had headed up to the head Kito family residence. At that time, Okatsu, Sanae, the sisters Tsukiyo and Yukie, Ryonen the priest and Ryotaku the apprentice priest had all been there. In other

words, Yukie had still been alive and at home. Shimizu had not only seen her, but had spoken to her too. It was about 6.30 p.m. when he arrived at the house.

2. At around 7.30 p.m., Doctor Koan, Mayor Araki and Takezo arrived. It was a long time before anyone noticed that Yukie was gone. Once again, Okatsu and Sanae searched the whole residence from top to bottom, and to everyone's consternation she was nowhere to be found. They split up and went out to look for her. Shimizu believed it was around 8.30 p.m. at this point.

3. This was how the search parties were made up: Sergeant Shimizu with Mayor Araki and Takezo with Ryotaku. Doctor Koan was pretty drunk as usual, and it was suggested that he stay behind at the house, but they found out that he had staggered off on his own later. Due to his old age and his having braved the terrible storm of the night before, the priest's chronic rheumatism was playing up. On top of that, if everyone had left to hunt for Yukie, the women of the house would have been left alone (bar the lunatic locked up in the back). Above all, Tsukiyo was terrified, so the priest stayed behind at the Kito residence.

4. The two search parties climbed up to the top point of the valley together. At this time it wasn't raining, but the sky was pitch-black and starless. When the four men reached the foot of the winding path up to Senkoji Temple, Takezo and Ryotaku said

they'd go up to the temple to check it out, and that's where the two groups split. Shimizu and the mayor continued along the same road and eventually reached the Tengu's Nose lookout point. The temple bell was there, and Shimizu had used his torch to look around its perimeter. At that time there had been no kimono sleeve protruding from underneath.

At this point in the account, Kosuke had to interrupt.

"Just a minute. You definitely came close to the bell at that time?"

"No, not right up to the rim. I just shone my light from the road up at the rock and saw the bell there. I shone my torch up and down and around it, and I am positive that the kimono sleeve was not there. Kindaichi-san, you saw it earlier this morning, so you are aware that the sleeve was sticking out from the side of the bell that faced the road. If it had been there, I would have been sure to notice it. And I wasn't the only one; Mayor Araki will swear too that it wasn't there. Whoever put the body under the bell did it after we had passed by. I can say that with the greatest of confidence."

"Thank you. Please go on."

5. There was nothing strange at the Tengu's Nose lookout point, so Shimizu and the mayor had continued down the hill to the branch Kito family's residence. It had begun to spot with rain, and the wind had got up, so the noise of the waves crashing

on the rocks below was loud. They found Gihei, Oshiho and Ukai at the branch family house. Gihei and Oshiho had been drinking sake together as usual. All three said they knew nothing of Yukie's whereabouts, that they hadn't seen her at all that day, and Ukai swore that ever since he'd returned from the temple that morning, he hadn't left the house again.

"Anyway, while we were standing at the genkan entrance hall, questioning the three, we suddenly heard a peculiar cry... from somewhere far off. It sounded like a voice calling for help. There was such a strong westerly wind last night that it was impossible to hear clearly, but the mayor and I immediately turned and ran out to the road and turned in the direction of the voice; Gihei, Oshiho and the young man Ukai all hurriedly put on *geta* sandals and ran out after us. The five of us stood stock-still in the wind, listening for any further sound, and it came, a second time, a third time: a voice crying for help. 'That sounds like Doctor Koan,' I said, and everyone seemed to agree. We'd told Koan-san to stay behind at the Kito house because he was so drunk, but he must have somehow come after us. His voice was slurred, and it was impossible to make out any actual words, but from the tone we knew it was something serious. The mayor and I went running in search of him, and the branch Kito family members, no doubt worried about Yukie too, came running after us."

"Just a m-minute. Who exactly followed you? Gihei, Oshiho and Ukai? All three of them?"

"Yes, all three. We'd stopped a moment in front of the main gate of the house and listened again, and decided the voice was coming from the bottom of the winding path. So we rushed up there as fast as we could."

"And so you must have passed by the temple bell again?"

"Yes, of course. There's no other way to get to the winding path."

"At that moment, did you happen to look at the bell again?"

"No, there wasn't time. We were in too much of a hurry."

"You said it was raining, so it must have been pitch-dark around there. I suppose you wouldn't have been able to see the bell properly without shining a torch on it."

"That's right. We'd only just checked the bell and, not expecting there to be any changes, we just ran on by in the direction of the voice."

"No, just w-wait, one m-more time. What time was it when you checked the bell? Approximately?"

"Hmm… well, I divided everyone up into search parties and left the head Kito house at about 8.30 p.m., so it must have been around 8.40."

"And then you went to the branch Kito house. About how much time did you spend there?"

"I'd say ten minutes at the most."

"And so if the distance from the branch house to the rock at Tengu's Nose takes two minutes, that's a round trip of four minutes. That means that from the time you examined the bell to the time you passed back by it, there was maybe a space of fourteen minutes. And you say it was now raining. About what time did the rain start? You said before that it

184

began on your way from Tengu's Nose to the branch family house…"

"Yes, that's right. Or maybe a little before that. While we were checking out the bell, I remember it began to spot with rain. We hurried down the hill."

"How was the rain at that time?"

"Hardly anything at all. Yes, that's right—I remember that when we passed the bell again later, it suddenly began to pour."

"And how long did it keep raining? Last night I slept so deeply that I—"

"It didn't let up until daybreak. I remember now—when Gihei, Oshiho and Ukai came to tell me they'd found the kimono sleeve, it was just easing off."

"What?! You mean to say that it was the three branch Kito folk who discovered the sleeve under the bell? No, never mind. Please tell me the events in the order they happened. But you are sure that it was still raining at that point?"

"Yes, it was. When I heard the news, I went out into the rain."

"Kindaichi-san?"

Inspector Isokawa had been listening in silence to the conversation between the other two, but now he cut in, sounding rather puzzled.

"You seem very concerned with the state of the weather. Is there some significance?"

"W-well, yes. It's because of this…"

Kosuke stuck his hand in his bird's-nest head and gave it a good scratch.

"As I was listening to Shimizu-san's account, something odd occurred to me. It's to do with Yukie-san's corpse.

When we lifted up the bell, the body was hardly wet at all. The sleeve that had been sticking out from under the rim was completely soaked, but the rest of her was almost completely dry. As we know, it had also rained the whole of the previous night, so the area all around that lookout point would still have been sodden the whole of yesterday. What's more, while the killer was performing that mechanical trick on the bell, he would surely have left Yukie's body lying on the ground. Now, the back of her kimono was quite damp, which bears out that theory, but the rest of it was completely dry. Her kimono, her hair... how on earth could that be?"

Inspector Isokawa and Shimizu stared at Kosuke. There was a long moment of silence, until finally Shimizu began to speak falteringly.

"Well, then... The corpse... it must have been wrapped in a kind of raincoat..."

"But the back of her kimono was damp. And not just with water—it was muddy too. And anyway, it doesn't matter how skilfully the killer managed to push that body underneath the bell, to get a corpse through that small gap would take quite a bit of effort. How on earth did he manage to avoid getting Yukie wet? Shimizu-san, you said the rain was fairly heavy?"

Shimizu nodded listlessly. The colour had begun to drain from his face.

"I see now why that's so strange. Kindaichi-san, what's your theory about that?"

"Well, let's see, there's only one possible explanation that I can think of. And that is that after you and the mayor had checked the bell and headed towards the branch family house—that's when the killer performed the stunt with the bell. We've already established there were about fourteen minutes before you came back again—I don't think it would have been impossible. You said that the rain was very light during that time."

"Right. Just gentle spotting. Like I said, it didn't really get heavy until we passed by the second time. But, Kindaichi-san, that means that the killer was close by, waiting for us to finish checking the bell."

"I think so. With the body."

With that, Kosuke's face turned grave. He sighed a deep, troubled sigh.

"The thing that bothers me is that according to Doctor Koan, Yukie-san was murdered long before that. Between 6.00 and 7.00 p.m.—that's the estimated time of death. For argument's sake, let's say Yukie was killed around 7.00 p.m. Why did the killer wait with the body until around 8.40 p.m.? But, no—an even bigger question is why on earth did he go to all the trouble and risk of being caught putting Yukie's corpse inside that bell?"

"Hmmm."

This time it was the inspector who let out an even deeper, more troubled sigh.

"You're right. Now that I think of it, the whole case is bizarre. The first murder and the second, they're both utterly insane."

"Exactly, Inspector. Nothing about them makes any sense... Sorry for interrupting your story, Shimizu-san. Please go on."

"Huh? Oh yes. I'm sorry—where was I now? Oh, right! So as we ran past the bell, the rain really began to fall… that's as far as I got. Yes, it was quite a downpour. We ran through that rain trying to reach the place where we'd heard the voice. We got to the bottom of the winding path and met Ryotaku and Takezo coming down from the temple. They'd also heard Koan-san's shouts and had come running down to see. So then, with the addition of those two, we were a party of seven. We kept going until we found Koan-san, stuck down in the valley, yelling for help. Takezo and I climbed down and helped him back up, but we saw right away that his left arm was dangling loosely and he was crying in pain and roaring and screaming something or other—it was impossible to make it out. It scared us half to death."

"I understand. That was when Koan-san had seen the strange man. But before you tell me any more about that, first I want to know why Koan-san had decided to leave the Kito residence."

"It was because of the Aizen laurel."

"The Aizen laurel?"

The inspector and Kosuke were equally amazed at the mention of this fictional tree.

"Yep. The night before when Hanako had slipped out of the house, she'd found the letter from Ukai-san in the hollow of the trunk of the Aizen laurel. It seems Koan-san remembered this and wondered if Yukie's disappearance also had something to do with that tree. He ignored Ryotaku-san and Sanae-san, who begged him not to go out, and set off to look for the tree."

"I see. And then?"

"As you already know, Kindaichi-san, the Aizen laurel grows in the middle of a small valley. Koan-san climbed down there to examine it, but there was nothing there. The hollow in the trunk was empty—no love letters from Ukai-san. Anyway, it seems while he was down in the valley he suddenly heard footsteps up on the road, heading up from the head Kito house, and then turning in his direction. It gave him a fright."

"Just a minute. Was he sure that the footsteps were coming from the direction of the head Kito house?"

"He was. At least that's what he said. In fact, that's not all—he said that thinking about it he was sure that he heard the person come out from the residence's back entrance. As I said earlier, last night there was a westerly wind, and as the Kito place is situated on the north-west side of the valley, even the slightest of noises could have been carried on the wind."

"The Kito residence's back door?"

Kosuke looked startled. An image of the lunatic locked away in the back of the Kito home flashed like a bolt of lightning through his brain.

"Yes. That's why Koan-san thought it was so strange. The only people left in the house at that time were Ryonen the priest, Sanae-san, Okatsu-san and Tsukiyo-san. And of course the lunatic. None of those people were likely to have ventured out from the house alone. And what seemed even stranger was that the person walking seemed to be wearing Western-style shoes or boots. So Koan-san crept up from the valley and waited in hiding by the side of the road as the footsteps came closer. Then, when they were right by him, he called out, taking the person by surprise and causing him to turn around and flee. Koan-san, being the stubborn fellow he is, took off after them."

"Interesting. And then they got into a scuffle?"

"They did. And that's when we heard Koan's voice shouting for help. It seems they struggled with each other for a little while, but as you know Koan is getting on in years, and isn't all that strong. On top of which, he'd been drinking. It was always going to be impossible for him to win in those circumstances. His arm was twisted behind his back, and as he was thrown down into the ravine, he heard his left arm snap."

When he got to this part, Shimizu suddenly stopped talking and looked at the two detectives. Kosuke was also silent, thinking over what Shimizu had told them; Inspector Isokawa the same. They shared an awkward moment of silence as they each considered the story. It was finally broken by Kosuke.

"Did Koan-san happen to see the man's face?" he asked gently.

"No, it seems not. Last night it was completely dark. What he could tell during their struggle was that it was a man dressed in Western clothing, and that he was well built. I'm afraid that's about all the information he could give us."

"In what direction did the man escape afterwards?"

"I'm sorry to say that Koan-san has no idea. It was the shock of being thrown down into the valley, and the pain of his broken arm—he was really only semi-conscious, and he doesn't remember much of anything after that."

"This mysterious man didn't happen to be carrying a dead body on his back, by any chance?" said Inspector Isokawa.

"You know, I thought the same thing. But Koan-san says there was no way he was carrying anything like that. But…"

"But?…"

"Well, he did say something about the fellow's hand. When they were fighting, he says that the man was carrying something under his arm which seemed to be wrapped in a *furoshiki* cloth."

"Something wrapped in a furoshiki?"

Kosuke frowned in disbelief.

"That's what Koan says. Anyway, I've worked out for myself what that was. I went up to the Kito house myself. When they heard me coming, the priest and Sanae-san came running out of the entrance hall of the main building. They'd heard all the commotion. I asked them to look after Koan-san, and set off again with Takezo."

"Just a moment. What had happened to the three from the branch house?"

"Ah yes, those three had followed us all the way to the head Kito residence. And would you believe, for once they actually stayed for the rest of the night. They'd got soaking wet from the rain, and they seemed to be worried about Yukie-san. Or maybe they had some other motive—I don't know—but they kept vigil together all night."

"Oh, really!"

Kosuke's eyes grew wide, and a great rush of happiness seemed to engulf him. His fingers began to grind and scratch and tear at his scalp.

"Th-that means that all of the relevant parties were gathered last night at the Kito residence. Besides the remaining members of the head Kito family, there were the priests,

Ryonen and Ryotaku, from Senkoji Temple, Mayor Araki, Doctor Koan, Takezo-san and you, Shimizu-san. And then also all three members of the branch Kito family were present. Everyone was there. And you say that they all stayed until morning?"

"Yes, they were all there. As I said, after we'd rescued Koan-san and taken him back to the house, Takezo and I went out again right away to look for this suspicious man, but we gave up almost immediately. It was too dark outside to see anything and the rain was getting heavier, so we decided it was hopeless."

"And you stayed at the house until morning?"

"I did."

"In that case, can you tell me, did anyone leave during that time? I mean not just the room, but leave the grounds of the residence altogether?"

"Definitely not. Everyone was in that large ten-mat sitting room. Of course, people got up to use the toilet at various times, but nobody at all went outside the building. The women brought us dinner, poured us tea, so they were in and out of the room constantly, but I'm sure they never went out of the house."

"And yet… let's say… there was the period of time when you and Takezo were out looking for the mysterious man. Are you sure everyone was at the house then?"

"I think they were. I'm pretty sure I would have known if anyone went out. And anyway, Takezo and I gave up almost right away. It was only a very short time that we were gone."

"So then, let me double-check one thing: the first time that you divided up into search parties and went out to look

192

for Yukie-san, besides the drunken doctor who followed you out, the people left behind at the Kito house were Ryonen the priest, Sanae-san, Okatsu-san and Tsukiyo-san? Just those four? None of them went outside at any time?"

"That's right. They didn't. I also wanted to make absolutely sure of that at the time. I am perfectly sure that no one at all ventured outside."

"All right. Thank you."

A broad grin on his face, Kosuke turned to Inspector Isokawa.

"And so you see, the alibis of all the concerned parties have been corroborated."

The inspector shrugged. At which point, Kosuke immediately backtracked.

"But that's not the case at all, is it? There is still one person who does not have an airtight alibi."

"Still one person? Who? I can't—"

"The patient in the cell. Shimizu-san, he was not included in your group last night. I can't imagine that you stood watch over him from beginning to end."

"Kindaichi-san!"

The rate of Shimizu's breathing began to increase.

"You believe that madman—"

"No, no. That's not what I believe at all. I'm simply thinking of all the possibilities. And we can't rule him out completely just because he is a lunatic."

Kosuke stopped speaking and a chilled silence fell once again between the three men. This time it was born of fear.

Shimizu had suddenly seen a picture in his mind of an escaped lunatic roaming the dark roads of the island. In his arms, he carried the freshly strangled corpse of his daughter Yukie. It was a shocking image—the contrast of Yukie's brightly coloured kimono sleeve against the black form of the madman. In Shimizu's mind, the expression on the lunatic's face was one of malice and hatred. It was the incarnation of evil itself. Clutching Yukie's lifeless body, the lunatic ran and ran and ran into the night. Through the driving rain, the howling wind, across pitch-black Gokumon Island...

"I'm sorry, Shimizu-san, for interrupting you so many times. Please continue with your story."

Shimizu was jolted back to reality by the sound of Kosuke's voice. He shivered and blinked hard several times, attempting to shake off the image of hell that haunted him.

"Ah yes, sorry. I seem to have got distracted by my own thoughts... Anyway, as I was saying, we all stayed together in the sitting room at the head Kito house until daybreak, without even so much as a quick nap. And when it finally got light to the east, the three branch family members left and went home. At that time it was still drizzling, like mist in the air. Anyway, those three came back almost right away, their expressions changed once more. They said there was a woman's kimono sleeve under the bell, and of course we all rushed to see. And that's the full account of everything that happened from yesterday evening through to this morning."

Shimizu let out a long sigh much like a whale expelling water from its blowhole. The horror of the previous night had been a dark ball of angst deep in his stomach, and he had finally managed to spew it all out.

"I see. Do you think it might be possible that the three

194

branch family Kitos had shoved the body under the bell right then and run back to the main house?"

"No, that is pretty much impossible. It was a very short period of time between them leaving and returning. There is no way they could have raised the bell and put a corpse inside it in that length of time. Besides, it was already quite light by then, and that lookout point is in clear view of both the sea and the bay. Fishermen are morning folk, and if anyone were to attempt something like that, they'd run the risk of being seen. I'm sure they couldn't have done it."

Inspector Isokawa gave that troubled sigh of his once more. The second prefectural police launch was due to arrive at the island any minute. This boat would be carrying Doctor Kinoshita, of the prefectural forensics division, his assistant and other members of the forensics team. The corpses were going to undergo full autopsies.

"*Gokurosama*—thank you for coming," said Inspector Isokawa when the police pathologist arrived. "I've got Maeda coming from Kasaoka to help inspect the body."

"Really? That's a stroke of good fortune," said Doctor Kinoshita. "I'll need all the help I can get. I hear there are two victims."

"Yes, they're sisters. It's a terrible case."

Kosuke was only vaguely listening to the conversation on the quay between Inspector Isokawa and the others. The party then set off for the head Kito residence, but on the way, Kosuke, who was deep in thought, his eyes to the ground, suddenly looked up. He turned to Shimizu, who was walking beside him.

"By the way, Shimizu-san, you said earlier that you arrived at the head Kito house last night at exactly 6.30 p.m.?"

"Yes, that's right. I happened to look at my wristwatch right as I arrived. I remember clearly."

"Does your watch keep accurate time?"

"It's usually correct. I adjust it every day from the radio. Even if it was off, it couldn't be by more than a minute or two. Why do you ask?"

"Fine. So you got to the Kito residence at exactly 6.30 p.m. Did they have the radio on when you arrived?"

"The radio?" repeated Shimizu. "I'm not really sure."

"At that house, if they have the radio on, you can hear it right away from the entrance hall. How about last night? Did you hear it?"

Shimizu thought about it.

"No, I didn't. The radio wasn't on."

"Then, you said you left to search for Yukie around 8.30 p.m. Did anyone turn on the radio at all between 6.30 and 8.30 p.m.?"

"No. Nobody turned on the radio."

Puzzled, Shimizu stared at Kosuke.

"Why are you so interested in the radio, Kindaichi-san?"

"You're certain?"

"Without a doubt. If someone turned it on, I would have heard it. But, Kindaichi-san, what is the significance of whether someone turned on the radio or not? What does it have to do with this case?"

Even Inspector Isokawa, walking just ahead of them, stopped in his tracks and turned to look at Kosuke. Kosuke vaguely shook his head.

"It's a little odd that nobody switched on the radio at 6.35 p.m. That's the hour that the repatriation news is broadcast. Sanae-san listens every day without fail for news of her brother, Hitoshi. But then somehow last night she either forgot to listen, or she purposely didn't. Either way she did not touch the button on that radio. I can't help feeling there is something significant about that."

Kosuke Kindaichi's eyes were staring at the inspector without seeing him. He had gone into some sort of daze.

MANHUNT IN THE MOUNTAINS

The latest team of investigators completed the autopsies and left Gokumon Island just around the time the sky began to turn red, and night's dark shadows began to fall. After they left, Doctor Kinoshita and his assistant Maeda-san finished up their work and left the island too.

There were no new discoveries as a result of the autopsies. While unconscious following a heavy blow to her head, Hanako had been strangled; Yukie had also been strangled by something similar—probably a cotton hand towel or tenugui—then her body stuffed under the temple bell. The times of death were also confirmed to have been the same as Doctor Koan's estimates. Yukie had been killed shortly after sundown on the previous day.

The moment the autopsies were concluded, preparations began at the head Kito house for the double funeral. It was a whirlwind of activity. By rights, Hanako's funeral should have already taken place that day, but to hold funerals on consecutive days would have been too much of an imposition on people, so the family had decided to wait until the next day in order to bury her along with her sister. Another new coffin was delivered, and the young men of the village hurried to dig a second grave for Yukie, alongside the one they had already made for Hanako. On Gokumon Island, everyone was interred rather than cremated, and the gravestones towered up behind Senkoji Temple. Gokumon Island's graveyard was on the side of Mount Suribachi.

Inspector Isokawa had just about concluded his interviews with all the families and other witnesses. Investigating this murder case was like trying to clutch at clouds, which had left the veteran detective extremely frustrated. His only hope had been that he would be able to find out more details about the mysterious man whom Doctor Koan had encountered, but even after very intense questioning, it was hopeless. There was no more information to be had beyond what he had already heard from Koan himself and Sergeant Shimizu.

The only things they could be certain of were that the man had exited the back gate of the Kito residence, and that he had been carrying some kind of bundle wrapped in a furoshiki cloth. He had questioned Sanae and Okatsu of the head Kito household, and separately both had stated the same thing. They were asked whether it was possible that someone had crept into the house while they weren't looking and taken something. Sanae in particular was insistent that nothing was missing. Okatsu seemed nervous and flustered throughout the questioning, and had no idea whether one or two articles wrapped in a furoshiki were missing or not, so that Kosuke completely discounted anything she said at all.

"Kindaichi-san," said Inspector Isokawa, "it looks as if we're going to have to set up a manhunt to search the whole island. I'm thinking that maybe the escaped pirate gang member is the man that Koan-san encountered last night, and that he murdered both of those girls. Maybe the girls witnessed him coming onto the island or found out where he was hiding…"

"Inspector, I agree with the theory that he's the killer. However, I don't believe his motive was that simple. Whether the killer is that man or not, there must be some much more dreadful, deeply hidden motive. By the way, Inspector, what are your plans now? Are you going to stay here on the island or go back to the mainland?"

"No, no. Of course I'm going to stay here, and not only because of this murder case. There's still the matter of the escaped gang member. And then I want to look at the crime scenes again. And it's so much trouble to travel back and forth from the mainland."

"Yes, that would be better. The Kito residence is really spacious. There should easily be room for five or six to sleep right here. The detectives and everyone can stay here together… In fact, I think I'll get them to let me stay here too from now on. I'll go and talk to Sanae-san about it."

"I'd be really grateful if you would…"

There was no objection from Sanae. After the violent deaths of her two younger sisters, the terrified Tsukiyo was relieved to hear that the police would be staying with them, as was the spineless Okatsu; in fact Tsukiyo's delight was like that of a small child.

"Oh, everyone's going to stay here? I'm so happy. I love it when the place gets lively. I hate it when everyone's all gloomy."

"Tsukiyo-chan, don't get so happy that you accidentally wander off out somewhere," Kosuke warned her.

"I'm going nowhere. Yukie-chan and Hana-chan were dumb. Going for a walk after the sun's gone down! What were they thinking?"

"Be absolutely sure not to go anywhere. Even if Ukai-san asks you to."

"Stop it, Kosuke-san!"

Tsukiyo giggled flirtatiously and made as if to swat Kosuke with her long kimono sleeve.

"I'm not going outside. I'm not. Not even if someone comes and asks me to. Life is too precious."

She may have been foolish, but it was still a pitiful sight to see her aware that she was the next target.

"Good, I'm glad to hear it. Not even for a short stroll. For now, it doesn't matter who comes to this house, nobody is to go outside."

"No, I won't. Instead, I'm going to curse the murderer to death."

"Curse the murderer to death?"

Kosuke stared at Tsukiyo, but she seemed perfectly calm and composed.

"Yes, that's right," she said, her eyes unfocused. "Whenever I'm worried about something, or there's something I don't like, then I always say an incantation. It works really well. Anyone who does bad things to me ends up cursed by the gods."

Seeing Kosuke's confused expression, Sanae gave a light laugh.

"You remember seeing a plain wooden building at the end of the garden? That's our prayer house. Whenever Tsukiyo-chan finds something that doesn't suit her, she shuts herself away in there and chants. It's well known throughout the island that Tsukiyo's invocations are always answered."

"That's right. And you believe in my powers too, don't you, Sanae-san? If I say my incantations as hard as I can tonight, I bet you that bad man will get what's coming to him."

Apparently this was Tsukiyo's speciality.

Kosuke recalled how the priest, Ryonen, had told him that the Kito estate had a prayer house. It was a building at the end of the garden on a slightly raised bit of land, just across from Yosamatsu's cell. Kosuke had wondered why a family home would have something called a prayer house, but he had never dreamed that Tsukiyo might be famed for summoning the gods.

Kosuke would have liked to give this topic more thought, but right then Inspector Isokawa looked at the clock.

"Kindaichi-san, I'd like to take another look at the crime scene. If we dawdle too much then it'll start getting dark. Let's get going."

This was how the conversation was interrupted, and never revisited. Kosuke did not realize how much he would come to regret it later...

Kosuke also looked at the clock. It was just about 6.40 p.m. He looked at Sanae expectantly, but she appeared to be lost in thought, and didn't notice. It seemed that tonight, too, she had forgotten all about the repatriation news.

When they got outside, it was just beginning to get dark. As soon as the sun set, the air on the island turned chilly. Kosuke hunched his shoulders against the cold.

"Do you want to go up to the temple? Or—"

"No, I want to go to Tengu's Nose."

The bell still hung there, suspended on the rocky lookout point where Yukie had been killed. Two detectives were undertaking a painstaking search of the grass around it. Autumn had set in and bush clover blooms dotted the grass and clothed the edges of the rock in pink finery.

"Have you found anything?"

"No, nothing…"

"Where are the rest?"

"They went looking for the fugitive up on the mountain. They haven't got back yet."

With Sergeant Shimizu and the young men of the village as their guides, some of the detectives had gone up Mount Suribachi in search of the pirate gang member.

Inspector Isokawa bent down to look under the bell.

"She was completely covered by this bell? So do you think that when Shimizu and Mayor Araki first passed by here last night, the killer may already have been hiding over there beyond the bell?"

"I believe it's possible," Kosuke replied. "When Shimizu-san and the mayor came by, they only shone their torch on the bell itself. They never tried to look around the vicinity. But as you can see from the way it's hanging here now, the bell had been placed right at the edge of the cliff. There were barely ten inches behind it. The killer, whether he was working alone or not, must have carried Yukie's body… let's see…"

The two men walked to the edge of the cliff and looked down. The rocky area they stood on jutted out from the cliff. If they stretched out on their bellies and peered carefully over, they could see the curve of the road about twenty feet or so below them. And all around, there was about 150 feet or so of sheer precipice. In other words, it would have been impossible to climb up the cliff this way. It was a simple conclusion to draw from looking down at the foot of the cliff and gauging the state of the sea, the strength of the wind, and observing the seaweed and other debris that clung to the rock, all at the mercy of the surging waves.

"Clearly he didn't climb up this way. Even if he were some kind of lizard man, there's no way he could have got up this cliff face."

Then, just as the two men were standing up and dusting off their clothes, they heard voices coming from further up the road. There was loud cursing and the stomping of many feet. They turned in surprise, to see a bunch of young men from the village careening down the hill, hoes and shovels over their shoulders. They were on their way back from the Kito family grave plot on the side of Mount Suribachi where they'd been digging Yukie's grave. As soon as they spotted Inspector Isokawa, they began to call out excitedly.

"Ah, Inspector, we saw him! We saw him!"

"Saw who?"

The inspector began to breathe a little faster.

"Some weird-looking guy. Thick beard all over his face."

"Wearing an army uniform."

"With scary eyes."

"You saw him? Where?"

"Right behind the Kito family burial site."

"But behind the burial site is nothing but a cliff."

"We were digging a hole right there. The rock is pretty rough in that area. We just turned around and—"

"This weird guy was watching us from a clump of bushes. With this terrible expression in his eyes."

"Yeah. He definitely wasn't from these parts. Never set eyes on him before. Gotta be that one who ran away and he's hiding on this island."

The young men were so worked up they could barely get the words out.

"All right then, so why didn't you capture this man?" asked one of the detectives. The mood changed abruptly, and they all fell quiet.

"Well, sir, because we heard he had a weapon…"

"When I spoke to him he got defensive and looked like he was ready to fight."

"And so you all just scuttled away like baby spiders?" sneered the other detective. "You island boys all make out you're so tough with your saying 'no more than an inch of plank between you and a watery grave', but you sure chickened out quickly."

"Yeah, I guess you're right—I can't explain it. But you know, it was so unexpected… hey, who was it who ran away first?"

"Not me. It was probably that son of a bitch, Gen. No way were we running away before—we just followed him."

"You bastard. You can talk! Who was it who was screaming and squealing like a little girl?"

As the young men began to squabble among themselves, there was another sound of heavy footsteps hurrying down the road. Sergeant Shimizu appeared, with the rest of the detectives close on his tail.

"Oh, this is where you lot got to. What was all that fuss just now?"

"Sergeant, we saw him. That devil guy. We saw him! We came back here to report to the inspector."

"Shimizu, how did it go with your team?" asked Inspector Isokawa.

"Oh, Inspector, it's true, for sure. There's definitely been someone hiding on the island. Up at the pirate fortress, we found the remains of a bonfire. And then there was this furoshiki…"

Shimizu produced a dirty, rain-soaked cloth that was obviously a furoshiki wrapping cloth that had seen better days. He opened it up to reveal the white face of an *oni* demon on a yellow background. Above it was printed the character "hon" meaning "main", also in white.

"The family crest?…"

"Yes, it's the Kito family crest. The branch family also uses the face of a demon, but theirs has the character for 'branch' above it."

Inspector Isokawa turned to Kosuke.

"This means that Doctor Koan was telling the truth. This fellow stole into the Kito residence last night and escaped with something wrapped in a furoshiki."

"Yes, he may have done."

Kosuke's response was less than enthusiastic. Inspector Isokawa gave him a puzzled look.

"*He may have done*? But it's clear that's what happened. We have the Kito family's furoshiki right here to prove it."

"Yes, yes. We do. But if that's the case, how come Sanae-san didn't notice anything missing?"

"Well, obviously because it's such a big house that it's not out of the question that someone could steal a furoshiki or two—or even a furoshiki full of food and no one would notice. Besides, right now they're preoccupied with all sorts of other things. But, Kindaichi-san, what are you thinking?"

Kosuke vigorously shook his head.

"Nothing important… but anyway, Inspector, at least we know beyond a doubt that there is a strange man hiding on this island. Let's get everyone together for a manhunt."

"I agree."

The inspector looked around. Twilight had completely given over to darkness, and it had become impossible to make out the identity of anyone standing nearby. Night had fallen over the Seto Inland Sea, and the first stars of the evening were growing brighter in the sky.

"If we wait until tomorrow, it may be too late," Kosuke added. "Luckily we have the light of the moon tonight. Perhaps we should give it a go right away."

"Right! Let's give it everything we've got!"

That night, Gokumon Island was a sight worth seeing. From that early part of the evening and throughout the rest of the night, the island was impressive, almost stately.

Inspector Isokawa's party headed first to the head Kito residence, and hurriedly ate an evening meal, kindly prepared by Sanae and Okatsu. Meanwhile, the young men headed back to the village and gathered together as many islanders as they could, appealing to them to join the manhunt. Of course these were daredevil fishermen, so as soon as they heard the call, they began to converge on the Kito residence in great numbers.

Thus, at around eight that evening, outside the Kito house, dozens of fishermen were awaiting Inspector Isokawa's orders. They each carried a torch or a lantern, and some kind of improvised weapon. They looked as if they were about to start a riot.

While Inspector Isokawa was organizing them into groups and giving each team directions, back in the sitting room, Kosuke approached Sanae and began to ask her some questions.

"Sanae-san, did you really have no idea that this furoshiki had been stolen?"

"I, er… No. Why do you ask?"

Undeterred, Sanae looked Kosuke straight in the eye. She was filled with an almost frightening determination. She somehow managed to keep her expression calm, but Kosuke could sense that deep in her heart there was a torrent of emotions. After a while she started to look frantic, as if trying to repel Kosuke's gaze, until eventually her eyes began to dart around as if hiding something.

"Sanae-san?" said Kosuke with renewed energy. "Tonight, everyone is going off on a manhunt."

Sanae didn't respond.

"With that many hunters, there is no way that anyone could escape. He's going to be captured. Sanae-san, do you really not mind?"

Startled, Sanae looked up, then glared at Kosuke. It was a glare of pure anger—one that could almost have concealed a murderous impulse.

"Kindaichi-san! What are you implying?"

"Don't you know?"

"I don't know. I have absolutely no idea. You're talking in riddles. How am I supposed to understand? I—"

Right at that moment, the tide master, Takezo, came rushing into the room, interrupting Sanae in mid-sentence. Takezo had come at the request of Inspector Isokawa to fetch Kosuke.

"Ah, I see. I'll be right there," Kosuke said. "Oh, Takezo-san?"

"What can I do for you?"

"Could you tell me where Tsukiyo-san is? I haven't seen her this evening."

"Hello? I'm right here."

Cackling with laughter, Tsukiyo scuttled into the room. But the moment Kosuke set eyes on her, he stiffened in shock.

She wore an outfit reminiscent of a traditional Heian Era courtesan of a thousand years ago: a glossy white silk robe with a long, trailing hakama skirt in bright crimson. On her head was a gold-coloured *eboshi*—a pointed hat. She was carrying a small golden handbell.

"Tsukiyo-chan, your outfit?"

"Oh, Kosuke-san, did you forget? I'm going to the prayer house to say an invocation. You're all off hunting, aren't you? I'm going to make a prayer that you capture that bad man. I'm sure you'll get him. My incantations always work."

She cackled once again, and then pattered off again out of the sitting room. Dumbfounded, Kosuke watched her leave. When he thought about it later, he realized that was the last time he ever saw Tsukiyo alive.

Takezo had come back a second time to summon Kosuke.

"Er… sorry—I'm on my way. Sanae-san?"

"Yes?…"

"I'm asking you to look after Tsukiyo-chan. Please keep an eye on her."

Sanae's face had turned rather pale, and now she raised an eyebrow at Kosuke, as if to indicate that his request went without saying.

"Takezo-san, you're joining the hunt, aren't you?"

"Yes, I am."

"I'd like you to stay here."

"But the inspector told me to lead a team. It's too late to make changes at this point."

At that moment, from deep within the compound came the dreadful roar of the lunatic. Sanae started at the sound.

"I'm sorry, I have to go. My uncle is rather unsettled by all the activity around here tonight."

And with that she hurried from the room.

As he watched Sanae leave, Kosuke was left feeling very uneasy, but he gave in to Takezo's urging and turned and walked towards the front door. On his way he glanced into the sitting room, to see Ryonen and Ryotaku reciting a sutra in front of the family altar. Mayor Araki and Doctor Koan were there too, along with Gihei and Oshiho and the pretty boy Ukai-san—the latter three all seemed meek and restrained. Even the branch family members were unable to ignore the activity that surrounded them.

The mayor spotted Kosuke.

"Ah, Kindaichi-san, are you joining the manhunt?" he said in a solemn tone.

"Yes, I'm just going."

"Thank you. I really ought to go to, but tonight is the wake... After it's over I'll come and catch you up."

"Whatever is best for you, sir."

The sound of the bowl-shaped gong gently vibrated through the air of the sitting room. The priest didn't turn around.

Kosuke could see from the entranceway that most of the hunting party had already departed. Only the band led by Takezo, and the inspector's team, each consisting of six or seven men, remained in the Kito family's compound.

"Kindaichi-san, let's get going."

"Just a moment. I'd like to leave three or four men here."

"Why?"

"Just in case the man we're hunting runs to this house to get away. I don't want to be unprepared, so let's leave three or four people to keep watch around the perimeter of the residence."

The inspector quickly picked two men from each of the bands and charged them with guarding the Kito house.

"Right then, time to go."

Kosuke checked his watch. It was exactly 8.30 p.m. Beyond the walls of the Kito residence, the sky seemed to be dripping with stars. The ten-day-old moon lit up the mountain behind Senkoji Temple. They climbed uphill from the Kito residence and, as they approached the road from the other side of the valley, they could see the winding path up to the temple dotted with the torchlights of the hunting teams that had gone ahead.

"Inspector, don't you think all those lights will alert the target to our presence?"

"No, after the bands carrying the lanterns and torchs, there are other groups approaching stealthily with no lights at all. The plan is for the light carriers to flush out the prey right into the nets of the stealth teams."

"I see."

Inspector Isokawa and Kosuke's band and the one led by Takezo carried straight along the road beyond the valley. They arrived at the Tengu's Nose point and took a left, climbing the hill that earlier the gravedigger band and the team of detectives had come down. There was no other way besides this path to climb Mount Suribachi.

Takezo's band of hunters were each carrying a lighted torch and purposely making a lot of racket as they climbed. About a hundred yards behind them, Kosuke and the inspector's stealth unit followed in silence. Normally the land above Tengu's Nose didn't get many visitors—the path was narrow and the slope precipitously steep. There was a bright moon in the sky, a whole shower of stars, and yet the tree branches that stuck out seemed to be determined to trip the hunters.

They passed around the jutting edge of the mountain and suddenly the view opened up before them. They were able to look up at the slopes of Mount Suribachi, leading the way up to the pirate fortress on the very tip.

Here and there on the rising ground were the lights of the advance hunting parties, floating in the air like will-o'-the-wisps as the men made their ant-like ascent of the mountain. Voices chanting as they marched could be heard both near and far. At this sound, a memory surfaced in Kosuke's mind of the small gong ringing back at the Kito house… All of a sudden, Kosuke was seized by an inexplicable feeling.

Before him was a manhunt; behind him, a wake. And then he pictured Sanae's distressingly pale complexion, Tsukiyo dressed like a courtesan, the lunatic locked away in his cell with his bestial screams, and then finally his mind went further back to Chimata Kito's dying wish. Before his eyes, the line of lanterns all of a sudden began to sway back and forth as if about to envelop the whole island in flames.

CHAPTER 5

Sayo the Shaman

As I mentioned before, all the homes on Gokumon Island were concentrated on the west side of the island, to make it easier to mount a defence in the event of a pirate invasion. This was customary on such small islands, but in the case of Gokumon Island, the geography also made it necessary. Apart from the western end of the island, there was no level ground suitable for building on.

Mount Suribachi wasn't all that tall a mountain. Apart from its western face, the other three sides seemed to leap straight out of the sea. There was no place to anchor a boat—nowhere to gain a foothold between land and sea. This is why the searchers knew that after they had gone over the west end of the island with a fine-toothed comb, the escaped killer would be cornered on the mountain, stuck, as one might say, between the devil and the deep blue sea.

The almost half-moon sat on the shoulder of Mount Suribachi. The twinkling stars seemed to multiply by the second. The smoky white tail of the Milky Way stretched across the sky. Gokumon Island was bathed in a misty silver light. In the midst of this scene, the pinpoints of lanterns, shimmering in mid-air, crawled up the mountainside. At the peak of Mount Suribachi, the ruins of the pirate fortress were visible. The battle cries of the marching islanders echoed here and there off the peak, sounding like distant thunder.

Kosuke followed Inspector Isokawa up the mountain path in silence. He spotted Seiko the barber in the middle of the column of men.

"Hey, you're here too!"

The two men grinned at each other.

"Hee-hee. This manhunt is the biggest thing that's happened here for a while! Seiko the barber hates waiting around for things to happen. But, sir, such terrible goings-on on the island!"

"Yes, really terrible. What are the islanders saying about it?"

"Hmm, well, they're saying all sorts of things. But that's no matter. They can never keep themselves from gossiping. But I was surprised—and the islanders were all surprised too."

"Surprised by what?"

"Well, about you, sir. At first they were all saying you were fishy—you know, to them you were a suspicious stranger. No one knew where you came from—you are a self-described drifter after all. You were an obvious suspect. Everyone was going around saying that Kosuke Kindaichi is really dodgy—they were all worked up about it."

"You don't say! But why did they imagine I would kill Hanako and Yukie?"

"Ah, well, they thought you were trying to embezzle the Kito family fortune. Don't be angry, sir, but that was the gossip. Don't worry, though, nobody believes that crazy story any more. I was surprised to discover that you were

Japan's number-one private detective… The islanders too, well, they were flabbergasted, sir. I was always telling the boys, 'Hey, don't misjudge him. He may look weird but he's a true Tokyoite.'"

"Ha ha. Thanks for that. I'm glad to hear it. But how did they think I was going to embezzle the Kito fortune? Even if I killed Hanako and Yukie, the fortune wouldn't be mine."

"Oh, of course, that was all meant to be part of the plot. I'm skipping ahead, but to summarize, after killing Tsukiyo, Yukie and Hanako, you would seduce Sanae into becoming your wife and insinuate yourself into the Kito family. That's the plot that they came up with. But I told them, 'Don't talk crazy. This guy is Tokyo born and bred.' I explained that you wouldn't choose such a roundabout, complex way to go about it. If you really wanted money, you would just get a pistol or something, and then rob them. But the biggest proof is that a Tokyoite could never choose to live here and put up with this island's boiled barley and rice for so long. Sir, I've been your supporter from the get-go."

This was quite the supporter indeed. Still, when Kosuke realized that everyone had seen him as some kind of dangerous character, it made him uneasy.

"Seiko-san, this whole plot sounds like a made-up drama about some ancient family feud. And my role was that of the evil daimyo lord."

"Rather it was the role of the seducer. You know, like Judayu Kurahashi of the Kuroda rebellion, or one of those other roles taken by the good-looking actors."

"Seiko-san?"

Kosuke's tone changed. He began to breathe faster.

"The inhabitants of this island, do they all think this way—as if everything's like some kind of drama?"

Even Sergeant Shimizu had believed in the past that Kosuke was a master criminal. Kosuke was very interested in the minds of these islanders, fond as they were of a good story.

"Well, they haven't always been like that. But I must admit they all love to watch a good play. I heard that the late Kaemon-san was very fond of the theatre. I don't know if you've heard of it, sir, but there's a Shinto shrine, Konpira Shrine in Sanuki City in Shikoku. There's an old theatre building on the grounds of that shrine, built back in the Tempo or Kaei Era, around the middle of the nineteenth century. They made it an exact replica of a theatre in Ohnishi in Osaka. It's still standing now. It was probably the smallest theatre building in the whole of Japan. Constructed in the traditional style and it has a great history. Much of it is still there. Many Kyoto-based actors would come and perform there. Kaemon-san was quite a patron of the theatre. If he heard about a good play, he would use his huge boat to take all the islanders over to Shikoku to see it. It was a magnificent spectacle. He would buy up the tickets in the private seating area, and all the fisherfolk were treated to a lavish spectacle. I was one of his favourites. He'd always take me along. It was wonderful, like a dream. We'll never see times like that again."

"Interesting. So that's why you're a fan of the head Kito family. What did you do to get in his favour like that?"

"No, no. It wasn't like that at all. It's because I was interested in *zappai*. Zappai... have you heard of it? It's a kind

216

of poetry loosely based on haiku. I used to be very serious about it—it wasn't all just comic and humorous stuff that I would write. Mine were quite tasteful—some of my better ones might even be compared to pure haiku. Someday I'll let you hear some of my best ones... Well, no, never mind about that... anyhow Kaemon-san was like the great Toyotomi Hideyoshi, and he had all kinds of hobbies. He would compose haiku, but he was the kind who much preferred to write zappai. He used to give himself the penname Gokumon."

Oh, so that was what it meant... For the first time Kosuke felt he understood. Those shikishi—the square poem cards on the folding screen back in his room at the temple, the ones he had taken so long to decipher because of their awful worm-like squiggles—those were the handiwork of the late Kaemon-san.

"Gokumon... Because he was like the ruler of Gokumon Island... Anyway, he held his own poetry salon and of course they all said that no poetry club would be complete without Seiko. Because of course I'm from Tokyo, the centre of poetic culture, so I was kind of their instructor. And that's how I came to be honoured with Kaemon-san's special attention."

"I see. So Kaemon-san had artistic tastes? I heard he loved theatre performance so much that even his own son, Yosamatsu-san, took an actress for his second wife."

To tell the truth, Kosuke had been dying to ask this very question. To find out about the mother of Tsukiyo, Yukie and Hanako. Since this morning, the desire to know the identity of this woman had been burning a hole in his brain, but he hadn't known whom he could possibly ask. Framing it as part of an interview or interrogation would have been much less

217

effective. Particularly because his real status had now been discovered. Whatever question he asked, the interviewee was bound to be cautious, and he couldn't be confident any more of getting a truthful response. Right now, although he'd been waiting a long time for his chance, he phrased it casually as part of the conversation, and sure enough, Seiko the barber played right into his hands.

"No, that's not it. It's true that it happened because Kaemon-san loved the theatre so much, but Sayo-san—that was her name—Sayo-san. I don't know what her stage name was. Anyway, Master Yosamatsu took this Sayo-san as his mistress. Kaemon-san was furious about it and opposed it vehemently."

"Did you know this Sayo-san personally?"

"Yes, when I first came to Gokumon Island she was still alive, but she passed away not six months later, so I couldn't say I knew her well. Although I did hear a lot of rumours about her."

"The one whose speciality was *Dojoji Temple*? They say that Yosamatsu-san saw her perform in that and fell in love, and that's when he made her his mistress."

"Yes, *Dojoji Temple* and *Tadanobu the Fox*, and *The Kudzu Leaves*, and... well, all those sorts of roles where the actor transforms into an animal were her forte, so they say. She had formed her own troupe of travelling players, performing around the Chugoku region. Then Kaemon-san heard about their reputation and he paid for the troupe to come to Gokumon Island to perform a play. He even constructed a stage in the grounds of the Kito residence and had them perform *Dojoji Temple* right there. As a matter of fact, that was when Yosamatsu-san fell in love and began sleeping with the actress. But Kaemon-san was enraged by this. It was right after Yosamatsu's first wife, Chimata-san's mother, had passed away. His marriage bed was empty. Imagine a beautiful actress paying you compliments. It must have been too tempting to resist. Like offering dried fish to a cat. It was the biggest mistake of Kaemon-san's life."

"But what did Kaemon-san have against this woman?"

"Well, sir, it goes without saying. She was just a common actress of undetermined lineage. And the Kito clan was the most important and influential family on the island. Here, even if you marry someone whose family background is well known, the islanders still look down on them as an outsider."

"So it must have been terrible for this Sayo-san, being despised by Kaemon-san."

"It really was. If she'd been a shy, retiring type, it might have been bearable, but she was the most sly and stubborn woman. She influenced Yosamatsu-san so much, gave him so much advice and was a constant thorn in Kaemon's side. She really had Yosamatsu-san wrapped around her finger. He did anything she told him to. And so, living there in the same house, there was a feud between father and son, a never-ending quarrel. It got so bad that it was rumoured that Yosamatsu tried to usurp the leadership of the Kito family from his father. In the end even the tough Kaemon-san lost some of his power to that canny woman, and it seemed to age him by years."

"It seems that she was quite a woman."

"Yes, she really was. And if only she hadn't taken up that business, Yosamatsu-san would have become head of the

Kito family, and she, Sayo-san, the wife of an influential fishing boss."

"If she hadn't taken what business up, exactly?"

"Shamanism."

"Shamanism?"

Kosuke's eyes suddenly grew wide and his heart started to thud in his chest. The outfit that Tsukiyo had been wearing earlier flashed before his eyes.

"Right, right. I think you've probably seen it, sir—at the far end of the Kito residence, there's a weird-looking building, right? Yosamatsu-san built it for his wife. This Sayo-san, I've no idea where she learned it, but she used to chant all kinds of spells and things. If you ask me, it was more witchcraft than shamanism. Around the time I came to the island she'd become a semi-invalid and had stopped doing it, but some time before I heard that she had quite a vigorous energy and dressed just like Shizuka Gozen. She'd shake her bell and burn incense, and try to summon gods, chanting things like 'Shoten of Ikoma, Shoten of Kawachi, show yourselves, show yourselves. I am a woman born in the Year of the Tiger...' She'd do all that sort of stuff."

Kosuke let out a deep breath.

"What the—?"

"What's the matter?"

"Well, it doesn't even make sense. Shoten is a Buddhist deity, but you said she started to practise shamanism, and it sounds like she dressed like a shaman too."

The outfit Tsukiyo had been wearing earlier had also made her look more like a Shinto shrine maiden than a Buddhist nun.

"Does that matter? Whether it's chanting, praying or saying an incantation, the more self-important you appear, the more belief others have in you. Sayo-san somehow had picked it up on her travels around the country with her theatre troupe. She claimed it was all dedicated to Shoten anyway. It turned out it worked rather well. Or rather it was rumoured to have worked. People would come to her with stomach complaints or strange pimples, plus there are a lot of young people here who suffer from all kind of strange diseases. These people had Sayo pray for them—you know, with this 'Shoten of Ikoma, Shoten of Kawachi, Come and show yourselves to me,' blah blah blah. And she would give them some sort of suspicious-looking water, a miracle cure, and indeed miraculously they would be cured, or so rumour had it. And so it wasn't only Yosamatsu-san who doted on her. She gained more and more believers throughout the island. By the end of it, there were even people coming from other islands to get her to cure them. Business was really flourishing. But this proved in the end to be Sayo's downfall."

"Sounds like she managed to build herself a very successful sideline."

"Well, it really looked that way, but that Sayo got all puffed up with her own success and started to push her luck. She failed to consult with the priest of Senkoji Temple."

"Oh, I see."

"The priest was not impressed by any of this. All the people who used to visit the temple to pray for their fortunes had somehow become followers of the great Sayo the Shaman. But you know our priest—having such a big heart, he just gave a wry smile when all this started up, and pretended not to notice any of it. But as Sayo's fortune business began to prosper, and she got more and more arrogant, and more and more influential, she ended up rather like some kind of cult leader, a real hoaxer. She began putting herself on a level with Buddha or God, and that was too much of a slight to the temple. At some point the priest decided enough was enough. He was a very large-hearted person but once somebody like that gets angry, it's terrifying. He decided once and for all to get rid of Sayo the Shaman."

"This is all fascinating. Seiko-san, you really tell a good story."

"Oh, you flatter me! Anyway, as I said, making an enemy of the priest was Sayo's downfall. She'd poached his believers, and disturbed a long tradition. The power and influence of a temple is not something that can be overcome in a matter of days. No matter how smart and cunning that woman may have been, her big mistake was to underestimate that power. Up until that point, the priest had taken a neutral position in the family feud between Kaemon and Yosamatsu, but suddenly he became a firm ally of Kaemon. In other words, they formed an alliance, against which Sayo, no matter how canny, had no hope of victory. To come to Gokumon Island and get in a fight against the temple and the chief fishing boss, that was the end of her. And so, Sayo's position became weaker and weaker. And as it grew weaker, she got more and more desperate. She began to say the weirdest things. That soon a great tsunami would come and swallow up the whole island. Or that Mount Suribachi would split in two and rain fire everywhere... And with that, never mind how foolish or easily persuadable the islanders may have been, they began to find her too spooky and started to avoid her. In the end, she began to tell people that they had to repent or the prayers wouldn't be effective, and then there was some fuss about her using burning hot tongs on a follower's face. In other words, she'd gone mad. And without a moment's hesitation, Kaemon built that lunatic's cage and locked her up in it. And with that, Sayo the Shaman was finally defeated."

"What a story! What did Yosamatsu do about it?"

"Yosamatsu-san as a person was much weaker than Kaemon. He would never have opposed his father without the power of the great strategist, Sayo, behind him. But now his strategist was locked in a cage, and he was like a bird that had lost its wings, or a beast that had lost its fangs. He had no bite left to oppose Kaemon. He did try to help Sayo escape from her cell, and made some other futile attempts to assist her. But eventually Sayo died of her madness. Perhaps it was because his heart was broken, but Yosamatsu also went out of his mind. And that's how he too ended up in the lunatic's cell."

"And this Sayo-san was the mother of those three girls?"

"That's right. It's surprising that she could even have children though. Everyone said so. Travelling actresses with nothing to sell but their plays, many of them end up selling their bodies too and messing them up. It was amazing how Sayo-san kept getting pregnant. I'm not sure whether having children was a joy to her or not, but anyway all three of them turned out to be girls. This Sayo was said to be quite a looker—a harsh kind of beauty, but nevertheless, her nose was long and straight, her eyes were big, and at the height of her success, everyone said she was stunning. Unfortunately, I wasn't around to see her at that time. By the time I came to Gokumon Island, she was already imprisoned in that cell and I only ever saw her when she escaped once and ran riot around the island. By then her features had changed and she more closely resembled an old hag than an exquisite beauty."

"Thank you. That really is quite a tale."

Just as Kosuke had thanked the barber, the sharp sound of a pistol shot, then a second, and then a third, rang out somewhere on the mountain. This was followed by a battle cry which echoed through the valleys.

THE PIRATE FORTRESS

"Hey, Kindaichi-san! They've found him!"

"Wow, let's go and see. With luck they'll take him unharmed."

Inspector Isokawa's party had already made their way almost to the peak of Mount Suribachi. They could see the pirate fortress right above their heads. Gasping for breath, they stumbled on rocks and tree roots along the moonlit mountain trail. Someone panted out a warning to the inspector at the head of the party.

"Sir, be careful. This is where the anti-aircraft base was. The whole area was dug up to make an underground air-raid shelter."

Right around this point the incline suddenly became gentle and turned into a smooth plateau. Here and there were protruding rocks and skinny pine trees and, underneath everything, a spider's web of underground dugouts, some of them open to the air, and others covered tunnels.

"Ugh. So he's burrowed under here and it's going to be a pain in the neck to flush him out."

"The pistol shots came from somewhere further up," said Kosuke.

"I wonder what's going on. It's gone very quiet," said the barber.

"Let's go up and see," said the inspector. "Just take care—he's got a firearm."

They'd just made their way a little further up the mountain, when all of a sudden several men jumped out from behind a large rocky outcrop.

"Who goes there?"

"Ah, Shimizu!" said Inspector Isokawa, recognizing the police sergeant. "Was it you who fired your pistol a moment ago?"

"Ah, it's you, Inspector. Yes, he fired on us from over there, so I fired back."

"And then what happened to him?"

"Then all of a sudden he disappeared… I think he must have gone down into those tunnels. Oh, by the way, I found something strange. Hey! Come and show that stuff to the inspector!"

The men in Shimizu's band stepped forward with what they were carrying. There was a cooking pot, a bag of rice, a jar of miso paste, several daikon radishes, dried fish, a cooking knife, a rice bowl and a pair of chopsticks. Inspector Isokawa stared in amazement.

"Where on earth—?" said the inspector.

"In one of the air-raid-shelter tunnels."

"No, that's not what I meant. I meant where on earth did he get all this stuff from?"

"Inspector, I think you must know," said Kosuke quietly. "They're from the Kito house."

"But if all this stuff went missing, then surely they would have noticed."

"Well... of course they'd notice. The question is, why didn't they tell us about it? Oh, someone's climbing up."

They turned towards the path that Kosuke and Inspector Isokawa's group had just come up. The climber was a lone man.

"Who goes there?" yelled Shimizu, squaring up.

"Oh, hello, Shimizu-san. It's me. I came to see how things were going. I heard a gunshot just now. Did you catch the bad guy?"

It was Mayor Araki. Typical of him, he strolled up, looking totally unperturbed.

"Ah, Mr Mayor, is the wake finished?"

"It is."

"And is Tsukiyo-san all right?"

"She's fine. When I left I could hear her at the prayer house. Koan-san and Ryotaku said they'd wait at the house until you all got back."

"What about the priest?"

"His rheumatism was playing up again, so he went back to the temple. The branch house Kitos all left too. But don't worry—the young men from the village are all on guard around the entrance."

Kosuke suddenly felt alarmed. His heart began to beat hard in his chest.

Right at that moment, they heard several gunshots, followed by voices shouting.

"There he is!"

"Over there!"

Everyone had already started running, Whooping and shouting, they surrounded the pirate fortress, torchlights moving this way and that.

"Where is he? Which way did he run?"

"Oh, sir, he went that way. Look—you can see him running along the ridge. Be careful. Gen already got injured."

They heard voices in the distance.

"Is he injured? Was he hit?" asked the inspector.

"Yes, but it just grazed him. It's nothing serious."

"Right, take care!"

The pirate fortress was two storeys high, and if you looked carefully, there was a figure bent over and running on the top of the upper wall, which followed the mountain ridge. Along the ridge were many large rocks and pine trees, so that the figure would disappear and reappear constantly.

"If he keeps going that way, he'll come to a dead end. There's a deep gorge at the end of that ridge. He's like a rat in a trap."

With Shimizu at the head, the men climbed up to the top of the fortress. It turned out that it had indeed been built in a perfect location. If you stood up on the wall, you had an unbroken view over the sea to the east, the dark shadows of islands dotted here and there in the moonlit water. The little fires lit to lure the fish flickered dreamily in the hazy night mist.

"Hey, he's reaching the end!"

"Shimizu, look out! Don't get too close. A cornered rat will bite a cat."

Before Inspector Isokawa had even got the words out, another pistol shot rang out, and a bullet ricocheted somewhere nearby.

"Aaagh!"

It was Seiko the barber who had screamed. Everybody flung themselves to the ground and lay flat in the grass. Taking cover behind rocks, they could see about twenty-five yards away a man crouched down behind a large boulder, pointing a gun in their direction. Because of the boulder and the cover from the low shrubs, it was impossible to make out either his face or his outline clearly. There was a deep gorge just to his left. There was nowhere left for him to run. He was trapped.

"Hey! Drop your weapon! Come quietly!" shouted the inspector.

As if in response, the man immediately fired the pistol once again. The bullet flew right over the heads of the prone men.

"Shimizu, take a shot. But make sure not to kill him."

Shimizu fired his pistol. The fugitive immediately returned fire. Several of the policemen came rushing to back Shimizu up, and fired two or three rounds at the crouching man. A high-pitched scream tore through the sky, and the figure of the man seemed to somersault through the air, disappearing into the valley to his left.

"Damn!"

Everyone ran to peer down into the gorge. The man's body spun like a ball, bouncing through the scrub and dislodging small stones. From the other side of the gorge, a cheer went up.

"Well, we'd better go down and take a look," said Inspector Isokawa.

The band of men searched for a way to get down into the valley. Clinging to rocks and tree roots, they gradually descended the steep rock face. Their side of the valley was well lit by moonlight, so it was not quite as dangerous as it could have been. There was no river at the bottom, as was common in gorges like this; instead the valley floor was filled with thick scrub.

"Where is he?"

"He must be over this way."

"Aaagh! There's someone over there!"

It was Seiko the barber who called out. In the bushes about twenty yards away someone was standing, a silhouette in the darkness. The person wasn't moving, and seemed to be looking down at their feet.

"Who goes there?" Inspector Isokawa called out, but there was no response. The person stood rooted to the spot, looking down at the ground.

"Who are you?" the inspector demanded once more. "If you don't answer we are going to have to shoot you."

The figure responded with a faint shake of the head, but Kosuke immediately jumped up.

"Inspector. Don't shoot!"

He ran towards the figure, holding his hakama skirt out around him like some sort of parachute.

"Sanae-san!"

At this, the figure tottered forward a couple of steps forward, as if blinded by light. Kosuke swiftly grabbed her in his arms.

"What are you doing? What are you doing in a place like this?"

Sanae's bloodless face stared back at Kosuke. She looked him up and down with wide eyes, but in reality took nothing in.

"Sanae-san?" Kosuke leaned in and spoke close to her ear. "Sanae-san, do you know this man? Is he your brother?"

Kosuke was looking down at the dead body of the fugitive, lying at Sanae's feet. As soon as he spoke, her face twisted like that of a crying child.

"No, he isn't! This isn't my brother!"

Her voice sounded as if she were spitting blood. She buried her face in both hands.

Inspector Isokawa had followed Kosuke and was kneeling down, examining the body. Now he got to his feet and pulled a wry face.

"I don't get it. There's no sign of a bullet wound anywhere. This man wasn't shot."

Instinctively, Kosuke looked up at the pirate fortress, but the edge of the crag wasn't visible from where they stood. The moon was directly overhead...

Just about that time, back at the Kito residence, a crime was being committed.

A HORSE TIED TO A TREE MAKES THE BLOSSOMS FALL

Back in the sitting room at the Kito residence, a pre-dawn chill permeated everything.

It had been bearable to sit here during the wake, but when it came to an end, the branch family Kitos left and went home. Mayor Araki was worried about how the manhunt was going, and he left the house too. Even Ryonen the priest had returned to the temple, complaining that his rheumatism was playing up. The only people left were Doctor Koan and Senkoji Temple's apprentice priest, Ryotaku, who was left feeling as exposed as a plucked chicken. He shivered with loneliness.

"Koan-san, Koan-san, should you really be drinking so much? Won't it affect your injury?"

"It's fine, it's fine! I'm all right. When I get drunk I forget. I forget pain too. I forget sorrow and heartbreak. Don't be stingy with the sake. It's not going to burn a hole in your wallet, is it? Ha ha."

"No, I'm not being stingy. I was just worried about you. Also, tonight is no ordinary night."

"No ordinary night... Ha ha. No need to tell me that. Tonight is Yukie and Hanako's wake. Isn't it? That being the case, Koan here is drinking to them and wishing them all happiness in the next world... Right? Ha ha."

"No. That's not right. That's not what I'm saying."

"That's not right? Well, if that's not right, what is right?"

"Koan-san, have you forgotten? Right when the police inspector and Kindaichi-san were leaving, what they asked us to do? They asked us to take special care of Tsukiyo-san."

"Ha ha. Is that what you're on about, Ryotaku? No need to worry yourself about that. Koan here, he has those words engraved on his heart."

"But if you drink that much—"

"It's fine. It's fine. Never fear, you can rely on me. Whether I drink or I don't drink, I can take on any role... Ha ha. Ryotaku-san, please, I ask you, I beg you, ask Okatsu-san for another bottle... Look—this one's empty. One like this. I promise this will be the last one. Come on, one more bottle. No, no—just half a bottle. I beg you, I implore you. Please, Ryotaku-san."

This was the classic talk of the heavy drinker. There was no need whatsoever to drink any more, but he couldn't just stop after he'd drained the last drop from the sake cup. Just one more cup, just half a cup more, becomes just one more whole bottle, just half a bottle, and the drinker ends up passing out with no recollection of any of his actions. Koan needed to take it that far in order to feel as if he had been drinking.

"Hey, Koan-san, are you serious? Do you really want to drink more?"

"I certainly do. I certainly do. I have every intention of drinking more. Look, Ryotaku, stop gawping at me with that heartless face of yours. Just pop to the kitchen for me. Be my special envoy. Go on—go on. His Imperial Highness Koan of the Goatee Murase, this very evening desires by all means possible the speedy delivery... eh? Ha ha. What's your problem, Ryotaku? Why are you pulling that scary face? Oh, I get it! You're going to gang up with Okatsu and cut off old Koan. Never mind. It's fine. I won't ask you again. If you two begrudge me a drink that much, Koan will go and get it himself. I'll go and drink directly from the barrel."

Koan placed his one free hand on the tatami floor and attempted to push himself up, buttocks first. However, he was already so drunk, not to mention that his left hand was tied up in a sling, that he was unable to gain his balance. He thought he was up, but his feet got entangled and he fell on his backside with a loud thump.

"Ow, ow, ow, ow."

Ryotaku sighed.

"Koan-san, you really are pathetic. When you're not drunk, you're such a good person too… All right, you win. I'll go. But if I do, you're only getting one bottle. That's it—just one bottle. No matter how much you might try to wheedle it out of me again, I'm not going to give in again…"

You cannot win against a crying child or a drunkard. Grudgingly, Ryotaku picked up the empty sake bottle. The kitchen was filled with dirty cups and dishes from the funeral wake. Okatsu was in there, wandering about, apparently searching for something.

"Okatsu-san, are you all right?"

"Oh, Ryotaku-san, have you seen Mii?"

Mii was Okatsu's pet cat. Never having had children of her own, Okatsu loved her pet like her own darling baby.

"Mii? No, I haven't. She must be out playing. Okatsu-san, I'm sorry to bother you, but could I possibly have another bottle of sake? Koan-san keeps demanding more."

"What? Should Koan-san really be drinking that much? He's going to get completely inebriated again. He's going to be no use at all to keep watch here."

"I know. I've told him the same thing, but he won't listen to anyone when he gets this way. He's like a stubborn child. I'll make sure he stops after this one."

"He's incorrigible, that one."

Muttering to herself, Okatsu set about preparing another bottle of sake. Ryotaku looked around the dimly lit kitchen.

"Where's Sanae-san?"

"Sanae? I thought she was in the sitting room."

"No, she's not."

"Hmm, I thought she was in the sitting room this whole time. Well then, she must have gone to bed, even though she knew how busy I was back here. I wish she'd come and helped me a bit first."

As she spat out her annoyance, Okatsu began to wash the dishes, banging them around with unnecessary vigour.

Ryotaku felt a pang of anxiety in his chest. Sanae wasn't the kind of young woman to go off to bed without saying anything to anyone.

"Okatsu-san, how long is it since you last saw Sanae-san?"

"When was it?... Oh yes, when the priest left she saw him off at the door. Stepped outside with him... And then I haven't seen her since. I could have sworn she was in the sitting room the whole time. Ryotaku-san, did you want her for something?"

It didn't seem to bother Okatsu at all that Sanae had disappeared. It was as if she cared more about her pet cat. She continued to fret about it.

"I wonder where Mii has got to. Why would she go out playing at this time of night? She must have caught a whiff of a tomcat in the neighbourhood. Humans and cats—they're all the same. Ah, Ryotaku-san, the sake's ready."

Ryotaku came back into the sitting room with the sake bottle awkwardly balanced on a tray to find Koan lying flat on his back on the floor with his legs outstretched, snoring loudly.

"Hey, Koan-san, I've got your sake. Hey, Koan-san! Koan-san!... Fast asleep, huh? You really shouldn't have pestered me so much for this..."

Ryotaku put down the sake bottle and seated himself on a zabuton cushion. However, the chill in the large empty room soon began to seep into his body. He pulled the sleeves of his robe together and tried to bring the brazier a little closer, but there was very little unburned charcoal left in it. He poked around in the embers with a pair of tongs, but the only effect was to put out the fire completely.

Ryotaku felt really guilty about this and quickly glanced around to check that no one had seen what he'd done. Koan-san was still fast asleep. Along with the doctor's snoring, in the distance Ryotaku could hear the dinging of a bell. In the prayer house at the far end of the garden, Tsukiyo was still chanting.

The sound of that bell filled Ryotaku with such a feeling of desolation that he felt as if something ice cold had been dropped down the back of his neck. He reflexively adjusted the collar of his robe.

"Koan-san! Hey, Koan-san! Wake up! Don't you think you've slept enough? Koan-san!"

Ryotaku was becoming more and more uncomfortable. He was unable to stay still. Ding! Ding! It was the most gloomy, depressing sound. It continued echoing from the far end of the garden. Ryotaku couldn't stand it any longer—he got up and headed out in search of the source of the sound. He came out of the front door and right away ran into the young men ordered by Kosuke Kindaichi to guard the house.

"Hey, Ryotaku-san, what's up? You don't look good. Did something happen in there?"

The men were warming themselves around a brazier placed between the main entrance gate and the house, drinking sake and snacking on bowls of pickled daikon. It felt to the young apprentice priest as if, wandering within the gates of hell, he'd come across Buddha. He rushed over to join them.

"No. It's that… Never mind… By the way, have any of you seen Sanae-san?"

"Sanae-san? No. Why? Has something happened to her?"

"No, no. Nothing in particular. It's just that we haven't seen her for a while."

"What about Koan-san?"

"He's drunk too much and is out for the count."

"Ha ha ha. I thought as much. So, Ryotaku-san, with him asleep, didn't you try to get Sanae-san to yourself?" suggested one of the lads.

"Ha ha. I reckon you've hit the nail on the head," said another. "I bet she turned you down flat, didn't she? Is that why you're looking so deflated?"

"Stop joking about it!"

"Ha ha. Ryotaku-san, you've gone red in the face. Why don't you give it a try? Tug on her kimono sleeve a little, whisper sweet nothings? You and Sanae-san go well together;

you were childhood sweethearts, weren't you? I remember well back in school you were quite the crybaby. You were good at studying but you had no backbone. I remember how you used to burst into tears at the drop of a hat."

"Yeah, yeah, that was funny. We used to tease him about it all the time. And then that Sanae-san... She was a scary, tough girl. If we were teasing you, she'd come running and tell us all off. She was really fond of you. To tell the truth I was a little jealous. I remember getting into an argument with her one time and she slapped me right across the face. Yeah, she was harsh."

"Do you remember how we gave her the nickname Wildcat? Well, times do change, but now that I think about it, she's been fond of you since way back then."

"Don't talk rubbish."

"It's not rubbish. Back then you were writing your names in a love heart together. Ryotaku, you're just too much of a coward. Back in the day Buddhist priests weren't allowed to go near women, but things have changed. Now any old guy with a shaved head can drink sake and sleep with women. It doesn't matter if she refuses you. That's a woman's tactic. You can't just give up and go home with your tail between your legs. You need to put some work into that too."

"Yes, that's right. That's right. The ones who say 'no, no, please, no!' They're the best. That's the height of pleasure. I have this woman over in the Sanuki region—"

"Don't start going on about her again!"

"Yeah, all you ever want to do is talk about your woman. I bet that's why you started this conversation."

The young men of Gokumon Island had no other topic besides sake and women. But their outspokenness and tendency to call a spade a spade were in some ways easy to listen to. Their speech wasn't vague and suggestive like an erotic novel, full of complex emotions. As Ryotaku listened to their flights of imagination, he found the effect strangely calming. On some level he admired their world of sexual and lustful yearnings. He hadn't visited this world of human warmth and desire for a long time, and strangely it warmed his heart.

"So how about it, Ryotaku-san? Drink just one cup with us?"

"No, I really shouldn't."

"What's stopping you? Because alcohol's not allowed on temple grounds? All those signs at the gates of temples about no sake... But everyone knows that each priest has his own secret stash. Well, except for our priest, Ryonen-san, he's totally different."

"Yeah, Ryonen-san. He's too strict. But he's an old man, so it can't be helped, but right now I feel sorry for you, Ryotaku-san. Hey, Ryotaku, come on, have a drink with us. And then come down to the village sometimes. Don't sit up in that temple reciting sutras all day and night—come on down to the village. Come and hear our stories about the whores we've bought. You might learn something—it'll be an education for you. Ha ha ha."

But no matter how much they urged him, Ryotaku steadfastly refused to drink any sake. Despite not drinking a drop, he was nevertheless intoxicated, drunk on their stories. It was a pleasant sensation for him. And while he was feeling guilty about neglecting his duties, he still didn't feel like leaving the side of these fellows. And before he realized it, he was glued to the spot. No matter how many more years the good and honest Ryotaku would live, one thing was certain—he would never stop regretting his actions, and blaming himself for what occurred that night. That his one tiny dereliction of duty had led to that great tragedy was something that haunted his nightmares for the rest of his life.

This is what Ryotaku's nightmares were made of.

The young men had got totally carried away telling their lewd stories, and Ryotaku was listening, utterly intoxicated, when suddenly from the back of the house he heard a woman screaming. He leapt to his feet.

"What the hell was that?"

Ryotaku was not the only one who had heard the cry. The young men broke off mid-tale and put down their sake cups. The screaming continued—a mixture of screaming, crying and some phrase being repeated over and over—although it was impossible to make out anything clearly.

"That's Okatsu-san's voice I think."

"Yes, Okatsu. Something must have happened."

Okatsu was always getting frights and having to sit down. However, it wasn't only her feet that got away from her; it was usually her tongue too. She would cry loudly and completely unintelligibly. Right now, she probably knew what she was saying, but it was as if she had lost control over her tongue and no kind of meaningful language could escape her mouth.

Ryotaku turned pale and began to shake.

"Better go and take a look. We should all go together."

Closely followed by the young men, Ryotaku went back into the main house. They followed Okatsu's voice through to the main sitting room, where they found Doctor Koan sitting up and blinking in bewilderment. Next to him sat Okatsu, blubbering uncontrollably and lamenting loudly.

"Okatsu-san, what is it? Koan-san, what happened?"

"I've no idea," said the doctor. "Okatsu-san shook me awake, but I can't make out anything she's saying."

Koan was staring at Okatsu, dumbfounded. Drool trickled down through his goatee.

"Okatsu-san, calm down. What has happened? Oh... your cat? Has something happened to your cat? Come on, Okatsu-san! Try to pull yourself together. We're worried about you. Is it your cat? What? Back there in the cage?... Something to do with the lunatic?"

Everyone looked at one another in bewilderment. Ryotaku turned even paler.

"Okay, Ma-chan and Gin-chan, you both go back there and check the cage. You know it, right? The lunatic's cell back there?"

The two men rushed out of the sitting room. Ryotaku turned back to the blubbering Okatsu.

"Okatsu-san, you shouldn't cry like this over a trifling matter. Even if he has got out of his cell. In good weather like this, even a lunatic might feel like stretching his legs sometimes. What? That's not all? Did something else happen? Your cat? What about the cat? It's in pain? No?... Tsukiyo-san in the prayer house?..."

Ryotaku and the remaining young men exchanged looks, and stopped talking to listen. They could hear a bell ringing.

"Okatsu-san, what is that? Isn't it Tsukiyo-san in the prayer house ringing her little bell?"

In response, Okatsu emphatically shook her head from side to side. She frantically tried to say something, but the more distraught she became the less able she was to articulate, and the less comprehensible she became.

At that moment the two men returned from checking the cell. They looked alarmed.

"The cage is empty and the lunatic is nowhere to be seen!"

"Let's check the prayer house too. There's definitely something going on there."

Ryotaku was the first one out of the sitting room, followed by the four young men. Koan stayed where he was, looking bewildered. Okatsu continued to cry, collapsed on the floor.

I've mentioned before that the tiny prayer house was at the end of the garden on a raised piece of ground. Built in a style that was neither Shinto nor Buddhist, it had three walls and then a door in the front with steps leading up from the connecting passageway. Right now the cedar door was slightly ajar.

Ryotaku ran to the base of the steps.

"Tsukiyo-san! Tsukiyo-san!"

There was no response. Instead, the ding-ding of the bell seemed to get louder.

"Tsukiyo-san, come out. Everyone's worried about you. Please stop doing that and come out."

He waited again for a reply but there was none. None, that is, except for the ringing of the bell that filled the air. A shadow of fear began to spread inside him.

"All right then, I'm coming in. I don't care if you get mad at me, I'll just apologize."

One of the young men ran up to the top of the steps and pulled open the cedarwood door. The interior of the prayer house was about ten tatami mats in size. At the far side facing the entrance was a large platform, apparently serving as an altar, about three feet in height. On this altar were placed grotesque-looking Buddha statues of various sizes, in between which were incense burners and incense-stick holders, tubes for holding funeral flowers, candlesticks, miscellaneous gongs and handbells. All of these were old and faded and ghostly-looking. There were two very pale votive lights burning, which the sudden wind from the open door caused to bob around as if in some sort of panic. The little prayer house was thick with incense smoke, heavy enough to cause their eyes to burn.

"Tsukiyo-san, Tsukiyo-san! Where are you?"

Nobody could make out much in the gloom and the smoke.

"Hey, does anybody have a match on them?"

"I've got one."

"Do you? It would really help. There are candles over there on the platform. Go and get one."

One of the youths began to shuffle forward through the swirling smoke, but then suddenly cried out.

"Wh-what is it?"

"Tsu-Tsukiyo-san's here."

"Tsukiyo-san? What are you talking about? Hurry up and light the candle!"

Trembling, the youth pulled out one match after another. But no matter how many times he struck them against the side of the box, his hand shook too much and they went out immediately.

"Spineless you are. Okay, look—there are some votive lights over there. We can use those to light the candle."

They finally got the candle lit and, in the flickering light, they began to make out more in the gloom.

"Oh my—"

Ryotaku clasped his hands together in prayer and ground his teeth. The young men all froze to the spot. The one who was holding the candle couldn't keep his hand steady and the light flickered constantly.

There was a good reason for everyone's reaction. The scene was the most bizarre any of them had ever seen. On the floor at their feet lay Tsukiyo, face up. She still wore the white robe as well as the red hakama skirt. The gold-pointed hat was still attached to her head. She was wearing make-up too, with her hair in a traditional style. Her face was so beautiful that you would not have thought it of this world.

But the beauty of her appearance was marred by a horror that would be the stuff of nightmares. A tenugui hand towel was wrapped tightly around her slender neck.

"That stool—"

One of the men began to speak, before fear stopped his mouth. However, a glance in the direction of his gaze told everyone what he'd been about to say. Just in front of the altar was a kind of stool, about one and a half tatami in area, and about a foot high. It was clear that Tsukiyo had been sitting on this stool, chanting her prayers, when someone had come up behind and strangled her, and then her body had tumbled to the floor. It appeared she had struggled quite hard against her attacker, the proof being the nails of her right hand, which were dug deeply under the edge of the tenugui around her neck. It looked almost as if she'd strangled herself…

"Ryotaku-san! Ryotaku-san!"

One of the men, who'd been turned to wax as he looked at the body of Tsukiyo, now grabbed Ryotaku's arm and shook it.

"It's all right. It's all right. We were saying in the village that Tsukiyo-san would be killed soon. Everyone was saying it down in the village. That it was Tsukiyo's turn now… So, you see, it's not a surprise. No surprise to see that Tsukiyo's been murdered. But what's that? What's that sprinkled all over her body?"

A different one bent down and picked something up between his finger and thumb.

"A bush clover blossom."

"I know! I know! I'm not blind. But I want to know why a bunch of bush clover blossoms have been thrown all over Tsukiyo-san's body. Ryotaku-san, there's no bush clover growing anywhere around here. The killer had to have brought it with him. Why did the killer bring bush clover?… Ah!"

Everyone suddenly jumped as if a thunderbolt had struck the whole group simultaneously.

Up until now they had totally forgotten about it, but that bell began once again to ring. Everyone's eyes grew wide as if they expected the source to be some sort of evil spirit.

Attached to the lintel above the platform were half a dozen or so colourful streamers, which hung down to the floor. Dangling from the middle of one of these streamers was Tsukiyo's handbell, and then tied to the end of that streamer, desperately trying to escape, was Okatsu's pet cat, Mii.

Ryotaku couldn't help thinking of the famous old song.

When a tied horse pulls on the tree, blossoms fall.

Only the lyrics had now become:

When a tied cat pulls on the streamer, a bell rings.

The sound that they'd been hearing was a cat ringing a bell.

Presently the hunting party arrived back at the house…

CHAPTER 6

All Cats Are Grey in the Dark

Kosuke Kindaichi's mind was in such a state that he thought he would go mad.

On that suffocating troop-transport ship, in the final throes of death, there was one specific request his comrade, Chimata, had repeated over and over: "Go to Gokumon Island. My three sisters will be murdered. Go to Gokumon Island in my place. Save my sisters."

That had been his earnest wish, spat out with the last of his breath, and yet he, Kosuke, had been unable to grant his friend even that. He hadn't been able to save even one of the three daughters of the head Kito house.

Kosuke's face was haggard from worry. He seemed to have aged ten or twenty years overnight.

"Sanae-san?"

There was no strength in his voice. Sanae's face too was devoid of life. She was lost in thought and didn't respond.

Three consecutive nights of tragedy had taken their toll. Inspector Isokawa and the other police officers could be seen going in and out of the prayer house. There was heavy tension in the air; even the imposing buildings of the Kito residence seemed to be holding their breath and trembling with fear.

Fortunately, search parties had soon managed to round up the escaped lunatic, Yosamatsu, and he had been returned safe and sound to his cell. Unused to roaming outside, he had made it halfway up the winding path to Senkoji Temple before running out of breath. He'd been found collapsed on the ground just in front of the little shrine to the harvest god. Yosamatsu was unaware of what was going on this strange night. He was excited by his adventure and was bellowing uncontrollably. This was heard as far as the prayer house, and seemed to demonstrate all the more the linked fates of father and daughter. Kosuke went to examine the prayer house, but he was overcome with nausea and returned quickly to the sitting room, unsteady on his feet.

Sanae sat alone, utterly dejected. The shadow of the unknown man's horrific death was engraved on her face. The fugitive must have been around thirty years old. His face overgrown with a heavy beard, he had been a brutal-looking man. His military uniform had been soaked in sweat and grime; his faded old boots bore the telltale bat-shaped mark on the sole.

"Sanae-san?" Kosuke ventured a second time. "You believed that the dead man was your brother, Hitoshi, didn't you? You thought that Hitoshi had returned to the island secretly and was hiding out up on the mountain."

Sanae flipped around to look at Kosuke. Her expression was that of a child on the point of tears. Kosuke continued.

"It was the night before last—when Hanako disappeared during Chimata's wake. You and Okatsu-san went out back to search for her. It must have been then: when you went to the room with the cage, you screamed. We heard the

247

patient throwing a fit immediately afterwards, so everyone in here thought the lunatic had done something to alarm you. What's more, when you came back to the sitting room, you acted as if that was the case. But really you were pretending. Your scream had nothing to do with the patient at all. Right by the caged room you had seen a suspicious man wandering around. Am I right? And it was the same man as just now on the mountain."

Kosuke's expression was dark as he stared blankly out at the garden.

"Why didn't you speak up right there and then? Why did you let us think your distress had been caused by the patient? Because you believed the man was Hitoshi-san, didn't you? There's a proverb in English: *All cats are grey in the dark.* Ever since that war buddy of your brother's visited to tell you he'd be repatriated soon, every single war veteran has looked like him to you. And therefore when you saw a man loitering in the gloom by the lunatic's cell, you were sure he must be Hitoshi. But when the man saw you looking at him, he ran away. Why would he run away? Or more importantly, why would Hitoshi return to Gokumon Island secretly? You were confused. But for the time being you decided to pretend it was the patient who had scared you. However…"

Kosuke paused a moment to draw breath.

"That night, there was a murder at Senkoji Temple. The victim was Hanako, and near her body they found the same boot prints you saw near the caged room. I can imagine it must have been quite a shock to you. But at the same time, you were even more convinced that the man was your brother. That the reason your brother had returned to the island without letting anyone know was to kill Hanako and her sisters…"

Sanae burst into tears. It was the painful, heart-rending sound of someone whose very soul had been crushed.

"No, no," she replied through her tears. "I wasn't completely convinced it was him at all. At first, I couldn't be sure that the person I'd caught a glimpse of was Hitoshi. As you say, all cats look grey in the dark. For a moment I thought it was my brother. In fact, when I saw him I called out 'Hitoshi?' But he immediately turned tail and ran. I wondered constantly about it. Was it my brother? Was it someone who happened to resemble him? I can't tell you how tormented I was…"

"But why didn't you just confess this to me before? If I'd known you were suffering from these suspicions, I could have helped you find a way to solve the mystery. When I observed your behaviour, I came to the conclusion that the man must have been Hitoshi. You'd stopped listening to the repatriation news, you were secretly giving him food…"

"Well, no, I never handed over the food directly. I was too afraid to confirm with my own eyes whether the man was my brother or not. But if it was my brother then he might come back again. And so I wrapped up some food and eating implements in a furoshiki and left it in the kitchen where it would be easy to spot right away."

"And he did sneak back in. You didn't see his face that time?"

"No, I was too afraid… Just the back of his head."

"And you still thought it might be Hitoshi. That's why you followed the manhunt onto the mountain. But that wasn't all you did, was it? It was you who unlocked the cage and let the patient out."

Sanae was momentarily taken aback, but right away she nodded yes.

"You're very clever," Kosuke said. "If the man turned out to be your brother, you needed suspicion for the murders to fall on somebody else. So you let the lunatic out of his cell and sent him wandering. But rather than setting up that clever trick, if only you had checked whether the man really was Hitoshi..."

Kosuke looked grim.

"If only you had confirmed that point, at least tonight's murder could have been prevented. Tsukiyo's life could have been saved... I was convinced from your behaviour that the man was indeed Hitoshi-san. What's more, I think the priest, the mayor and the doctor thought the same thing, and they believed you were protecting Hitoshi-san too. That's what led me up the wrong street."

"Kosuke-san!"

Sanae looked up at him, her eyes full of tears.

"Tell me, who was that man?"

"As the inspector said before, the man was one of the pirate gang who raided a storehouse on Mizushima Island. When the gang was chased by the police launch, he jumped into the sea and swam to Gokumon Island. Then, when he snuck in here in search of food, you caught sight of him and mistook him for Hitoshi-san. In other words, you were protecting a man who had no connection to you whatsoever, and I was chasing a complete stranger."

Kosuke gave a wry laugh.

"So Hanako and Yukie's killer…" Sanae began.

"I thought it must have been that man," said Kosuke. "A brute of a man like that, finding himself in a desperate situation, is perfectly capable of committing murder, but I didn't understand why he hung Hanako from the branch of the plum tree, or stuck Yukie under the temple bell. By the time Tsukiyo-chan was killed, he had already fled up the mountain to the pirate fortress."

"So who—?"

"That's the question. I'm going to have to rethink the whole case. Now that I know the man wasn't Hitoshi, and that he couldn't have killed the three girls, the killer must be someone else. But, Sanae-san, perhaps the man had some kind of connection to the case after all. I think he might have known who the killer was. He may have seen the killer's face. And therefore he may have been murdered by the killer…"

A startled look crossed Sanae's face.

"When we found the man's body down in the valley, you heard what the inspector said, didn't you? That there wasn't a single bullet wound on him. He hadn't fallen from the cliff edge because he'd been shot. There was a huge laceration on the back of his head. His skull had been crushed. And yet down there in that gorge, there was not a single rock that could have made an injury like that. And that's not all…"

Kosuke took a deep breath.

"The appearance of that wound was remarkably similar to the one found on the back of Hanako's head. In other words, that man was struck and killed by the same weapon that was used to knock Hanako unconscious."

"Oh, that's terrible!"

All of the light had drained from Sanae's complexion. Her skin had turned to gooseflesh and every hair on her body was standing on end.

"Yes, this is a vicious murderer. One victim a night, for three nights in a row. With precision... in cold blood... without even a hint of madness, this killer carefully executed his plan. By the way, Sanae-san? The inhabitants of Gokumon Island have an odd way of thinking, don't they? They expected that if Chimata-san, the Kito family heir, were to die, then his three sisters would be murdered to allow Hitoshi-san to head up the family... Tell me, Sanae-san, even you shared this way of thinking to some extent, didn't you? That's why you went so far as to mistake a complete stranger for your brother, and to believe that he would kill the three girls. That's the problem, right there, Sanae-san. What is the origin of that belief? That with Chimata-san dead, the three sisters would be murdered... Is this something that people have been talking about for a long time?"

Sanae stared at Kosuke, wide-eyed. He caught a glimpse of some kind of turmoil deep within.

"To tell the truth, Sanae-san, that was why I came to the island in the first place. Chimata-san thought that way too."

"What?" The word came out like a high-pitched shriek. "Chimata? The heir to the Kito house... He said that? Are you sure? Chimata did?"

"Yes, he did. Did you never wonder why I came to such a small, remote island? I came at the request of Chimata-san. I thought I could prevent this tragedy happening before it started. This is what he said to me. 'If I die, my three younger

252

sisters will be murdered. Go to Gokumon Island. Save my three sisters.' And therein lies the problem. With Chimata-san dead, who would want to murder those three girls? No, before that, I'd like to know how he even knew they were going to be murdered."

Sanae was growing more and more pale. Her parched lips had faded to a kind of violet blue.

"Sanae-san, do you have any idea who?"

"None."

It seemed to take all her strength to muster a response.

"This whole ghastly affair—I don't know anything."

And with that she seemed to be struck dumb.

Inspector Isokawa came into the sitting room.

"Sanae-san, does this belong to the house?"

He held up a tenugui hand towel, opening it out to show the demon's face with the character "hon" above it. Sanae's gaze moved from the inspector to the cloth and back again.

"Is that the tenugui that you found on Tsukiyo?..."

"Right. Tsukiyo-san's right hand was clutching the inside of this cloth. While she was absorbed in her prayers, she was strangled from behind. I was surprised by how dirty this tenugui was, even though it doesn't seem to be particularly old. See—in contrast this end of it looks completely new. Has anyone recently used a tenugui like this?"

"I don't know."

Her response was abrupt, but then she went on.

"I don't remember using any brand-new tenugui recently. Nor do I recall giving one to anybody. But anybody on the island could have one of these in their possession. Before

253

the war, when cotton was freely available, we'd distribute them all the time. Not only for the New Year's celebration or the Bon festival in the summer, but if anyone was having a personal celebration or if there was a death in the family…"

"Do you have any more of these in the house?"

"Yes, we have two or three rolls of them. When my grandfather heard that cotton was going to be rationed, he had lots of cloth dyed. Then, when it became difficult to get hold of, we stopped giving them away. We became frugal with them and were careful not to use any new ones."

"Oh, so this tenugui comes from a dyed roll of cloth?" said Kosuke.

"Yes, the tenugui we give away are all like that. We just cut off from the roll what we need."

Kosuke Kindaichi took the cotton hand towel from Inspector Isokawa. He'd been busily investigating this and that, but for now he stood stock-still in thought.

THE WALKING TEMPLE BELL

The tragedy was over. There would be no more gruesome murders. The inhabitants of Gokumon Island were sure of that much. Apologies to the victims, but everyone was rather relieved.

But even if there were to be no more murders, the case was far from over yet—or rather, the true nature of the case was still to be revealed. Everything that has a beginning also must come to a proper ending. The islanders knew too that ending must be near.

The signs were very obvious. First of all, the comings and goings between the island and mainland Japan had really been stepped up. Police boats arrived one after the other at the harbour, the police officers on board always with grave expressions on their faces.

Meanwhile, Kosuke Kindaichi appeared to be grieving. He spent a sleepless night, and all of the next day absent-mindedly watched the police activity. However, his mind was not at all inactive. He was furiously chasing a solution that seemed to be dangling right before his eyes, and yet was frustratingly out of reach. Every time it seemed to be in his grasp, it would slip away again into the mists of confusion. He had to do something. There must be a way… It felt as if he were trying to light a fire with damp wood. Slow and frustrating.

As he passed the sitting room at the head Kito house, he could hear the priest, Ryonen, chanting. Mixed in with his strong resonant voice were the high-pitched, wavering tones of the apprentice, Ryotaku. Mayor Araki, Doctor Koan and the three residents of the branch Kito house were surely there too…

Kosuke slipped on some geta sandals and headed out into the garden. Like some sort of lost soul he drifted towards the back gate of the house and left the grounds. His head throbbed and burned. Perhaps the cold sea breeze would make him feel better.

He made his way down the sloping road into the island's commercial quarter—by which I mean a single row of about five or six shops. As he passed by, someone called out to him.

"Hey, where you heading?"

It was the barber, Seiko, sitting on a chair by his open door. There were several customers in his shop.

"Come and join us, sir. We have another shocking incident to report."

Kosuke slowed down a little.

"Come on!" Seiko urged. "Sen-chan here just told us something very odd."

"Something odd?"

The words stopped Kosuke in his tracks.

"Seiko-san, please! No need to—"

The speaker must have been the man called Sen-chan.

"Right, no need to get into all that again," added a different man. "I'm sure it must be a mistake anyway. A temple bell getting up and walking! No way. With all these murders happening, there has to be all sorts of gossip. People say all kinds of things. Right, Seiko-san?"

"A walking bell?"

Kosuke felt a stab of excitement in his chest.

"Yes, Sen-chan said it and we were all just laughing about it. Come on, please join us."

It was a source of great pride to the barber to be seen to be on friendly terms with the famous detective. He continued to usher Kosuke inside, which proved easier now that his curiosity was piqued.

"Well, I suppose I could drop in for a minute or two…"

"Make room for our esteemed guest!"

None of the men assembled in the barber's shop was actually there for a haircut. They had heard about the deaths the night before and had all stopped by to chew the fat. They had invaded the tatami-matted waiting area; some were perched on the edge, others sat cross-legged, still others sprawled out, but when Kosuke came in they all straightened up and made space for him to sit.

"Thank you for all your help last night," Kosuke began.

"Not at all, not at all. And we hear that you, sir, were involved in all the fuss after that up at the Kito place. What a terrible thing. It just never stops, does it?"

"Yes, well... By the way, what you were saying before... About the temple bell walking or not walking or something? What's that all about?"

"That story... Hey, Sen-chan, come on and tell him about it."

Egged on by his friends, Sen-chan blushed.

"Well, it's... it's a really weird story," he said, scratching his head. "Everyone was laughing at me just now when I told them, but I still believe that I saw that bell walk... It was two nights ago—the night that Yukie-san was killed. I was out at sea and on my way back to port—I'm not sure what time it was—but it was already dark. Anyway, I was rowing back towards the island and happened to look up, and I saw something unusual on the slope just below the Tengu's Nose lookout. I screwed up my eyes and tried to make it out, and it turns out it was the temple bell... Well, it was pretty much completely dark by then, and I couldn't make it out in detail, but I had no doubt at all about the shape of it. But of course at that point I didn't think anything much of it. I mean, I knew that just the other day the young men carried it on their shoulders up to Tengu's Nose. And from that spot I didn't have a clear view of the lookout point anyway."

257

"Huh. So, you're saying that the bell wasn't sitting on Tengu's Nose when you saw it?"

Kosuke sat up a bit.

"Right. Right. That's what's so strange. And then, after rowing some more, I happened to glance upwards again. This time I was at an angle where I could see the sticking-out-nose bit of the point, and what do you know? The bell was sitting there right where it should have been."

Kosuke was watching Sen-chan fixedly. It was clear from his expression that he found the man's story fascinating. Sen-chan was encouraged by his reaction.

"I was really taken aback," he continued. "A temple bell is big and heavy. It's way too heavy for a couple of people to pick up and walk with. For people to carry it from the place I first saw it up to the lookout point there would take quite some doing, and they'd be bound to make quite a racket. The time I saw it was during the evening calm. If there'd been any noise, it would have carried as far as my boat, but I never heard a thing. And so that's why I believe that bell went wandering around by itself."

"And at that point the bell was no longer visible on the slope below where you first saw it?"

"Well, the thing is, from the position of my boat, I couldn't see that bit of road any more. Now that I think about it, perhaps I should have turned around and rowed back to where I'd been to check. But I was a bit freaked out so I just went home."

"But you are absolutely sure you saw the bell partway up the hill, on the road below Tengu's Nose."

"Yes, I am sure about that. It may have been dark, but

there was no mistaking the shape. It was definitely there on the hill."

"Are there two temple bells on this island?"

"Of course not. And during the war we didn't even have one."

"That bell is pretty old, isn't it?"

"Yes, very old. One time it got a crack in it, and Kaemon-san of the Kito family paid to have it fixed."

"That's right," chimed in one of the others. "I remember that. It was about fifteen years ago. They carried it all the way to Hiroshima or Kure or somewhere like that and brought it back all fixed up. Sir, it's not possible that there are two bells on the island. Sen-chan must have been dreaming. Probably because of all the excitement of that night—"

"Idiot! I saw all that long before the manhunt or the fuss over Yukie-san!"

Kosuke's own mind was full of turmoil. There was something there. There was a clue somewhere that could be the key to the whole mystery.

He turned to Sen-chan.

"By the way, you just mentioned Kaemon-san. Was this Kaemon very rich?"

"Oh yes. He was like the Toyotomi Hideyoshi of the island. And he was at the height of his prosperity around then. These days you can't find anyone who has reached those levels."

"And yet the way he died was very pitiful, I heard," continued Kosuke. "He'd been worrying that the Kito branch family was going to steal it all away from him. They say he was unable to depart from this world in peace."

"He died of a stroke or something," said Sen-chan.

"Yes, it was what they call a cerebral haemorrhage," explained another man helpfully. "He had one right at the end of the war, and one side of his body didn't work properly any more. I'm pretty sure that his left hand didn't work at all and used to hang down. The second time, he was bedridden for a week, and then succumbed. You know, now that I think about it, the first anniversary of his death is coming up."

"He couldn't use his left hand?..." Once again, Kosuke felt that stab of excitement.

"Yes, one half of his body wouldn't work so he was even more irritable than usual. Then, when he was struck down a second time, that lively old man became nothing more than a senile old shell of himself. It was a pitiful sight. At the height of his power he was like Toyotomi Hideyoshi, but he also resembled the great man in the way he died too."

As Kosuke reflected on all this new information, Seiko joined in the conversation.

"By the way, sir, please tell us about last night. About what happened to Tsukiyo-san. Rumour has it she was strangled in the lodge on the estate. Is that true?"

"The 'lodge'?"

"Well, the prayer house. We call it the lodge."

Lodge... lodge... again Kosuke felt his mind run up against something horrifying that pricked at his consciousness.

"That was the name that Kaemon-san gave it. You know, back when he was locking horns with Tsukiyo-chan's mother, back when everybody used to call her the demon hag of the lodge. That's how the prayer house came to be known as the lodge."

Lodge. That was where he'd seen that phrase before! That haiku...

In the same lodge sleep courtesans—moon and bush clover.

A fearsome force seemed to drag Kosuke to his feet. It had such a tremendous strength that it startled everyone in the room. All heads turned to look at him.

"S-sir, what's the matter?"

"Er... ah, thank you for such an interesting conversation. See you again soon."

And with that, leaving everyone staring after him in amazement, he staggered out of the barber's shop like a drunk leaving a pub.

"Wow. What's got into him? What's given him such a shock?"

"He must have had a brainwave about the case," said Seiko proudly. "He must have been inspired by our talk."

"Whoa. He's a bit creepy, don't you think?"

And indeed, Seiko was correct. Kosuke had understood something vital to the case. The dark clouds that had occupied his whole mind had finally parted enough to allow a single ray of sunlight to penetrate.

In the same lodge sleep courtesans—moon and bush clover.

Tsukiyo's name meant "moon child"! And her body had been sprinkled with bush clover blossoms. Was that meant to echo the haiku? And then the white robe she was wearing—did it make her one of the courtesans from the haiku?

261

What on earth? How utterly spine-chilling! What crazy antics were these? The very earth seemed to shake, the sea to boil, the sky to glisten...

Kosuke staggered back to the entranceway of the head Kito residence as if inebriated by some very cheap sake, where he ran into Inspector Isokawa, who was just about to step out of the house.

"Kindaichi-san!" he said. "What's up with you? You're as pale as a ghost."

The voices of the priest and his apprentice could still be heard from inside the house, continuing to chant. Suddenly Kosuke's teeth began to chatter.

"Inspector," he said in an excited whisper, "please come with me right now. There's something I want to show you."

Inspector Isokawa looked at him in surprise, but he didn't ask any questions. Without a word, he put on his shoes and followed Kosuke out of the Kito residence.

Kosuke set off up the hill to Senkoji Temple at a semi-jog. Of course, when they arrived, there was nobody there. Kosuke led the inspector straight to the study where he had slept.

"Inspector, please read what's written on the left-hand card on this byobu screen."

For a moment, Inspector Isokawa wondered if Kosuke Kindaichi had finally gone mad. What Kosuke was showing him was a folding screen of the type placed by a bed in order to shelter the sleeper from the cold night-time draughts.

"You see, Inspector, I wasn't able to read this one of the three poetry cards attached to this screen. If only I'd been able to make it out, I would have been able to see the truth of this case much more quickly. Please read it. Hurry up and read it for me."

Kosuke was practically stamping his feet with impatience.

Looking rather perplexed, the inspector turned his attention to the poetry card Kosuke was indicating.

"Oh! This is by Kikaku."

"That's right. But what particular haiku, is it?"

Inspector Isokawa stared at the verse awhile.

"The handwriting is terrible... Hm, I see. This would be impossible for someone unfamiliar with haiku to read. But this is a famous poem of Kikaku's. Hoitsu Sakai even wrote a parody of this particular haiku. Anyway, it reads,

"Bush warbler upended in its tree—first song of spring.

"Hoitsu parodied it by turning it into a courtesan on top of the steps in Yoshiwara, the old red-light district, calling to a new apprentice courtesan."

Kosuke began to tremble.

"That's it! Insp-sp-spector!"

A cold sensation ran up his spine.

"Hanako had been hung upside down from the branch of the plum tree as an allusion to that haiku. And Yukie was hidden under the temple bell. That was a reference to this haiku here:

"How tragic—beneath the helmet, a hidden cricket.

"And then last night's murder was a reference to this final poem card here:

"In the same lodge sleep courtesans—moon and bush clover."

The inspector was speechless.

"That's right. That's right, Inspector, I know what you're going to say: 'But that's crazy.' But everyone here on Gokumon Island is crazy. They're all out of their minds—it's beyond reason!... Out of their minds. Beyond—"

Kosuke suddenly broke off in mid-sentence and glared at the screen, his eyes almost popping out of his skull. Then, unexpectedly, he grinned.

"Out of reason!"

Kosuke began to tremble again, but this time it was with laughter. He held his belly, and tears began to pour down his cheeks. It seemed he couldn't stop.

"Out of reason. Of course! It wasn't that at all. Ah, I was such an idiot!"

He was thinking of that moment right after Hanako had been killed, when he and the priest, Ryonen, had been standing by the old plum tree, and the phrase that the priest had muttered.

"Out of reason, but it can't be helped."

The true meaning of that phrase had finally become clear to Kosuke.

THE TWELVE SCENES OF CHUSHINGURA

"You'd like me to tell you about Kaemon-san, I expect."

Gihei, head of the Kito branch family, took a sip of his high-quality green tea, set down his expensive ceramic teacup from the famous *inbeyaki* pottery, and gazed calmly at Kosuke. He seemed completely relaxed.

The deep line that ran from his nose to the outer corner of his full lips still gave him the image of a rather cruel and heartless character. The supporters of the head Kito family loathed him, seeing him as a contemptible louse. But now that Kosuke was sitting face-to-face with him, he was fully convinced that he was in the presence of a powerful fishing chief.

They were in the guest sitting room at the branch house. Through the windows, the shingle roofs of the main Kito house were visible across the valley. A fresh morning breeze blew between the two men.

The previous night, Kosuke had not caught a wink of sleep. He'd spent the night turning the clue from the haiku folding screen over and over in his head, revisiting the very beginning of this case from page one. And in doing that, some of the lines of text appeared in a much more vivid light, with some shocking implications.

When the dawn came, Kosuke looked haggard and pale, his eyes gleaming with a kind of madness.

"Kindaichi-san, are you feeling ill? You look as if you have a fever."

Kosuke had arrived at breakfast to find Inspector Isokawa already eating. (Kosuke had continued to stay along with the police at the Kito residence.)

However, Kosuke had had no reply for the inspector. He had simply gulped down the bland-tasting food, and tried to avoid the inspector's gaze. Then he'd come straight to the branch family home.

"There's something I really need to ask Gihei-san."

Oshiho-san had greeted Kosuke at the door and immediately noticed that he didn't look well. She'd flashed him her usual fake smile but it had faded immediately when she had seen the gravity of his expression. And now Kosuke sat face-to-face with Gihei.

"Kaemon-san was a remarkable man. The islanders all compared him to Toyotomi Hideyoshi, and in fact he did have something of that famous leader about him."

Gihei had a deep, resonant voice. He spoke very deliberately, paying careful attention to intonation and grammar. His speech wasn't flamboyant; it was steady and revealing of his character. He appeared as calm as the Buddha himself.

"Before coming to Gokumon Island, you must have heard all of the rumours associated with this place. And then when you arrived, no doubt you didn't find it as different from other places as you were expecting. However, twenty or thirty years ago, when I was a youngster, it was awful. It truly lived up to its name of Hell's Gate Island. They say we're all descendants of pirates and exiled prisoners, and so it really couldn't be helped. We were a feral lot, full of bad manners and customs. That the island has became the place it is now is all due to Kaemon-san. He wasn't a learned man, nor was he any kind of teacher. I'm not saying that he made a huge effort to change the manners and customs of the island. What he did was to make the island wealthy. He improved the living standard of the islanders. Poverty is the mother of crime. If people are poor, they lose all sense of shame, and behave appallingly. But thanks to Kaemon-san, the residents' quality of life gradually improved, and naturally they began to acquire some self-control. Formerly they had given up all hope of being as wealthy as those on other nearby islands, but in the end they actually became more prosperous. The islanders then became anxious not to be inferior to their neighbours in any other sense, so they made an effort to improve their manners.

"This was how Kaemon-san was able to change the whole character, the ethos of the island, even though it has to be said that none of the work that he did was ever specifically to benefit the people. He hadn't set out to make them wealthy. It was from his own greed, his own desire to get rich, that he worked his fingers to the bone. But on an island like this, if the fishing boss is rich, then it trickles down to the fishermen who work for him. In addition, if one fishing chief is doing well, then the others become competitive, and do their best not to lose out to him. Kaemon-san had a good eye—he could see the future. Also, if he got it into his head to do something, he would always find a way to get it done. After the first great war, he found a way to ride the wave of prosperity. He really expanded his operations, and ended up being the owner of almost all of the fishing operations in the area. I mopped up his leftovers—that's what it had come to. But I really understood him—I knew what he was all about."

Gihei's faded eyes looked on Kosuke. Neither proud and arrogant, nor self-effacing, his eyes were full of candour.

"Thank you," said Kosuke. "I see now why everyone held him in such high regard. And yet, how did someone so great spend his final years in such misfortune? I heard especially the anguish he suffered on his deathbed was terrible to behold…"

Gihei continued to regard Kosuke with complete calm. Then, with a grave timbre to his voice, he continued.

"Most of the islanders claim that it was my fault. I'm sure you have heard the same thing. To be honest, the charge isn't completely without foundation. It's true that in recent years Kaemon-san and I were estranged. And that became worse over time. However, it was something that couldn't be helped. I was able to make the greatest effort to keep up with him in matters of work, but as for his tastes, his indulgences if you like, there was no way I could keep up. It really put him in a bad mood."

"It seems that he had a lot of very extravagant tastes."

"That's right. He had a generous disposition, he loved to make money but he also loved to spend it. When business was good, he spent money like water. At those times, when someone important wouldn't participate in his get-togethers, he would be very bad-tempered, but I just couldn't keep up with that level of indulgence. It wasn't fun for me, and I couldn't just join in to curry favour. I was still a fishing boss and head of the branch Kito family. And so I began to absent myself more and more from the get-togethers, and this made Kaemon-san furious. Eventually he began to see me as scheming and malicious. But despite what people said, in the end it was simply about a difference in temperament."

"I heard that towards the end of his life Kaemon-san got into composing humorous haiku."

"Yes. As you can see by the fact that Kaemon-san was satisfied with a woman like Okatsu-san, he wasn't really interested in affairs or anything like that, but from way back, how should I put it, he liked to think he had refined taste. He used to compose haiku with the priest of Senkoji Temple. But then the barber, Seiko-san, got involved too. One time, I couldn't find a way to refuse, and I joined a poetry circle meeting. But talking of difference in temperament—to me it was all tasteless and not the least bit amusing. When it comes to matters of taste, I believe, just like the haiku by Basho, that even a simple glass of water is enough to welcome someone. Kaemon-san and Seiko-san would make everything so fancy and pretentious that I begged not to be obliged to participate, but then after that they started to get caught up in parodying things."

"Parodies?"

Kosuke must have looked startled. It was as if in the darkness he had unexpectedly stumbled into something that he'd been searching for.

"Well, it's finding a whole slew of things to compare something to. Of course, I only attended that one meeting, so I don't really understand much about it, but the time I was there they were likening things to food. The topic was the twelve chapters of the *Chushingura* epic tale, from the prologue through to the raid scene. Two or three verses per person had been allocated before the meeting and each person had to rewrite them with an allusion to some kind of meal. I had the chapter about the raid and I was struggling. Seiko the barber came over and explained that because there was a reference to snow, and it was white, I could change it to a kind of tofu. And everything went like that: the barber went around 'teaching' everyone else. Kaemon-san and Seiko were just messing about in the most trivial and meaningless way, and it just turned completely ridiculous. So I had to leave."

Parody… parody… so Kaemon-san was fond of that kind of contrivance…

"I see. So not the most tasteful of poetry circles. By the way, as well as the priest from Senkoji Temple, were the mayor and Doctor Koan also part of this group?"

"Yes, of course. They were regulars. Despite the priest being younger than him, Kaemon-san treated him like a kind of senior member. Kaemon-san looked up to him, and in return, the priest acted towards him as if he were indulging some kind of spoiled child; if Kaemon came up with an idea, he'd always say, 'Yes, yes, very good.' On the other hand, the mayor and Koan-san… well, I would have to say they sucked up to him. I hated it."

This was the first moment that Kosuke detected any emotion in Gihei's voice. It was barely noticeable, but there was a hint of disgust in his tone.

"Kaemon-san put a lot of trust in those three, didn't he? Did he also entrust his affairs to them after his death?"

"Oh, I should think so. Especially after he and I became estranged, they were his best buddies. However, believe me, Kindaichi-san, the agony and grief that Kaemon-san suffered on his deathbed—that had nothing to do with me at all. If things had been going well for him at home, nobody would have even thought of me as a threat, but then there was the whole business with Yosamatsu-san. Looking back on it, the moment that Yosamatsu began his affair with Sayo-san was the beginning of the downfall of the Kito house."

"Oh yes, I wanted to ask you about this Sayo-san…"

"Sayo-san. She was utterly crazy. I don't know if you've heard, but our region is full of what they call drumbeaters—people claiming to be magicians and fortune tellers and those types. The Shikoku region with its dog spirits, Kyushu's snake spirits—those stories are a little different. Those beings are said not to be able to mix with ordinary people. Now this is an ancient tale, but it is said that when the sorcerer Abe no Seimei came down to visit our Chugoku region, all of his attendants died. So Seimei-san granted life to the weeds along the roadside and bade them be his entourage. But when he returned to the capital, and was about to cast the spell to turn them back into weeds, the attendants begged him not to change them back. The sorcerer took pity on them and let them remain human. But they were, after all, basically weeds and had no idea how to live as human beings. So Seimei-san taught them the art of sorcery. For generations, this story has been told and in some people's minds has somehow become an established fact. There are some who believe that the Chugoku region actually has weed people, otherwise known as drumbeaters, and that they are practising sorcerers. Their literal roots are grass, so they don't know how to build relationships with regular human beings. Ordinary people abhor them. They say that Sayo-san was one of those. I can't tell you if that's true or not. Araki-san, who's the mayor of the village now, somehow investigated her and passed the information on to Kaemon-san, which made him detest her even more strongly."

"The mayor? But why did he meddle in that affair?"

Gihei laughed bitterly.

271

"It's a thin line between love and hate. Makihei Araki has the position of mayor now, and shows the most serious of faces to the world, but in the past he wasn't exactly a worthy candidate. At one time, he was a rival with Yosamatsu-san for Sayo's affections."

Once more, Kosuke felt as if he had stumbled into something in the dark. His eyes lit up with surprise.

"The mayor?"

"Yes, indeed. Never judge a book by its cover. But it wasn't only the mayor who hated Sayo. The doctor, Koan, had a great number of his patients stolen away by that woman. It seems she spread malicious gossip that he was some sort of quack, and he nearly lost his living completely. It was mostly Sayo who was to blame. I didn't really have a lot to do with her, but I disliked the woman. I still feel deeply sorry for Yosamatsu-san, for having got entangled with a woman like her."

Kosuke was silent for a while, thinking over what Gihei had told him. Then, as if something had just occurred to him:

"By the way, I heard that Sayo-san performed *Dojoji Temple* here on the island. I wonder if you know what happened to the temple bell she used for the play?"

"The bell?"

Gihei looked puzzled. He knitted his brow.

"The temple bell she used was just a theatrical prop. It was made of bamboo and covered in paper…"

"Yes, exactly. That prop bell—what became of it afterwards?"

"I see. Well, I think it used to be kept in the storehouse on the Kito estate… I wouldn't know what's happened to it since. The trick was that it was designed to split exactly in half, vertically down the middle."

A temple bell that would split down the middle... That had to be it. It felt to Kosuke as though something had got lodged in his throat.

"Thank you so much," he said, in a rather gloomy voice. "You've been the greatest help to me."

"Not at all. I know that your job must be very tiring," replied Gihei equitably. "Always thinking, always trying to work things out."

"Not really," replied Kosuke, with a polite laugh. "The police are on the job now, so I'm sure the killer's identity will be discovered sooner or later."

Gihei raised an eyebrow.

"Now that the police are on the job? Are you sure? I have to say, I was aware of your identity from the beginning."

This information was a bolt from the blue to Kosuke.

"You kn-kn-knew who I was? Wh-who told you?"

"The mayor. Well, I didn't hear it directly from the mayor. It was one of his assistants who told me. Kindaichi... Well, it's an unusual name. The mayor immediately... right from the start... what was it called?... That's it—the Honjin murders. It seems he remembered the case. He pulled out some old newspapers from the store cupboard in the village office, and looked it up. His assistant saw him. It seems the mayor told him never to tell a soul what he found out, but the assistant told me in secret. But it's strange that you never realized."

So the mayor had known who he was. And that meant that Ryonen the priest and Doctor Koan—well, at the very least the priest—also knew.

But what did it mean? Yes, this was a bolt from the blue indeed!

CHAPTER 7

The Overlooked Fragments

"Ryotaku-san! Ryotaku-san! There's something I need to ask you."

"Yes, Kindaichi-san?"

"The night that Hanako was killed was the same evening as Chimata-san's wake, wasn't it?"

"Yes, that's correct."

"That evening, the priest, Ryonen, asked me to run an errand for him to the branch family house. And then after that, when I was on my way to the head Kito house, I met you and the priest and Takezo-san coming down the winding path from the temple. You remember that, don't you?"

"Yes, of course. What would you like to ask me?"

"Could you tell me whether the three of you walked together all the way down the path from the temple before meeting me? Were you together the whole time?"

Ryotaku looked puzzled.

"I'm not sure why you want to know, but now that you're asking, to tell the truth, no, we weren't."

"You weren't?... So you are saying you weren't with the priest and Takezo all the way down the winding path to the end?"

Kosuke sounded rather impatient, which made Ryotaku even more confused.

"The Reverend Father and I left the temple together, but right after going out of the main gate, he realized that he'd left something behind, and asked me to go and fetch it for him. It was a pile of papers, all his funeral chants, which were written down and wrapped up in a silk handkerchief. He said he'd left them on the table in his quarters, so I immediately turned around and headed back into the temple to get it. But it wasn't there, so thinking that he'd just forgotten exactly where he'd left it, I looked everywhere around his chambers. However, the bundle of papers was nowhere to be found. Eventually I had to give up looking, and set out again down the winding path. When I got almost to the bottom, I came across the priest and Takezo-san waiting for me. The Reverend Father apologized right away, laughing and saying that the bundle of funeral chants had been in his breast pocket the whole time, and then that's when you came along, Kindaichi-san."

Kosuke looked troubled.

"And was Takezo-san with the priest the whole time? I met him on the winding path. Did he go back into the temple with you?"

"No, no. When the priest and I set out from the temple gate, he was right there. But then I turned right around and went back in to look for the papers, so of course Takezo-san was with the priest."

"I see. Thank you. By the way, where is Ryonen-san right now?"

"He said he was going to the branch family house."

"The branch house?... I wonder what he wants with them?"

"He got the official letter of approval from the head temple in Tsurumi. Tomorrow he says he's going to hold the ceremony to pass the priesthood of Senkoji Temple over to me. And because the branch Kito family is now the head fishing family on the island, he's gone to ask for their formal approval."

Ryotaku looked as if he was about to cry.

"Handing over the temple? What is Ryonen-san planning to do after officially giving up the running of Senkoji?"

"There's a temple for retired priests up in Sakushu in Okayama. He says he's going to move there. He's been talking about it for a while, but I don't know why he's suddenly in such a hurry. I really don't know what to do."

Kosuke commiserated with him awhile and then left Senkoji Temple, feeling rather unsteady on his feet.

Halfway down the winding path he came to the tiny shrine to the harvest god. He stopped a moment and peered in through the wooden latticed doors. Suddenly his eyes grew round. He checked about him that no one was watching, and gave the doors a push. Apparently they were kept unlocked because they swung open with ease. Kosuke entered the dim interior.

It was clear that something had been stored inside the shrine very recently. The dust on the floor had been disturbed. Not only that, there was a single brightly coloured flower petal lying there. It was artificial, the kind of petal that came on the end of an ornamental hairpin. Kosuke picked it up and placed it in his notebook. Then he wheeled around and hurried out of the shrine.

He descended the rest of the slope and continued to the head Kito house, where the serious-faced policemen were still busily coming and going. There had been a temporary burial of the three sisters the previous night, but the official funeral was yet to be scheduled.

He recalled Okatsu's depressing lament the evening before.

"Chimata-san's funeral still hasn't taken place and already we have three more deaths... And then there's the one-year anniversary of Kaemon-san's death to be marked. It's all just overwhelming how everything's happening at once."

He went to the kitchen and was glad to find Takezo there. He called him over.

"Takezo-san! Takezo-san! There's something I need to ask you."

"How can I help you, sir?"

"It's about the evening that Hanako was killed. That night I was coming down the winding path from Senkoji Temple and I met you on the way. Do you remember?"

"Yes, I do."

"After that you climbed up to the temple, and you said you met the priest and Ryotaku-san near the temple gate. Right after that, Ryotaku was asked by the priest to go back into the temple and fetch something that he'd forgotten. I'd like to ask you about what happened next. Were you with the priest all of the way down the winding path to the road where you met me on my way back from the branch family house?"

"Yes, I was with him the whole time," Takezo said, although he was clearly puzzled by the question.

"Are you sure? You didn't leave his side even for one moment? Takezo-san, this is very important. Please think carefully and answer truthfully."

Now Takezo looked a little frightened. He thought for a while.

"Ah, now that you mention it, that's right... that's right. Partway down the path, the strap on the priest's sandal snapped. I offered to fix it for him, but he said it was fine and told me to go on ahead, so I went down to the bottom of the path alone. The priest got there a little afterwards, and while we were talking, Ryotaku-san showed up too. Then, just as the three of us started to walk on, you arrived from the direction of the branch family house."

Kosuke felt all hope leave him. His chest felt as if a great weight were crushing it.

"By the way, the point at which the priest's sandal snapped—was it above or below the shrine to the harvest god?"

"Actually it was right in front of the shrine. He sat down on the step to fix it."

Kosuke's heart grew even heavier. The spark was gone from his eyes. Eventually he spoke again.

"Oh yes, yes. I wanted to ask you one more thing. That night, the first time you and I met on the winding path, you asked me where I was going. And I responded that I'd been asked by the priest to go and inform the branch family about Chimata-san's wake. I recall you made a face at that. Could you tell me why that was?"

"Yes. Well... That was because I knew the branch family was already aware that the wake was that evening. Just the day before I'd been sent by the priest to tell them about it. I thought it was strange that you had been charged to deliver the exact same message. I assumed that you had some other reason for going, so I just let you continue on your way without saying anything."

"I understand. Thank you. By the way, is the police inspector on the premises? If he is, would you mind asking him to come out?"

Takezo did so.

"Morning, Kindaichi-san! How can I help?"

"Would you come with me, Inspector? Takezo-san, do you have any kind of long pole or rod here that I could borrow? Something with a hook on the end?"

Takezo went to look, and soon came back with something that matched that description.

"Would this do, sir?"

"Perfect. Takezo-san, could you come with us too, please?"

The three men headed downhill from the Kito house to the bay. Islanders they passed gave the three of them some strange looks, but Kosuke paid them no attention.

They walked down onto the quay. Kosuke turned to Takezo.

"I'd like to borrow a boat, if I may."

"Certainly," he replied immediately. "I'll bring one around right away."

He returned with a rowing boat and Kosuke and the Inspector Isokawa climbed in.

"Kindaichi-san, what on earth are we doing?" said the inspector.

"You'll know soon enough. Before your very eyes I am going to reveal the secret of a conjuring trick. Takezo-san, please row around to just under that jutting rock—the Tengu's Nose where the temple bell is sitting."

It was well into autumn, and the Seto Inland Sea was as smooth as a piece of jasper, polished to a sheen and glittering in the sunshine. Inspector Isokawa and Kosuke

Kindaichi sat in silence, but it was an uneasy, nervous kind of silence. In Kosuke's mind, he knew he was about to reach the truth of the case, and the solidification of everything in his mind. Inspector Isokawa could sense this.

The boat passed under the lookout point. This part of the sea was effectively a shallow tide pool, and drifts of seaweed gently bobbed on the surface. Kosuke looked up at the bell on the clifftop far above.

"Thank you, Takezo-san. Just about here will do. Could you stop the boat and try poking around with that pole under the water?"

"What am I trying to find, sir?"

"From what I understand, there should be weighted fishing nets around this area. But right now they seem to be fully submerged. I suspect that there is some fairly lightweight object tangled in the nets that is keeping them under the surface. Just try stirring the water up a bit."

Takezo took the hooked pole and splashed it around underwater awhile. Kosuke and Inspector Isokawa hung over the side of the boat, watching the pole's movements under the surface of the water. Kosuke could sense his friend's breathing getting heavier.

Suddenly, Takezo cried out.

"Did you find it? Okay then." Kosuke reached over towards the tide master. "Takezo-san, let me hold the pole for now. I'm sorry to ask this, but could you get into the water and cut the nets for me? I apologize for using you like this."

Kosuke produced a large military knife from the breast pocket of his kimono.

"Of course. That shouldn't be much of a problem."

Takezo peeled off his kimono to reveal a strong, muscular body. Wearing nothing but a loincloth, he took the knife between his teeth, and slipped into the sea.

He dove immediately underwater, leaving a pattern of gentle rings behind him. A short while later he re-emerged.

"Sir, could you grab this…"

Takezo passed over the edge of the net to Kosuke and pulled himself back up into the boat with ease. Kosuke gripped the piece of net nervously.

"Inspector, now for the big reveal. There's no telling what might appear."

As Kosuke began to haul in the net, a strange-looking object began to emerge, gently rocking and rolling its way from the depths. At first, the inspector and Takezo had no idea what they were looking at, but before long the full picture became clear.

"Oh… It's—it's a temple bell!" cried the inspector.

"That's right. A temple bell… Except that this one is a papier mâché version of a temple bell. A bell that splits in two vertically right down the middle. The same bell that the mother of Tsukiyo, Yukie and Hanako used to perform the stage play *Dojoji Temple*. And this very bell that the mother used as a prop in her play was used again a prop, this time in the murder of her daughter."

There was deep melancholy in Kosuke's voice. He showed none of his usual glee on uncovering the secret to a trick.

Right at that moment, Ryonen the priest had just left the branch family house and was approaching the lookout point. He walked calmly up to the edge of the cliff and looked down at the sea below him. Maybe there was some kind of unconscious connection between the priest and Kosuke, because Kosuke looked up at the exact same moment. Their eyes met.

"I put my trust in you..." Ryonen pressed his hands together and began to chant.

AFTER THE BUDDHIST CEREMONY

The following day...

On Gokumon Island it had been drizzling the whole day. In the main hall of the mist-shrouded Senkoji Temple, there was a solemn ceremony underway.

The head priest, Ryonen, was passing over charge of the temple to his apprentice, Ryotaku. In the Soto school of Zen Buddhism, this ceremony normally lasted for a week.

A red curtain had been hung in the main hall, behind which the teacher and pupil were in isolation. Such ceremonies are the first time a teacher communicates the true secrets to his pupil—importance, inheritance and bloodline—and the pupil must write everything down in scrupulous detail. After the pupil writes down each character, he must get up and bow three times. It is no wonder that the ceremony takes so much time. What's more, the successor is not permitted to leave his place for any reason before the completion of the ceremony, except to use the toilet. If he needs any food or water to sustain him, then the teacher must fetch it. For once, the master must serve his apprentice.

In performing this ceremony, the successor learns to put all worldly thoughts out of his mind as he becomes one of the direct receivers of the Buddha's teaching. He is now considered on equal footing with his teacher and the Buddha himself.

However, for some reason, Ryonen didn't bother with any of that. He performed the ceremony to pass over the guardianship of the temple to Ryotaku in a single day. And just like that, Ryotaku became the eighty-second generation of head priests of Senkoji Temple.

When the succession ceremony was over, and the two men came out of the main building, Ryonen wore a weary expression on his face. He visited the toilet, and as he washed his hands, he looked around the temple grounds. Out of the gloomy mist, the figures of armed police officers began to materialize.

Ryonen saw this and let out a deep sigh, but he was not one to lose his composure quite so easily. He strode purposefully towards the study and went inside.

"Thank you for waiting."

And with that briefest of greetings, he sat down heavily on a zabuton floor cushion.

There were two visitors in the study: Kosuke Kindaichi and Inspector Isokawa. It seemed they had been waiting a long time. The ashtray on the table between them contained a veritable mountain of cigarette butts.

"Not at all," said Inspector Isokawa, shifting his position on his floor cushion. "Did the ceremony go off smoothly?"

His voice was tense.

"Yes, thank you."

"Ryonen-san, where's Ryotaku now?" asked Kosuke.

"Ryotaku? He's gone down to the branch family house to pay his respects. Whatever happens, from now on he will have to ask for Gihei-san's support and protection. Of course, properly I should be asking Gihei-san to come up here, but I hear from you that you have something you need to discuss with me... Kindaichi-san, would you mind telling me what it's all about?"

"Ryonen-san?"

Kosuke broke off. His voice was unsteady; his lips trembled in a kind of spasm. He held his breath for a moment as he searched the priest's face for any kind of expression. Then he quickly looked away.

"Ryonen-san, we are here to arrest you. You have offered me much kindness, shown me much hospitality. I am so sorry that it has come to this."

Kosuke sounded close to tears. The priest, for his part, didn't reply right away. Inspector Isokawa sat observing the faces of the two men. The silence was deafening.

"To arrest me?... On what grounds?"

The priest was totally calm. The words were not so much an actual question, but rather a test of Kosuke.

"On the charge of murder... Ryonen-san, it was you who killed Hanako."

"Killed Hanako? Is that all, Kindaichi-san?"

"No. There's more. It was also you who killed the pirate gang member up at the fortress."

"Killed a pirate up at the fortress... Hmm. And what else?"

"That's all. Hanako and the unidentified pirate... You murdered those two people."

Inspector Isokawa looked at Kosuke in utter shock. It seemed he hadn't heard the whole story yet.

"Is that all?" said the priest once again, with utter indifference. "Kindaichi-san, what about Yukie and Tsukiyo? Weren't they my victims too?"

"No, they weren't. Ryonen-san, those two murders were not your handiwork. Yukie-san was killed by Mayor Makihei Araki, and Tsukiyo-san by Doctor Koan Murase."

"Kindaichi-san!"

Inspector Isokawa cut him off, but then found he could get no more words out. The shock had been too great for him.

"Is th— Is that true?" he said after a long pause. His voice was barely audible.

"Yes, it's true. Inspector, it was Ryonen-san who killed Hanako, the mayor who killed Yukie, and then finally Tsukiyo was killed by Doctor Koan. No other explanation makes any sense whatsoever. It's a truly unusual and, likewise, a truly horrifying case. The priest, the mayor and the doctor murdered Hanako, Yukie and Tsukiyo one by one. And yet, Inspector, it would be a mistake to think of these three men as accomplices. These three separate murderers were each committed single-handedly. And so, depending how you look at it, you could say there were three separate cases, which took place one after the other."

"But that's ridiculous! Three sisters, all murdered in order, one after the other? How can you call that three separate cases?"

"I know. But there was, of course, one person who was directing the whole thing. A person who used the priest, the mayor and the doctor to do his will. That person is the real culprit behind this string of murders. Compared to that person, Ryonen-san, Araki-san and Koan-san are nothing but instruments of murder."

"But who? Who is that terrible person?"

"A man who passed away one year ago. Kaemon Kito!"

Inspector Isokawa's body went stiff as if a lightning bolt had just passed through it. His cheeks had lost all feeling and began to twitch. By contrast, the priest remained perfectly calm. His eyes half-closed, he didn't move a muscle.

"That's correct. This whole thing was born of Kaemon-san's obsession and the influence he wielded over the people of the island, even after he was dead. I was an idiot. I should have noticed the moment I arrived on Gokumon Island. No, I should have realized even before I got here."

Kosuke had lost his usual vitality. He turned his despondent face towards Inspector Isokawa and the priest.

"Ryonen-san, Inspector, shall I tell you why I came to this island? I was requested to come by the heir of the Kito family, Chimata-san. He asked me to prevent this very thing happening. Which meant, of course, that Chimata knew beforehand that these killings were likely to occur. This is what he said to me: 'If I die, my three sisters will be murdered... Go to Gokumon Island... My cousin... My cousin...' And that's as far as he got before he took his last breath. However, long before Chimata-san got so sick, he had recommended that I visit Gokumon Island, and had even written me a letter of introduction. The problem was who this letter of introduction was addressed to. It was addressed to the priest, the mayor and the doctor—all three of them. Why had Chimata-san chosen these three as the addressees? Or rather, why had he not chosen someone closer to himself? A family member? Well, of course, his father, Yosamatsu-san, is in such a condition as to render him unsuitable to receive such a letter. But then, why did he not address the letter to Kaemon-san? Why did he not write this letter to his grandfather?... Well, if I'd thought about it, I could have solved the riddle of this case right away."

A faint shadow seemed to pass through Kosuke's eyes. It was a cloud of anguish and self-reprimand.

"Of course, Kaemon-san was an old man, and he might not still have been alive. This may have been what Chimata-san was thinking. But then again, that was also the case with the three men whose names did appear on the envelope. All of them are getting on in years. Maybe that was the reason he addressed the letter to all three of them, rather than just one. If any of them had passed away, at least one of the others would hopefully be available to receive the letter...

"But that does not answer the initial question: why did Chimata-san not write the letter to Kaemon-san? After all, this was his own grandfather. And on top of that, he was essentially the ruler of Gokumon Island. Anyone would choose Kaemon-san as the recipient of a letter of intro-duction, and then just in case, after that, they might write another one addressed to the priest or the mayor or the doctor. And yet Chimata-san didn't do this most logical of things. He kept his distance from Kaemon-san. Why was that? Was it possible that Chimata was afraid of Kaemon-san? Was it that he knew that his grandfather was the ring-leader of a group that intended to kill his three sisters?"

Kosuke took a break from speaking to light a cigarette. The hand that held the match shook. But once the cigarette was finally lit, he simply let his fist rest on his knee, forgetting to smoke it.

"As soon as the war started, Chimata-san was called up to serve in the army. In the beginning he was deployed to China. And after that, he passed through the southern islands on his way to New Guinea. He had no correspondence with home for a very long time. And even if he had done, there certainly wasn't anyone who was likely to have sent him a letter warning him that his three sisters might be killed. And yet, somehow Chimata-san knew that if he were to die, his three sisters would be murdered. How did he know this? Because before he ever left Japan, before he ever left his house, this had already been discussed."

A length of ash broke off from his cigarette and tumbled softly into his lap, but Kosuke didn't notice. His eyes were cast down, staring at the tatami flooring.

"In my mind I can see the following scenarios: in that tatami sitting room, deep in the Kito residence, three men are assembled. One is an old man by the name of Kaemon. The other two are the old man's grandsons, Chimata and Hitoshi. Chimata has already got his call-up notice. And it's almost certain that Hitoshi's will arrive soon. Yosamatsu, the man who is supposed to be the head of the Kito family after Kaemon's death, has gone mad. Furthermore, the Kito branch family, on unfriendly terms with the head family, is getting stronger and becoming a rival to the main family. One of his grandsons is about to go to war, and the other grandson will also soon be taken from him. Kaemon-san feels nothing but despair. So what did Kaemon-san tell his grandsons? It was probably something along these lines… If

Chimata, the heir to the Kito family, were to survive the war and return home, there would be no problem at all. However, were Chimata to die and only Hitoshi to survive, then the line of succession should pass to Hitoshi. But the problem was Chimata's three sisters, Kaemon's granddaughters. They would be in the way of Hitoshi's inheritance. And therefore they would have to be killed..."

Kosuke's voice, already shaky, suddenly gave out. He found himself unable to finish the sentence. Inspector Isokawa watched him, still enthralled by the story he was being told. The priest still hadn't moved; his eyes remained half-closed.

Kosuke cleared his throat.

"It's a horrifying thought. Not the feelings of a human being. Inhuman feelings rather. Well, islanders often feel differently from other people. For Kaemon, the future of the Kito family was of overwhelming importance. If any one of the three girls, Tsukiyo, Yukie or Hanako, became his successor, that would be the end of the powerful family... And that was Kaemon's greatest fear. Another factor was the hatred that he had once had for the girls' mother. If Chimata died it had to be Hitoshi who inherited. And if both Chimata and Hitoshi were to die, Sanae-san could inherit. Whichever the case, the three girls had to die first."

"No. That's incorrect."

It was the voice of the priest. His eyes still half-closed, he continued.

"So sorry to interrupt your story, but you've got that part wrong. Kaemon-san couldn't have cared less about girls. Whether it was Tsukiyo, Yukie, Hanako or Sanae made no difference to him. It was six of one and half a dozen of the other as far as he was concerned. If both Chimata-san and Hitoshi-san had died, there would have been nothing for it but to adopt the oldest girl, Tsukiyo, and have her succeed him. He would never have killed the three girls for Sanae's sake. That had never even occurred to him."

The expression on Kosuke's face was one of complete surprise, tinged with sorrow.

"Ryonen-san! Are you saying that if Chimata-san died but Hitoshi-san managed to survive, then these murders were to be committed? But if both grandsons had died, the three girls could have survived?"

The priest silently nodded. Kosuke and Inspector Isokawa exchanged looks. And in those looks was a sadness that the priest could not have understood.

"It's fate. Everything is fated."

The priest murmured this, his eyes still half-shut.

"I went to pick up Senkoji Temple's bell. It turned out that the bell had not been melted down and was still in one piece. And then, on the boat back to the island, I was informed by Takezo that Hitoshi-san was still alive. Then, right after that, you told me, Kindaichi-san, that Chimata-san was dead... Everything is fate. Chimata-san's death and Hitoshi-san's return alive, and then the temple bell... I vividly felt Kaemon-san watching over us, expectant. If any one of those three elements had been lacking, the three girls would not have been killed. But everything came perfectly together. The conditions were right: Chimata-san's death, Hitoshi-san's survival and the temple bell."

Kosuke and the inspector exchanged another glance. They both sighed deeply. The priest was still perfectly calm.

"Kindaichi-san, I may be a Buddhist priest, but, as I am sure you are aware, I am not one to hold superstitious beliefs. Still, when these three events happened at the exact same time, a kind of thrill ran through me. I truly felt that there was some kind of invisible power controlling all our movements. Besides, my duty was to Kaemon-san."

With that he broke into a dreadful smile.

"Those three girls deserved to die. I knew I would never regret killing them. Ha ha ha. Oh, but I interrupted your story, Kindaichi-san. Do go on."

The priest was beyond human emotion. He'd reached a point where he had managed to liberate himself completely from all materialistic and earthly desires. Right now he was simply experiencing the sense of peace and fulfilment that came from completing an important task. He felt no guilt and was making no attempt to deny his involvement. He was completely secure in himself.

"Inspector, Ryonen-san, please listen."

Kosuke began again in a grave tone.

"I said something impertinent just now. I may have led you to believe that I was aware early on of the shadow of Kaemon-san hanging over this case. However, that is not true. I didn't realize it until everything had already happened. And now that I've seen it, I realize what guided me to that conclusion was none other than you, Ryonen-san. You knew who I was and where I had come from. And in the spirit of fair play, you placed the key to solving the puzzle right under my nose. In other words, you got out that folding screen with the haiku poems just for me. However, I wasn't able to recognize that clue for what it was until long after the murders were committed. That was in part due to my own ignorance, but also in part to having fallen for your great hoax, Ryonen-san."

The priest raised his eyebrows. It was the first time they had moved at all since the three men had sat down together. Puzzled, he looked at Kosuke.

"Let me rephrase," said Kosuke hurriedly. "It was never your intention to have me fall for your hoax. Rather it was I who completely misunderstood. And until the eleventh hour it had me stuck in a blind alley, wondering how to get out. However, before I explain what I'm talking about, let's return to that first murder—that of Hanako. I don't think you know all of the details of that night yet, Inspector."

Kosuke tipped the dregs of his tea into his mouth. The brownish leaves that had been floating in the bottom of his cup were bitter on his tongue. The priest got up and fetched the iron kettle and teapot from his chambers.

THE DELUSION OF REASON

"Hanako was murdered on the night of Chimata's wake. That night, she left the house around 6.15 p.m. and from that time until Ryonen-san found her hanging upside down from the old plum tree in the courtyard of Senkoji Temple, nobody had set eyes on her. I found that extremely problematic. If Hanako had left the house at 6.15 and headed straight up to the temple, then she must have encountered somebody along the way. And yet nobody saw her. So where did she go? And at what time did she go up to Senkoji

Temple? I have a confession to make. I jumped to certain conclusions, which left me with a huge blind spot. One was that the young girl hanging from the branch of that plum tree at Senkoji Temple had been killed right there in the temple grounds. The second was that the culprit had killed her and then strung her up. Because of those two suppositions, I assumed that Hanako had been killed and then immediately hung from the tree. It was this blind spot that led me to miss the truth of Hanako's murder. And yet neither of my two assumptions were justified. In fact, Hanako was killed at another location and later carried up to Senkoji Temple. Consequently, there was a substantial interval between the time of her death and the time she was hoisted up into the tree, and it took me a long while to realize it. And so as soon as I did realize it, it felt as if someone had suddenly rinsed the dust from my eyes, and the truth of her murder was as clear as day to me."

Kosuke stopped speaking and took a sip of the fresh tea that the priest had served him.

"That night Hanako left the house at around 6.15 p.m., and set out right away up the winding path towards the temple, but she stopped at the little shrine to the harvest god, partway up the path, and hid inside, probably on the instructions of her killer—in other words, Ryonen-san. Of course, he had put Ukai-san's name on the letter he wrote and handed directly to Hanako. He probably claimed that Ukai-san had asked him to pass it on, or something like that, and poor Hanako was too innocent to suspect anyone's motives, particularly when that person was a priest. She had absolutely no reason not to trust him. So she slipped out of the house and, as the fake letter had instructed her, she hid in the little shrine, her heart beating with excitement, eagerly waiting for Ukai-san to come.

"When, at 6.25 p.m., I left the temple to run the priest's errand, and passed by the shrine, Hanako was already inside. Then, after I went on down to the bottom of the winding path, Takezo-san immediately came straight up the same path. He met the priest at the temple gate. At that same moment, Ryotaku had been sent back inside the temple on a bogus search for the 'forgotten' funeral chants. Ryonen-san then set off down the winding path accompanied by Takezo-san. In fact, the priest had not counted on Takezo-san turning up right then, and his plan was in jeopardy. It was precisely because he wanted to go down that path alone that he had sent me off on a fool's errand to the branch family house, and had sent Ryotaku to search for a non-missing item. But then Takezo-san turned up, and as a last resort he had to pretend to break the strap of his sandal to make sure that the tide master went on ahead. Anyway, Ryonen-san was finally alone, and able to knock on the lattice door of the shrine and call out to Hanako. As I've said before, Hanako didn't know how to be suspicious, and she must have stuck her head out of the door. At which point, Ryonen-san, you used your priest's staff as a weapon… and it really was the ideal shape… You took that staff and with one blow knocked Hanako out cold. Then, just in case she was still alive, you strangled her with a tenugui hand towel, and afterwards all you had to do was close that lattice door again, leaving her inside. The whole thing took no more than a couple of minutes.

"Next you strolled leisurely down the path and joined Takezo, who was waiting for you. Soon after, Ryotaku arrived, and just as the three of you set off walking together, you met me on my way back from the branch family house. Inspector, as you know, in the case of murder, the simpler it is, the greater the likelihood of it succeeding. In fact, this one is daring in its simplicity. From my point of view, when I ran into all three of them together at the foot of the winding path, Ryonen-san, Takezo-san and Ryotaku-san, I assumed they had all been together since leaving the temple. It would never have occurred to me for a moment that the priest had taken a detour to commit such a horrible crime."

The priest didn't say a word. His expression was utterly calm. Yet his silence could well be interpreted as acknowledgement of every word that Kosuke spoke. Inspector Isokawa found himself unable to stop himself from looking up to the priest, both figuratively and literally.

"And that is how the priest managed to kill Hanako. However, his task was not yet complete. Or rather I should say that the next bit was the most important. He had to take Hanako's body up to the temple and hang it upside down from the plum tree. If that part was omitted, as far as the priest was concerned, Hanako's murder was meaningless. And pulling off this part of the task was as daring in its simplicity—no, even more daring—than the actual murder. When Hanako's absence from the wake became a concern, and everybody split up to search for her, the priest naturally decided each person's role. He made sure that he was one step ahead of everyone else as he went up to the temple. The arrangements seemed so natural that nobody could have guessed at his real motive. When Ryonen-san rushed off to the temple as fast as he could so as not to be observed by anyone else, it set off no alarm bells. When I met Takezo and Ryotaku at the foot of the winding path, and the priest was still on the path above us, he was carrying Hanako's body over his shoulder."

Kosuke shuddered slightly; Inspector Isokawa looked amazed; the priest continued to look perfectly relaxed. Kosuke addressed the priest directly.

"Remembering that night, I have to pay you some kind of respect. It was pitch-black. Of course, we couldn't see you or the body that you were carrying. All that we could see was the light of your lantern. That said, for a murderer carrying a dead body to be able to walk at such a careful, measured pace? That's not a feat that just anyone could achieve. We... the distance between us and you was not getting any greater; rather I'd say we were closing in on you. But you got to the temple gate at just about the right moment and tied Hanako up in the tree. That was the main objective for you in that murder. If you hadn't been able to do that, then most of the reason for killing her would be gone. And why was that? Well, the haiku by Kikaku that was stuck to the byobu screen:

"Bush warbler upended in its tree—first song of spring.

"To turn Hanako's body into a parody of that haiku was important—no, more than that. To you, Ryonen-san, it was an absolutely vital matter. And at last, you managed to create that parody. Then all you had to do was to rush out of the gate of Senkoji Temple and call down to us, but when you went back into the kitchen, you became aware that there was an unexpected intruder on the premises."

Kosuke stopped and sighed. He turned back to the inspector.

"That intruder was, as far as the priest was concerned, an unexpected obstacle. And for me, the start of all kinds of confusion. Ryonen-san had seen the man was hiding in the Zen meditation hall, so he deliberately manoeuvred things to give him a chance to escape. At first I thought the priest must have recognized this man, and therefore allowed him to get away. In other words, that the intruder was the murderer… But in fact, I was mistaken. The man had no connection at all to either the priest or this case. He simply happened to witness the priest stringing up Hanako in the tree. Or even if he didn't actually witness that part, he may have seen Ryonen-san carrying a dead body into the temple. Either way, this was a threat to the priest, and he needed to be resourceful. First of all, it was vital that we didn't catch the man there and then, so he needed to do everything he could to prevent that happening. And so he found a way to let him get away. Then, two nights later, during the manhunt on the mountain, just as the man was on the brink of being captured, he lay in wait and smashed him over the head with his staff."

The priest remained calm, and now Kosuke's storytelling was equally calm. Between the two of them, the accuser and the accused, there was no sign that they were discussing such a gruesome topic. It was almost as if they were on a higher plane.

"But before this particular crime was even committed, the priest duped me completely by something he said. Well, to be honest, as I've said before, it was not exactly his intention. It was my unfortunate mistake, and because of it, I spent a long while fumbling around in the dark. It happened when we all gathered around the plum tree looking at Hanako's hanging body. At one moment, the priest muttered a phrase. It went like this: *'Out of reason, but it can't be helped.'* From his manner, and from his tone of voice, I believed that it was something that he just blurted out, that he was expressing true feelings of grief. There was nothing practised or polished about it. I saw a deep sorrow well up and be expressed in the moment. That was the only way to see it, and I took the phrase 'out of reason' to refer to Yosamatsu, locked away in his lunatic's cage. In other words, I wondered how Yosamatsu-san could be connected to this case. And once again, this error led me down the wrong path where I wandered aimlessly for several days. When I finally realized what the priest had really said, the murders had all been committed and it was too late… Inspector, the phrase that the priest uttered at that moment, was not 'Out of reason, but it can't be helped' at all. He said, 'Out of *season*, but it can't be helped.' In other words, I had simply misheard him. But then why, you may ask, that particular phrase? Well, he was comparing the flesh and blood of Hanako to the haiku:

"Bush warbler upended in its tree—first song of spring

"That haiku is undeniably a celebration of spring, and right now it is autumn. So when Ryonen-san said 'Out of season, but it can't be helped', he was lamenting that he had been unable to fulfil Kaemon-san's dying wish by perfectly recreating the image of the haiku."

Kosuke observed a smile cross the priest's face.

"Ah yes, I see you're laughing at me. But it isn't the first time, is it? Right after the incident, when we were searching for the intruder in the main hall of the temple, I questioned you about the meaning of your phrase. At first you didn't get what I was talking about, but then you suddenly realized my ridiculous error. You covered your face with both hands, and your shoulders began to shake. At the time, I thought my question had caused you some sort of pain. I thought you were reacting in a mixture of shock and horror, and I was so confident that I had spotted something clever, but now I realize you were laughing. That my comical mistake had you in stitches, and that you had to put both hands over your face to conceal that from me. At that moment, in the eyes of the great high priest of Senkoji Temple, I was nothing but an ignorant child."

"No, no, not at all, Kindaichi-san."

The priest controlled his laughter now, and was looking soothingly at Kosuke. There was something of the affectionate parent in his expression.

"I have never seen you as an ignorant child. You are truly great, an admirable person. You have managed to see through me completely. Stop feeling sorry for yourself. There was no way that anyone could have prevented these murders. Well, you seem to have pretty much cleared up the case of Hanako's murder, but what about Yukie and Tsukiyo? Can you explain those?"

Stumbling over words along the way, Kosuke set out to explain the second murder.

"The greatest challenge in solving Yukie-san's murder was working out when the body could have been placed under the bell. According to Sergeant Shimizu, at around 8.40 p.m., when he passed by the Tengu's Nose lookout point, he checked the bell with his torch, and there was definitely no kimono sleeve protruding from under the rim. From there, Shimizu-san and the mayor walked downhill to the Kito branch family house, and then about ten minutes later, turned around and came back. Shimizu-san reports that, this time, as they passed the bell it began to pour with rain. Accordingly, the body couldn't have been placed under the bell after that time. Why not? Because the body of Yukie, found in a sitting position under the bell, wasn't wet at all, apart from the kimono sleeve that had been left sticking out from the bottom. Well, her back was a little damp, but everywhere else was completely dry. This meant that her body had to have been put underneath before the rain began to fall—in other words, after Shimizu-san and the mayor first passed it on the way to the branch family house, and while they were there at the house. If we include the walking time between the lookout point and the house, that gave the killer a total of fourteen minutes. It would have been just about possible to perform the lever trick with the bell and put the body underneath within the space of fourteen minutes. And that is what I believed had happened. However, when I really, really thought about it, I found that theory rather far-fetched. According to Doctor Koan's estimate, Yukie had been killed between 6.00 and

300

7.00 p.m. If we say her time of death had been close to 7.00 p.m., why on earth wait an hour and a half and then use that precariously narrow time frame to hide the body under the bell? Moreover, according to Shimizu-san, the first time they examined the bell, it was already starting to spot with rain. By waiting for that moment, it was pretty much guaranteed that the body would end up getting wet. As I have said before, there was no sign that the body had ever been out in the rain. How was this possible? How?

"The more I thought about it, the more I was convinced that Yukie's body had already been there under the bell the first time that Shimizu-san and the mayor passed by. I was sure that this explanation was the one that made the most sense, but this called into question Shimizu-san's statement that he and the mayor had examined the bell by torch and there had been no kimono sleeve visible at that time. When the murder was discovered, the sleeve was sticking out on the side that faced the road, and it was dyed in bright colours. Even if the beam from the torch was rather dim, something like that would have caught their eye immediately. I was perplexed. There had to have been some sort of trick involved. But what kind of trick?… While I was still puzzling over the answer to that question, I heard at Seiko the barber's that there had been another bell spotted that same night, down the road from the lookout point. Then from Gihei-san I also learned that the mother of the three girls used to perform the Noh play *Dojoji Temple*, in the course of which she used a temple bell that opened up vertically down the middle, splitting into two halves. He told me that this prop used to be kept in a storehouse somewhere on the Kito family property, and that it could well still be there. These two pieces of information shocked my mind like a conjurer revealing the secret to his trick. I had no difficulty after that in fathoming how it was done. The real temple bell was raised and Yukie put underneath. Only her sleeve was purposely caught under the rim of the bell and left visible on the outside. In other words, the protruding sleeve was no oversight on the part of the killer. He deliberately placed Yukie-san so that her sleeve would be visible from the outside. Then he placed the papier mâché bell around the outside, concealing both the real bell and the sleeve. And that was how that night when Shimizu-san ran his torch over the bell to examine it, it was in fact the papier mâché bell that he was seeing."

Almost as if to save Kosuke from running out of steam, Ryonen-san took up the story.

"And you found that same bell yesterday and pulled it out of the sea, didn't you, Kindaichi-san?"

He moved over to pour Kosuke some more tea.

"That's right. Attached to the ring at the crown of the bell was a thick length of rope, and tied to the other end of the rope was a heavy rock. Then, right under the protruding ground of that lookout point, there were signs that there had been some slippage of rocks and stones. I believe that this is what happened: somebody placed the fake bell over the real one, then attached a length of rope to the ring on the fake bell's crown with a heavy rock as a weight on the other end. They took this rock down to the roadside below the cliff edge. After putting it there, they waited first until Shimizu-san had looked over the papier mâché bell and there had been no kimono sleeve to be seen. Then, they went down to the road below and pushed the rock over the edge. The weight of the rock on the rope pulled on the fake bell, the device opened up down the middle, and it was pulled neatly away from the real bell, falling over the cliff and into the sea. And now of course, Yukie's kimono sleeve was sticking out from under the real temple bell...

"Last night, I indirectly asked Shimizu-san about it, and he replied that the bell he'd seen with the torch had seemed somehow larger than the temple bell they'd examined the next morning. It could just have been an optical illusion—a difference between darkness and daylight, he thought. And that was when I guessed the trick. However, the question remains, why on earth did the killer even attempt such a complicated trick? Well, I think you already know. It was to create an alibi for himself. At 8.40 p.m., when Shimizu-san was passing the lookout point, the sleeve had to be invisible. It was vital that everyone believed Yukie to have been placed under the bell later than that. And so I needed to work out who would be the person to have their alibi most clearly established by this time frame? And at the same time, who had the greatest opportunity to push that rock off the side of the cliff? The horror of the solution—I drove myself almost crazy thinking about it. The person to whom these two conditions most applied was none other than the mayor himself, Makihei Araki. The mayor had been with Sergeant Shimizu when he'd examined the bell by torch. Along with Shimizu-san he had gone down that road where the rock weight on the end of the rope had been placed. The road was pitch-black that night: I'm sure there was some opportunity to surreptitiously push that rock over without Shimizu-san noticing… So again, last night, when I was speaking to Shimizu-san, I asked him about that night and got an interesting reply. He said that soon after they'd gone down that road beneath the lookout point, the mayor had suddenly needed to relieve himself. Shimizu-san had walked on at a leisurely pace, but he said that the place that the mayor stopped was directly beneath the lookout point. The same place where I found the traces of the weight and the slippage on the cliff side. And then Shimizu-san recalled that he thought he heard the splash of something falling into the sea. But with the sound of the waves, and because the wind had been strong that night, he hadn't been sure what he heard."

Kosuke broke off and stared absent-mindedly out through the window. Inspector Isokawa gave a little cough to bring him back to reality. Hesitantly, Kosuke took up the story again.

"That was a horrifying discovery. Utterly crazy. Hanako had been killed by Ryonen the priest, but Yukie's killer was the mayor. It was so utterly crazy that I was afraid to let myself believe it. And yet, however much my own morality told me to reject the possibility, it was an indisputable truth. The priest killed Hanako-chan. And then the mayor killed Yukie-chan. Was it then the doctor who killed Tsukiyo-chan?… Just thinking this was making me go out of my mind. But as I considered the possibility, I couldn't find any grounds for thinking Koan-san couldn't have been Tsukiyo's killer. No, quite the contrary, there was nobody besides Doctor Koan who had the opportunity to kill her."

"But that's a little unreasonable," said Inspector Isokawa. "Koan-san may well have had the opportunity to kill Tsukiyo-san, but it was physically impossible. He had broken his left arm and couldn't use it at all. Tsukiyo-san was strangled with a tenugui hand towel. How can you strangle someone with only one hand?"

"That particular tenugui, as you already know, was one from a roll that were dyed in bulk. There was a bunch of multicoloured streamers hanging from the lintel above the altar, the one that Tsukiyo-san was facing. You remember—the cat had been tied to the bell? Tsukiyo-san probably wouldn't have noticed a length of tenugui hand towels cut from the roll mixed up with the streamers. Koan-san took one end of the length of cloth in his right hand, and crept up behind Tsukiyo-san while she was deep in her incantation. He quickly wrapped the end around her neck, and pulled it tight—and because the other end was already attached to the lintel above the altar, it only required one hand to carry out the murder. And then, when he estimated that Tsukiyo-san had taken her last breath, he cut the length of cloth so that it left a hand towel of about the usual length around her neck. Inspector, you noticed yourself that although the tenugui was rather soiled, the end where it had been cut looked brand new. That's how the one-armed Koan-san managed to strangle someone with a traditional Japanese hand towel. He perpetrated an impossible crime."

Outside it was dusk. Inside the study there was a deathly hush. Inspector Isokawa's heavy breathing seemed to fill the empty space. He wiped the sticky sweat from his forehead and finally found his tongue.

"Thank you," he said, his voice hoarse. "What on earth? The priest, the mayor and the doctor? Was this some kind of meeting of all Gokumon Island's genius criminal minds?"

"No, not at all," said Kosuke quietly. "As I said before, Ryonen-san, the mayor and Koan-san were all no more than instruments of murder. The mastermind behind all these three hideous, macabre murders was none other than the late Kaemon-san, ex-head of the Kito family. Inspector, I'm sure you've heard it said that before he passed away, Kaemon-san suffered a stroke and lost the use of the left side of his body? Well, in order to properly honour his master in the killing of Tsukiyo-san, Koan-san hit on the idea of deliberately breaking his own left arm. Would you mind explaining that in some detail to us, Ryonen-san?"

Kosuke broke off and looked at the priest.

WORSHIP OF A PATRIARCH

Night closed in, and the shadows in the room lengthened. Outside, a fine rain fell. Inspector Isokawa got to his feet, and flipped the electric light switch. A cold, pale light flooded the study, reaching as far as the plants that grew at the edge of the *engawa* veranda.

The priest still had his eyes half-closed, so utterly dispassionate that he could have been a statue. His full lips began to move.

"Kaemon-san's final moments were utter misery. As I think you have already heard."

With complete detachment, his tone was as bland and colourless as water. His voice was low, but it reverberated in the room. He recounted the story in detail.

"His own son, whose role as heir to the family was so crucial in the line of succession, turned out to be a lunatic, and now in a bitter stroke of misfortune, his two beloved grandsons had been taken from him by war, perhaps never to return. All that were left were girls, and when it came to the three granddaughters who were his direct lineage, they were not even yet of age. To make matters worse, Oshiho of the branch family was using the young man, Ukai, to meddle in his affairs. Kaemon-san was about to die, but he was determined to the end not to give up. When in the last days of the war he had some sort of stroke and suffered from paralysis on one side of his body, there was something that could be done to help him. But at the beginning of October last year, he was struck again, and this time there appeared to be nothing anyone could do. Kaemon-san himself knew he had to be prepared for death but he was clinging to life and his obsession. Worrying about the fate of the Kito family caused him the worst agony—as if he were burning in the fires of hell. Too pathetic, too horrible to watch.

"Then, two days before he died, he had a brief moment of lucidity, and called the mayor, the doctor and me to his bedside. He said a very strange thing. Even now, whenever I shut my eyes, I can still hear that voice in my head. These are the words he spoke... 'Please listen to what I have to say. Last night I had a strange dream. In this dream, I killed Tsukiyo, Yukie and Hanako. Moreover, the manner of their deaths was most exquisitely beautiful...' That's what Kaemon-san said. And then he burst out laughing. Ignoring the way we all looked at one another, he continued talking. It was just as Kindaichi-san has described here, all three manners of death. Kaemon-san was terrifying in his relentlessness—he told us over and over again. But it wasn't true that he'd had a dream. Ever since his first stroke... no, long before then even... for months, for years, he'd been plotting this. If Chimata were to die and Hitoshi were to return from war, he was going to murder his three granddaughters himself. Now and then he'd let the odd hint slip to us, his three trusted associates, as if it were some kind of joke. But it turned out to be no joke. At the end of his speech, Kaemon-san told us, 'This deed should be done by my own hand, but with this body of mine I can't do it any more. I don't have much time left. I really ought to have carried it out when I still had my health, but I had no news of Chimata and Hitoshi, and I don't want to take someone's life in vain. I refrained until now, but now that the time of my death is near, I regret it so much. So, good priest, Mr Mayor, Doctor Koan, please take pity on me and do my will. If Chimata dies and Hitoshi returns, kill off those three girls in the manner I've described. That would be the greatest consolation to my soul...'

"Kaemon-san shed tears as he implored the three of us to do this for him. From under his pillow, he produced those three shikishi with the haiku written on them, and told us, 'Here are mementos for you to keep. When you look at these, you will always remember my final request.' And then he went over, time and time again, each of the methods of murder. 'I beg you, I implore you, if you disregard my dying wish, I will haunt you for eternity.' He handed to me the Kikaku haiku, to the mayor the cricket under the helmet and to Koan the moon and bush clover.

"Lately I had kept those three poem cards stuck to that folding screen that I had placed by your futon, Kindaichi-san. I'm sure you had a chance to take a look at them. You might wonder why I displayed them for you like that. Well, it was because the mayor told me about your background. He recognized your name. He searched out some old newspapers and was able to confirm that it was you. I heard that this man, Kosuke Kindaichi, was a famous detective, and got to worrying what you might have heard from Chimata-san. At the same time, I decided that it would be very unfair of me not to leave you some kind of clue. If you really were such a great detective, you should be able to solve the puzzle of the haiku poems. If you couldn't work them out, then it would show your ignorance. You would not deserve the title of 'great detective'. Well, anyhow, whether it meant victory or defeat, I decided that it would be cowardly to hide those shikishi. I overcame the opposition of the mayor and Koan-san and put them out for you to see. The result was of course total defeat for me. But I'm glad. I'm happy to lose. It's actually refreshing… Ha ha. But I've strayed from the subject… Anyway, regarding Kaemon-san's dying wish… I'm sure that if you had been there and seen how heartbroken the great man was, you wouldn't have been able to refuse him either. I shed tears myself. When I thought how that extraordinary man had been reduced to this miserable state, I couldn't help crying. My reply to him was thus: 'Sir, be at peace. If Chimata-san dies and

Hitoshi-san returns from war, then I promise I will do as you have requested. Even if it means I end up in hell, I will do my utmost to hang the body of Hanako upside-down from the branches of the old plum tree. By the name of the Buddha, I swear that these words are true.' The mayor and Koan-san recoiled at the gruesomeness of what they were being asked to do, but reluctantly they too vowed to carry out Kaemon-san's request. He must have felt relief or peace of mind after this, because just two days later he closed his eyes for the last time."

Kosuke and Inspector Isokawa had been listening to the priest in silence. But it was as if they were listening to the final words of a captured enemy commander. Their compassion was only fleeting.

The priest's spirits were gradually fading.

"After Kaemon-san's funeral, the mayor, Koan and I had a private meeting. At that time, Koan asked me, his expression sick with worry, 'Ryonen, you made that promise, but do you really intend to keep it?' I roared with laughter. 'Kaemon-san was out of his mind. There are details of his wishes that we can't possibly follow. The temple bell. Where is there a temple bell on this island? Kaemon-san must have completely forgotten that we've given away our bell for the war effort. 'How tragic—beneath the helmet, a hidden cricket' can't be done. And the mayor won't be the only one unable to keep his promise. If it's acceptable for the mayor to break his promise, then by the same principle we can surely break ours too.' And with that, the mayor and Koan looked as if a huge weight had been lifted from their shoulders... And yet... And yet..."

For the very first time, there was pain in the priest's expression.

"A year later, I got a message from the town of Kure to go and pick up Senkoji Temple's bell. I was stunned. I wasn't sure why, but a sense of foreboding came over me, which I found myself unable to ignore. I set out anyway, to find that the bell hadn't been melted down and was still in one piece. I completed the paperwork and set off on the return journey. As I have already explained, I was then hit by the news that while Hitoshi-san would return alive, Chimata-san was already dead. It was the same with the mayor and Koan—when they heard the news they trembled with terror. What to do? Well, the three of us met to discuss the matter. But by then I had already made up my mind. It had happened just as Kaemon-san had feared. And worse, in the year that had passed since his death, I had kept watch over those three granddaughters of his, and they had started to behave like cats in heat. They were completely vulnerable to that man, Ukai, and no doubt there would be a second Ukai or a third showing up before long. Anyone could see that coming. At this point, it was more merciful just to have them die. For their own sakes, and for the sake of society. And thus, this is what I said to the mayor and Koan: 'You two do whatever you want; I'm going to carry out the plan as I promised. If you want to go to the police, then go ahead. But if you do, then Kaemon-san's resentment and my own curse will fall on you.' The two of them weren't going to go ahead with the murders, but when I killed Hanako and strung her up in the tree, they were so horrified that they literally shook with terror, utter panic. It was the first time they had witnessed the real power of my determination. Those two were less afraid of the grudge that the spirit of Kaemon-san would hold against them than the divine wrath that I might bring upon them. And because I carried out my part of the plan, the two of them finally resigned themselves to their roles. First of all, the mayor performed his, then Koan his. I actually feel a bit sorry for them because they're so pathetic. If the moment ever arose, I planned to take responsibility for all the murders."

The priest sighed deeply and turned to Kosuke.

"Kindaichi-san?"

"Yes?"

"What's happened to the mayor and Koan?"

Kosuke and Inspector Isokawa exchanged glances.

"Last night, the mayor fled from the island. Ryonen-san, it was you who told him to flee, wasn't it?"

The priest gave a bittersweet smile.

"Yesterday, I saw you drag up the papier mâché bell from the sea, and I knew the game was up. I realized that I wasn't going to get away with a lie as big as admitting to all the crimes, so I went to warn the other two. Only Koan was predictably drunk so I gave up and came home. But it seems the mayor managed to escape. What about Koan?"

"Well, Koan-san…"

"He went out of his mind."

"Mad?"

For a moment, the priest's eyes looked as if they were about to pop out of his head, but then he looked depressed and let out the deepest of sighs.

"I see… Well, yes, I'm not surprised. He was rather a faint-hearted type after all. Always tended to fret too much over things."

"No, there was another reason. Today Sergeant Shimizu got a call from the prefectural police headquarters in Kasaoka…"

Kosuke's voice broke off. The priest frowned curiously.

"A phone call from Kasaoka police station?… Kindaichi-san, what did that have to do with Koan?"

"Ryonen-san," said Kosuke, taking a deep breath. "I wish I didn't have to tell you, but unfortunately I do. The call from the Kasaoka police was to inform Shimizu-san that a fraudster had been arrested in Kobe. It seems he was a repatriated soldier recently back from Burma. It appears he was walking from one end of Japan to the other, visiting all the homes belonging to his fellow soldiers. According to this fraudster, whenever he would tell families that their relative was still alive, they would be so overjoyed that they would treat him to lavish meals. If he told them their relative was dead, he wouldn't get much out of them. And so he hatched a plan to tell the families of comrades who had died in action that they had actually survived…"

The priest looked stricken. He began to pant heavily.

"Ki-Kindaichi-san, you m-mean that Hitoshi-san?…"

Kosuke could hardly bear to look at Ryonen's face. This single piece of information had mercilessly demolished the fortress of strength that the priest had carefully constructed around himself.

"I'm afraid so. He died in action. But if the fraudster had told the truth, then he wouldn't have got much in the way of thank-you gifts… Ah, Ryonen-san!"

The priest jumped to his feet so suddenly that Kosuke and the inspector both started. For a few moments, the priest stood utterly still. He looked like a lifeless glass marble that had lost its shine and turned dull and cloudy. He tried to say something, but his lips just opened and closed without a single sound escaping. He looked at Kosuke, then at Inspector Isokawa, slowly shaking his head from side to side… Then, all of a sudden, on both sides of his face, a vein appeared the size of a large wriggling worm, which began to expand and swell alarmingly. His complexion turned unpleasantly sticky and then he began to turn red.

"I put my trust in you… Kaemon-san!"

"Ryonen-san!"

Kosuke and the inspector rushed to his aid, but he brushed away their hands. And then he simply toppled over like a rotten tree.

And that was the end of Ryonen, former head priest of Senkoji Temple.

Kosuke Kindaichi Leaves the Island

Kosuke was getting ready to leave Gokumon Island. Sergeant Shimizu, the tide master, Takezo and Seiko the barber had all come down to the harbour to see him off. As was normal on the island, a light mist of rain was falling.

"Shimizu-san, have the police still not located the mayor?" Kosuke asked.

"No, not yet. The latest rumour on the island is that he found some isolated spot and killed himself."

"I see…"

That was the end of the conversation. They stood together silently on the quayside. An indescribable sadness had pierced Kosuke's heart, and seemed to spread through his body like a chill winter wind. The drizzle was constant and unending…

"Why? Why? Why?"

It was Seiko the barber who broke the silence.

"Why is everyone so down in the dumps? You are getting to leave the island, sir. You should be excited. Why so miserable? Sanae-san might be a great beauty here on the island, but get her back to Tokyo and you'd see that she's nothing special. There's nothing to be miserable about. Hey, Takezo-san, don't tell Sanae-san I said that, okay?"

Seiko's words were very much on target. The previous day, Kosuke had gone to see Sanae and asked her if she would like to come to Tokyo with him. She had been taken by surprise by the suddenness of the invitation and stared at him awhile with her big round eyes. After a few moments she realized his true intentions, and her gaze began to shift towards the floor.

"I'm sorry. I've decided to stay here. My brother and my cousin, who should have inherited the family name, are both dead. I know how difficult it's going to be from now on. If Japan is revolutionized, then Gokumon Island will be too. The system of having fishing chiefs controlling whole fleets will become nothing but a naive dream of the past. But however difficult the future may be, I need to be part of it. I can't stay still. The young men of the island are starting to return from war. I need to find myself a suitable husband from among them, and until I do, I need to protect the Kito family. If I don't do that, then my grandfather's soul will never be able to leave this house and rest in peace. Born on the island, die on the island. That's the rule around here... But thank you. I'm sorry that we won't meet again."

Sanae had turned her face from Kosuke's gaze. Then, a little shakily, she walked away.

"Takezo-san," said Kosuke, "please take care of the Kito family, especially now that the priest and the mayor and Koan-san are all gone."

"Sir, I will. Until my dying day."

Takezo wiped the corner of his eye with a sleeve.

At last, the familiar sight of the *White Dragon* entered the harbour.

"Well then, good health to you all!"

"Take care, sir!"

"Kindaichi-san, please drop us a line when you get settled. I'll let you know if we capture the mayor."

Just as the welcome barge was about to set out to meet the ferry, a figure came rushing down onto the quay. It was the young Shozo Ukai, dressed in his army uniform. He had no umbrella and was soaked to the skin.

"Ha ha. Ukai-san! I see you've finally been given the shove," said Seiko rather maliciously. "The lady of the branch family sure is a fickle one!"

Ukai blushed bright red and hunched his shoulders as if trying to disappear. He stumbled hastily onto the boat.

(Yes. That's just about right. This is not a place for outsiders to spend much time.)

The engine of the barge turned over, and the sound of a temple bell was carried to them on the mist.

Ryotaku, the new priest of Senkoji Temple, was bidding Kosuke farewell with the chimes of the temple bell. That bell with its gruesome memories...

Kosuke stood up from his seat in the boat and faced the island, enveloped in its usual layer of fog.

"Bless you."

He placed his hands together in a posture of prayer as he bade farewell to Gokumon Island.

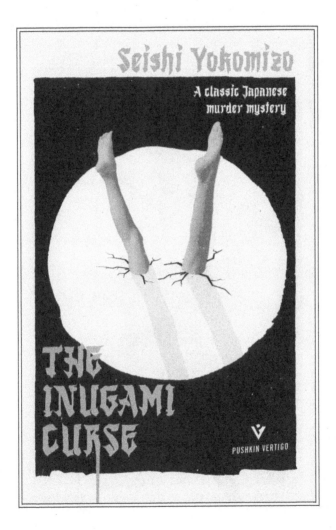

Seishi Yokomizo

A classic Japanese
murder mystery

THE
INUGAMI
CURSE

PUSHKIN VERTIGO

Seishi Yokomizo

A classic Japanese murder mystery from
the author of *The Honjin Murders*

THE
VILLAGE OF
EIGHT GRAVES

PUSHKIN VERTIGO